Dangerous Beauty

Anastasia Black

Ellora's Cave
Romantica Publishing

An Ellora's Cave Romantica Publication

www.ellorascave.com

Dangerous Beauty

ISBN # 1419952773

Edited by Pamela Cohen
Cover art by Syneca

Electronic book Publication April, 2005
Trade paperback Publication October, 2005

Warning:

The following material contains graphic sexual content meant for mature readers. *Dangerous Beauty* has been rated *S-ensuous* by a minimum of three independent reviewers.

Ellora's Cave Publishing offers three levels of Romantica™ reading entertainment: S (S-ensuous), E (E-rotic), and X (X-treme).

S-e*nsuous* love scenes are explicit and leave nothing to the imagination.

E-*rotic* love scenes are explicit, leave nothing to the imagination, and are high in volume per the overall word count. In addition, some E-rated titles might contain fantasy material that some readers find objectionable, such as bondage, submission, same sex encounters, forced seductions, etc. E-rated titles are the most graphic titles we carry; it is common, for instance, for an author to use words such as "fucking", "cock", "pussy", etc., within their work of literature.

X-*treme* titles differ from E-rated titles only in plot premise and storyline execution. Unlike E-rated titles, stories designated with the letter X tend to contain controversial subject matter not for the faint of heart.

Also by Anastasia Black

Forbidden

About the Author

Anastasia Black is the pen name for a writing partnership between two Ellora's Cave writers: Julia Templeton and Tracy Cooper-Posey. Anastasia Black writes Regency and Victorian historical romances.

The authors welcome mail from readers. You can write to them c/o Ellora's Cave Publishing at 1056 Home Ave. Akron, Oh. 44310-3502.

Dangerous Beauty

Chapter One

East End Docklands, London, 1838

A steam tug blew a mournful note, which echoed flatly across the water. Its passage and the wake of the ship it towed rocked the Artemis where it was tied up at the dock. The motion told Seth Harrow that he had indeed made it back on board last night. It also drew attention to his thick head, which began to thump at the motion. He swallowed dryly, keeping his eyes shut against the daylight filtering through the portholes of the captain's cabin, and remained perfectly still upon the mattress, riding out the subtle rocking of the ship.

With luck, this would be his last day in this stinking city. Last night had reacquainted him with the vices and venom of the fat, old broad of a town. Tucked away in fresh, feisty Albany, deep in the colonies, he'd forgotten how the double standards here could crush a man's spirits and break his back in all but body. Well, he'd been reminded, and now he was ready to leave. Just one last piece of business, and he could break out the sails and head for Ireland.

Home. The thought came with a deep longing, an ache for the familiar. And whenever he thought of home, he remembered Liam as he had seen him last, sitting in the courtroom with a stricken expression on his white face as the sentence had been passed down.

A warm, light hand slipped over his naked hip, and Seth opened his eyes, startled. He rolled his head to the right, slowly, and found himself staring at a sleepy-eyed redhead. She lay on her side, and she was smiling a little. He could see a sliver of dark green eyes showing under her lowered lids. Her hand was stroking his thigh, and his knees fell apart under her coaxing fingers, as they fluttered against the inside of his thighs.

A good deal of the previous evening's activities was restored to his memory then, and he smiled.

"And a fine mornin' to ye, too, Duchess," he said, rolling over to face her.

She smiled more fully, her excellent teeth flashing, and her eyes opened a little more. "Your Irish is showing, Seth." Her voice was deep, husky, but with an upper-class preciseness that had not slipped even when she had been deep in the throes of orgasmic passion—he remembered that much about her. She was a genuine blue blood.

She had been slumming last night, looking for a raw entertainment that cotillions and balls could not provide. The duchess had paused at the door of the dockside pub for a brief moment to lower the hood of her green velvet cloak, pulling off her gloves and assessing the men in the room. She had seen Seth, sitting on a stool, and had come straight over.

"You may buy me a drink, Captain," she had said, her voice throaty. She had given him a knowing smile he'd instantly understood. Like a gentleman, he'd stood and offered her the stool, and sent for another glass of rum.

He looked at her now, at the full breasts that he had played with last night. They were white in the dim light, tipped with rose-colored nipples that crinkled hard even as he studied them. "Ye had no objection to my Irish last night, I recall."

Her hand gripped his engorged and ready cock, and he drew a sharp breath.

"I recall listening to an educated man," she said. Then she relented, her grip on him loosening and her hand beginning to stroke with a practiced caress, the fingers sliding over the ridge of flesh at the tip. They felt soft, maddeningly arousing.

Seth swallowed. He dredged up habits of speech he hadn't used for years. "It is quite astonishing how one can be misled by appearances, is it not?" The rounded pronunciations were an echo of school halls and manorial estates.

"He sounds like a right proper gent, don't he?" another soft voice said. A small hand slid over his waist from behind.

Seth swiveled to look over his shoulder. A petite blonde with small breasts was sitting up behind him. Her hand caressed him.

Annie. Now he remembered all of it. Annie, the duchess' maid, who shared her adventurous spirit.

A flash of sense-memory came to him—lying on the bed, arms flung wide, as they had attacked him with their mouths and hands, the multiple sensations building a swift explosion of pleasure in him.

He growled and reached for the woman, bringing her over to the same side as the duchess. She shrieked and giggled as they sprawled together, and the redhead sat up, too. They both reached for him again. The look on the duchess' face was one of a predatory, hungry animal.

That was when the hesitant knock sounded on the door.

Seth frowned. "Go away!"

The knock came again. Firmer this time.

"That'd better be you, Harry, or I'll have your guts for garters, whoever you are."

"It's Harry," came the answer, muffled.

Seth looked at the duchess and gave a rueful smile. "A moment only," he assured her.

While Annie pouted, the redhead fell back against the pillow with an exaggerated sigh. "A moment only, Seth. My patience will only stretch so far."

Seth climbed over the duchess and looked around for his trousers, which he found beneath a pile of stiffened petticoats and a corset. A shirt, one of the tattered ones he wore at sea, hung on a nail driven into the wall. He threw that on, too. Not bothering to button it, he cracked open the cabin door.

Harry's sun-bronzed features, and the almond-shaped eyes, peered back at him through the crack. "There's a boy here, up on deck. Says he must speak to you. Says he has a message."

The news he had been waiting for. Seth nodded, and opened the door enough to slip through.

Harry craned his head for a glimpse. Seth shut the door firmly and smiled. "You'll just frighten them."

"Two?" Harry said, blinking.

"I'll wager neither of them has ever seen a Chinaman before." Seth gave the long braid hanging between Harry's shoulder blades a gentle tug and walked up the passage to the steep steps that climbed to the main deck.

"I ain't never seen a duchess before, neither," Harry said, following along behind.

"They're all the same, undressed." Seth stepped out onto the deck, taking a lungful of the thick, damp air. A fog hung about the *Artemis*, so thick he could barely see the ship docked next to them. He certainly couldn't see the far side of the river. It curled about the deck, thick strands about the rigging, making everything sound flat, muffled.

"Sodden old England… I'd forgotten what a miserable place this could be." He looked over at the gangway, where a small boy in ragged pants and dirty shirt stood clutching the bulwark with a death grip, his eyes wide, staring down at the dirty, oily water swirling between the sides of the ship and the stone dock. "You, boy," he said softly. "Don't be afraid. Come here."

The boy visibly swallowed and shuffled forward. He doffed his cap quickly, as if he'd only just remembered the custom.

"You have a message for me, lad?"

He nodded. He was staring over Seth's shoulder now, and his eyes grew even bigger. Seth glanced at Harry standing at his shoulder.

"This is Harry Hang. He won't hurt you. Give me the message, boy."

The boy reached inside his shirt and brought out a thick envelope with a red seal on the back. "'Is eyes are all funny-lookin'." The boy didn't take his eyes off Harry as he held out the envelope.

"I was born in China," Harry said. "A long, long time ago."

The boy considered this. Harry's western speech seemed to reassure him a little, and give him confidence. "My guv told me about them Chinamen. Ain't they supposed to wear funny white pajamas and round pointy hats, and have plaits down their backs?"

Seth laughed a little as he broke the seal on the letter. "Not Harry. Just the braid, now."

Harry turned his head to display the hip-length braid to the boy.

"Why?" the boy asked with innocent directness.

"So that when I die, God can pull me up to heaven," Harry explained.

The boy shook his head firmly. "God don't do that, 'e makes you take a boat."

"Like this one?" Harry asked, with a smile.

Seth tuned out their unconventional theology discussion and read the cursive script on the sheet. He frowned at the news it conveyed.

"You're to give me tuppence," the boy said to Seth, nodding at the letter. "'E said 'e'd put it in that there letter."

"That he did," Seth agreed. "Harry, fish two pennies out of the ship's purse for him."

"Aye, Cap'n," Harry said, and went below.

The boy was given his tuppence and skipped down the gangplank, delighted with his well-earned treasure trove.

Harry spread his legs, finding his balance on the gently rolling deck, and crossed his arms. "Good news?" He glanced at the thick, cream-colored sheet of paper in Seth's hand.

"In a way." Seth rubbed his chin, considering the matter, and heard the rasp of a day's growth under his fingers. "She'll be at the annual Sweet Pea Ball this evening."

"That doesn't sound too bad," Harry said judiciously.

Seth shrugged.

"So why do you look like you've bitten into whale blubber?"

"It's one of those height of the season, oh-you-simply-*must*-attend events that everyone on *the ton* dutifully turns out for and makes silly fools of themselves."

Harry laughed a little, even as puzzlement drew a furrow between his brows.

Seth took a deep breath and laughed at himself, too. "Harry, you have to see one of these things to believe them. The women will spend a year's worth of your wages on one gown, and they'll be dressed to within an inch of their lives, squeezed into corsets and weighed down with jewelry that would keep your six kids eating for five years. The men…" He shook his head. "The men will wear black broadcloth and satin, and white shirts with collars so stiff and high you can't tuck your chin to your chest. When they get to the ball they will take off their coats and hats and gloves, and they will immediately put on another pair of gloves."

Harry stared at him. "Why on earth would they do that?"

"So that when they dance with a lady they will not soil her gown, or her skin, with their bare fingers."

Harry thought about that one for a moment, then started laughing. "That's a good joke, Seth," he said between chuckles. "Very good."

"I'm not joking." A sigh escaped him. He truly was back in England, land of the aristocrat.

Harry wheezed out another chuckle, and took a breath. "And you're going to this thing?" His big barrel chest, powerful with muscles built from hauling wet canvas across rigging and belaying heavy ropes, bounced up and down, as the paroxysms of mirth rippled through him.

"*What?*" Seth demanded, spreading his hands wide.

Harry pointed at him, tears squeezing out of his eyes. "You. You will be a hare amongst rabbits—a big loping, patched, piebald hare."

Seth smiled a little, looking down at himself. The trousers were acceptable enough, but his big bare feet, the ripped and stained shirt that was once his best, but now hung in tatters around his shoulders. His calloused hands sported rope burns, and were a far cry from the bathed and pampered gentility he intended to move amongst tonight.

"There's a thing about them you don't know, Harry. Appearance is everything. If I look and sound like them, they'll assume that I *am* one of them." The thought reminded him of the two women he'd left to their own devices below decks, and he stirred, folding the letter and sliding it into his trousers pocket.

Harry was looking out over the bulwark at the cobblestones on the dock, and the stone lip. His good humor had faded. "It's a strange world, indeed."

Seth recognized Harry's sudden change in mood. Mild alarm touched him. "Don't get all superstitious on me, Harry." Harry sometimes drew upon his exotic eastern upbringing, bringing forth snatches of Oriental wisdom that often proved prophetic. "I go to the ball, I see her, we leave for Ireland. That's it."

Harry shook his head a little, studying the swirling fog. "Step off the ship and you step into a foreign land where nothing makes sense. Strange worlds can be dangerous."

Seth gave a little laugh and clapped Harry on his broad back. "I grew up amongst these people, Harry. I'll be fine. Just fine."

Seth turned and hurried back down the stairs, and pushed open the cabin door.

He was greeted by the sight of the duchess lying with her eyes closed, soft whimpers escaping her, as Annie knelt between her thighs, her tongue lapping at her mistress' folds. They were fully occupied with each other.

Seth's cock sprung to immediate attention, hard and ready. He closed the door softly, removed his shirt, and loosened and dropped his pants as he moved to the end of the bed. He grasped the hips of the maid and swiftly thrust into her from behind. She gasped, and her hips pushed back against him, encouraging him. He was reminded yet again of the previous evening when he had mounted the duchess and she had writhed against him in pleasure and whispered in his ear, "Fuck me hard, Seth."

Blue blood. Lower class. They were all the same in the end. The elite weren't any better than those they disdained. Everything that had happened in Seth's life confirmed it, even this moment of primal pleasure.

He came with a growl of defiance and rage, throwing his head back, his hips and pelvis thrusting hard against the girl as she wriggled with pleasure.

As soon as he had caught his breath he escorted both women out of his cabin and off his ship, into the waiting carriage. He extracted a dollop of satisfaction by ignoring the buxom Duchess' drawled protests that he had not taken care of her.

But the satisfaction quickly melted, and the rage burned on.

* * * * *

Natasha glanced at the giant papier-mâché swan floating overhead, as did the other four hundred and fifty-five guests at the Sweet Pea Ball. Their delight, however, was probably genuine. They swirled around each other, greeting and gossiping, taking the measure of each other.

Did these events never change? Just last week she had been at the Abernathy's annual ball, an elaborate affair for the daughter of the Duke of Devonshire, where cigars wrapped in pound notes had been distributed to all the men and heart-shaped chocolates direct from Belgium were presented to each woman. Natasha released a heavy sigh and looked out the window.

The lights in the garden below beckoned. *Escape*. What she wouldn't give to be a world away from this place! Or even at the townhouse, tucked in her favorite chair while reading John Polidori's *The Vampyre*. Her mother would be horrified if she discovered that the headache that had been forcing Natasha to retire to her room early each evening these last few days had been a ruse that gave her privacy to read the lurid, shocking novel, and shiver over the deliciously wicked passages.

"Natasha, dear, will you please bring me a glass of punch?" her mother asked, fanning herself exuberantly with the fan she had purchased just that morning. It had been the most expensive fan in Madame le Boutelliers' shop, and absolutely lacking in good taste. Natasha knew her mother had chosen it deliberately, for Aunt Susannah had been with them and such an expense, so casually dismissed, was a subtle way of reminding her sister how much she owed her better-off older sibling. The point had not been lost on either Susannah or Natasha.

"Hurry," her mother added, "for I fear this heat shall be the death of me."

Resisting the urge to roll her eyes at her mother's dramatics, Natasha nodded and walked toward a liveried servant in a bright red jacket. The bewigged young man remained expressionless, though his gaze drifted toward the low décolletage of her gown. The side of his mouth curved the slightest bit.

Natasha didn't bother pretending to be shocked. In truth, the servant's reaction pleased her. The gown had been the most daring at Madame le Boutelliers' small store—a creation of royal blue silk with an extremely tight bodice and scandalously low neckline that made her full breasts appear larger. Her mother had approved the choice, believing Natasha had the same aim as her in mind—attracting a wealthy husband. Natasha had bought it solely for the shock it would cause.

How she longed to ruffle these haughty people who didn't care about her beyond the perennial examination of her marriageless state!

At the age of twenty, she was on the verge of becoming a spinster, an old maid—or so her mother reminded her at every opportunity. Every reminder, though, sent uneasiness rippling through her.

So Natasha smiled prettily at the servant, a silent thank-you for his admiration, took two glasses from the tray and began her return journey through the assembled mass of London's finest.

The air was already stifling. Too much perfume mingled with body odor made drawing breath a challenge. Hopefully the host would soon throw open the four sets of doors that led out to the courtyard.

A tall, slender man was speaking to her mother when she returned. Her father had already departed. He'd made it a point to extract himself from the gaiety at the first available moment. The card room had always held more appeal to him than dancing.

On occasion, she had seen the man talking so earnestly to her mother, and remembered him for his effeminate movements and speech. It was apparent in the way he used his hands when speaking, the graceful steps and the overall way he carried himself. But mostly what she remembered was the large, watery blue eyes that stared at her without blinking.

"Ah, there you are, my dear," her mother said, taking a glass from Natasha. "I would like you to meet Lord de Henscher."

Natasha curtsied and extended her hand. Lord de Henscher's thick red lips pulled back in a thin smile, while his pale blue eyes raked her up and down. He took her hand in his and lifted it to his lips. "Sholto Piggot, my lady. It is a pleasure to meet one so fair. Your mother tells me you enjoy dancing. I would be delighted if you were to add me to your dance card."

"She would be honored, my lord," her mother blurted, looking quite pleased with herself. Natasha penciled Lord de Henscher's name on her card under a quadrille with sharp movements of the pencil. She would not give him a waltz. She wanted the waltzes left open to men more familiar to her.

"Lady Munroe," Sholto said to her mother in his nasally voice as she wrote, "You look so fresh and young, one would think you and your beautiful daughter were sisters."

Natasha hid her grimace. It was little wonder the man thought they were sisters, for her mother had to be nearly ten years younger than him. He was lifting a quizzing glass to his eye to inspect them. The glass distorted the watery blue eye, exaggerating the red veins, as he looked from Caroline back to Natasha.

"Indeed," he pronounced, "you could easily pass as sisters."

Her mother tittered gaily, while her hand encircled Natasha's wrist and squeezed. A liveried manservant stepped up to Piggot's side and whispered in his ear. Caroline took the opportunity to say to Natasha in an undertone, "Could you at least try to be personable?"

Natasha smiled prettily for her mother, and for anyone who might be watching. "I don't care who he is, or what title he possesses."

Piggot nodded at the manservant then turned his attention back to them. "Lady Natasha, would you care to take a stroll about the gardens? The air in here is quite stifling, is it not?"

"A lovely idea, indeed," her mother replied, stiff smile in place.

Natasha accepted his extended arm, feeling rough broadcloth beneath her fingers and a spindly forearm below. He led her toward the nearest pair of double doors, and she hoped there would be others in the dimly lit gardens. Her mother might have at least offered to act as chaperone!

"Your mother tells me that you will be spending the entire Season here in London," Piggot ventured. "Are you looking forward to the extended visit?"

Natasha glanced up at him, and caught him staring straight down her bodice. No doubt from his height he could see more than most. She lifted a brow, and he abruptly shifted his gaze. "I find the sights of London stimulating," she said stiffly.

"I can think of many stimulating opportunities." His thin lips stretched into what she assumed was a smile, but the expression was so distorted it made her shiver.

They were out on the long balcony now, and the night air *was* welcome. However, the light was considerably dimmed out here. There were quite a few people lingering on the balcony and on the pair of stairs on either end that swirled down to the gardens. Despite the witnesses, Piggot slid his arm around her waist, pulling her closer to him. She caught her breath as his long, emaciated fingers stroked the underside of her left breast. The indecency of the man! Torn between slapping him silly and kicking him between the legs—a position she had heard was particularly painful—she stopped in mid-stride, which tore his arm away from her. He spun to face her, and merely lifted his brow a little, watching her.

With her heart pumping in her ears, she gave him one of her most brilliant smiles, to disarm him, took a half step forward to bring him within range, then stomped on his instep with the heel of her dancing shoe.

She heard his choked cry of pain as he bent over sharply, but didn't wait for more. She stalked back inside, fury and despair swelling her heart. Her mother was determined to find her a husband and now, after Natasha had resisted for so many years, it appeared she would literally push her into any vaguely suitable man's arms, regardless of the proprieties, or the price it might extol upon her daughter.

The walls of the trap were starting to close in. She could feel them shuddering closer. In all these years of scheming and plotting…had she extended her parents' goodwill on the matter of a husband to breaking point? Would they force the issue now?

If only…if only she had not met Vaughn and Elisa Wardell, her life would be considerably simpler!

Chapter Two

The footman's brows lifted all the way to his hairline. "I am sorry, sir, but I can not allow you entrance without the invitation."

Seth counted to ten. Twice. The young man had no idea how close he was to losing his relatively straight front teeth. "As I stated before, I left the invitation on the bureau in my study. Now, let me through. Your stubbornness is causing all these fine ladies and gentlemen to wait."

There were a group of cloaked and hatted people standing behind him, but he knew they were more interested in his situation than in gaining access to the ball, and that galled him. It had been so long since he had attended one of these damned things he had forgotten that an invitation would have to be produced to be allowed entry. The doorman's insistence on seeing his invitation was drawing attention to Seth—attention he did not want. He could feel his frustration mount with each head that turned curiously to study him.

And, too, the peaks of his brand-new shirt collar dug into his chin in a most uncomfortable way. The new styles were irksome to wear, and with each scratch he thought longingly of his comfortable shipboard rags. However, judging from the appreciative glances he gained from some of the bolder ladies watching him, the new style suited him well enough.

He forced a smile to his lips and addressed the doorman again. "It's as cold as hell—heck, out here."

"Perhaps your man could fetch the invitation for you."

"In Yorkshire?"

"I am sorry, sir." The footman didn't look at all sorry.

Salt-black fury flowered in him. Seth gripped the man's lapels in both fists and drew him closer, feeling the rage pounding at his temples.

The doorman's eyes opened wide, his mouth too.

Seth had no idea what he was going to do beyond the overwhelming desire to shake the man until his head rattled.

"Hey! See here!" came an indignant cry from behind.

Abruptly, before Seth could do more than lift the doorman off his feet, many hands were laid on his arms and shoulders, and around his wrists.

A large, rounded face inserted itself in front of Seth's gaze, peering up at him. "You don't want to hurt him, sir. He meant no disrespect. Let him loose, and we'll discuss this civilly."

Behind Seth, the delighted audience of gentlemen and their ladies were making sounds of shock and dismay, while gobbling up the drama with pure delight. The hypocrisy made his temple thud even harder.

But he dropped the doorman back on his feet, anyway. Come what may, he must gain entrance to the ball, and letting his damnable temper loose would not assist him.

He took a deep breath. Another.

The doorman scurried backwards like a frightened chicken, straightening his overcoat.

Seth nodded at the man with the rounded face—a much older man in hotel livery. Butler? Concierge? No matter, he was someone who knew how to deal with gentry and diplomatic situations. The manservants who held Seth back now ranged behind him. Clearly, he was a leader of some sort.

"Now, sir, if I could simply have your name, and someone to vouch for you, then the matter is done with," the concierge said with a pleasant smile.

Seth almost laughed. Bitterness touched him. Who would vouch for him here? And his name! He shrugged his coat back into place, and ran his fingers through his hair, to give himself time to answer. He couldn't give his real name, yet his real name would give him instant access…

"Harrow," he said at last, but did not add the expected, usual tail of titles. Nor did he add his first name.

"Harrow?" The concierge frowned, struggling to fit the name into his knowledge of the upper-class families. Clearly, the name was not instantly recognizable. Seth relaxed a little. They wouldn't, of course, be used to including that name amongst society anymore.

"Did you say Harrow?" came another voice from behind the concierge and his ranked men.

Seth caught his breath.

A man stepped around the grouped servants, limping quite badly. He was a rail-thin anemic-looking fellow, with large, watery blue eyes that reminded Seth of a frightened doe. He was dressed in absolutely correct evening attire, but not the latest fashion.

He stepped up to the concierge and raised a quizzing-glass to his eye. "Harrow?" he repeated. "Seth Harrow?" He blinked at him.

"You can vouch for the gentleman, Lord de Henscher?"

The man just looked at Seth, waiting for him to confirm his identity. Hating the very public revelation, Seth nodded, barely moving his head.

The man de Henscher gave a small nervous smile and thrust out his hand. "So pleased to meet you at last," he said, as Seth shook his moist, spindly hand.

The concierge and his men moved away.

Seth frowned. "You know me, sir?" he asked warily.

"By correspondence only. Sholto Piggot, Lord de Henscher, at your service, sir."

And finally, Seth coupled up the names and titles and realized why Piggot knew him. "Piggot. Pleased to meet you," he said with formal stiffness. "I was pleased to receive your letter this morning, informing me of this affair."

Piggot was drawing him into the foyer of the grand building, past the doorman who had taken up his place once more. "A mere trifling matter," Piggot assured him.

Seth did not point out that the man had signed all his correspondence over the years merely as "Piggot", with no mention of his title, which was why Seth had not recognized him. For nearly ten years Piggot had been acting as Seth's agent in England, and clearly had no wish to advertise that he was a lord dealing in common business affairs. Seth kept his mouth shut now, because the man had just helped him.

Piggot was leading him down a wide, carpeted corridor. At the end were four sets of double doors that must surely lead to the ballroom. But halfway along the corridor, another set of double doors opened up, and men were entering and leaving in pairs and groups, and the odd individual.

The smoking salon, Seth assumed. Piggot turned into the room, and Seth stifled his protest. He wanted to get to the ballroom. Now. But Piggot, like most men, would rather linger in the salon and drink inferior hotel brandy.

Piggot made an extended fuss of trimming and lighting his cigar, and puffing on it until it was drawing smoothly, and Seth reined in his impatience. His gaze shifted over the man, from his thinning, lifeless, carefully brushed hair, the thin lips and the odd twisted way he had of holding them, to the slender, nervous fingers and almost emaciated body. The lapels of the man's suit jacket were the slightest bit shiny and showing a hint of threadiness, and the hems of his pants were just a little bit faded. The shoes were bright with polish, but showed deep creases in the leather from much wear.

Piggot, then, had little money to support his title. No wonder he was in trade.

Finally, Piggot drew on the cigar with satisfaction, then handed it to Seth.

Seth shuddered at the thought of smoking a cigar another man's lips had touched. Was this a new custom, then? One that had become all the fashion since he had been away?

He did not want to appear rude, particularly since the man's timely intervention had saved him from pummeling a footman. He drew on the cigar and swiftly handed it back. He did not enjoy smoking as many men did.

"You have made me a tidy sum over the years, Harrow," Piggot said. "For that I thank you." He took another long draw on the cigar, savoring it.

"And I have appreciated your services," Seth responded.

Piggot stood with his hip cocked, and leaned his elbow on the mantelshelf, his hand hanging loosely, and Seth marveled at Piggot's unexpected appearance. Seth had always envisioned him as a large, barrel-chested man, who cared little about his dress, with sharp eyes and a head for business. From Piggot's looks, Seth judged him to have spent hours on his appearance.

The man was taking Seth's measure, too. His gaze drifted over him. Did he imagine it, or did Piggot's gaze pause for a moment in the vicinity just below his waistcoat?

"So…what brings you to London after ten years?" Piggot lifted his gaze to Seth's.

Uneasy with the man's perusal, Seth shifted on his feet. "A small business matter. Then I'm off to Ireland."

"Ah, I thought I detected a bit of brogue." Piggot stuck out his tongue and removed an offending piece of tobacco, then ran his tongue over his lips. "Black Irish," he judged with a knowing gleam in his eye. "That would explain the tantrum I just witnessed out there."

Seth clamped down on a flare of irritation. "One could say that, I suppose." He kept his tone even. Polite. "I am most anxious to return." He held Piggot's gaze. "Return to Harrow," he added deliberately.

Piggot blinked, visibly coupling Seth's last name with his destination. His brow rose the smallest fraction, the most shock an English lord could be permitted to show.

After a moment, Piggot tapped his cigar into the heavy crystal ashtray next to his wrist. "While you remain on English soil we should get better acquainted…personally. To assist our business arrangements. Perhaps tomorrow. Would brunch be too uncivilized for you?" Piggot's voice was a casual drawl, but his eyes speared Seth, relentlessly assessing him.

He'd had enough of this strange little game. "Perhaps." Seth straightened his cuffs and nodded his head. "Thank you for vouching for me."

Piggot nodded. "Anytime, Harrow. I shall find you later?"

"Certainly." It was the polite answer, but Seth had no intentions of being found at all. He headed for the doors, feeling the man's gaze on him the entire way.

* * * * *

Natasha found a quiet corner of the room, as far from her mother as geography would allow and, thankfully, far away from Piggot. The baron had reappeared, his mouth pulled back into a thin, meaningless little smile as he scanned the ballroom, no doubt searching for her.

She shivered at the memory of his fingers so near her breast. All she wanted was to go back to the townhouse and hide away in her room for the night, read her book, and forget about men like Lord de Henscher.

There was a group of three debutantes giggling and gossiping behind their fans, just to Natasha's left. She glanced at them. Her own first season had been barely three years ago, but comparing herself to the girls made her feel very old, and oddly tired. She had giggled and gossiped just like them, once.

"Oh, my goodness me. Look at that one," one of them said, staring towards the grand entrance of the ballroom. Another of them turned her head to look, and her eyes opened wide and her lips parted with a sigh.

Curious, Natasha followed the women's gazes. At the top of the short, broad flight of steps down to the ballroom proper, a man stood visually searching the room.

Her heart gave a fierce, odd little tug as she stared at him, and something low in her stomach seemed to roll over slowly.

Even from across the vast ballroom she could tell he was not comfortable here. Though he looked like any other peer of the realm in his black suit and snowy white shirt and cravat, there was a ruggedness about him that told her he fit an outdoor environment more naturally. There was an animal-like restlessness in his pose, which was at odds with almost every other man she knew. It made him different from all of them.

He stood a good head taller than most of the men present, and his hair was quite black. He had a breadth of shoulder that spoke of a man who enjoyed physical activity. As Natasha watched, he spread his jacket so he could plant his fists on his hips, and the tight trousers clearly displayed a flat stomach and muscled thighs.

She could not see what color his eyes were, but they were striking even from this distance, piercing in intensity as he surveyed the crowd.

Who was he searching for? She felt a sudden jab of jealousy, as she wondered who it was. Then her breath caught as she realized that his roving scrutiny had almost reached her.

His gaze skipped past her.

Natasha let her breath out with a rush, venting her acute disappointment, even as she mentally chided herself. What had she expected? That he would cross the room, bow and ask her to dance?

No, I want him to kiss me. And more.

She felt a touch of shock at her own daring thought, but with the honesty she had been forcing herself to cultivate these last few years, she acknowledged that yes, one glance at him had reduced her to a carnal wantonness.

Oh, to be taken by a man like that! He would satisfy a woman in *all* ways.

And that was when his gaze checked…and returned to her.

Her heart stood still.

He was staring at her with frank openness, with no alleviating smile, no nod of acknowledgment, not even a bow. He just stared, his gaze pinning her like a butterfly to the mount.

She thought she could see a hint of puzzlement in his expression, but the idea faded under the onslaught of wicked thoughts flooding her.

Yes, much more than a kiss! Her books, the ones hidden in the secret drawer at the bottom of her bureau, had been frustratingly unclear on exactly what happened to a woman who was "taken", although many of the heroines she read about seemed to enjoy the process as much as the dashingly handsome heroes. She had supposed, when she puzzled over the lack of details, that she might draw parallels from the rutting sheep and other farmyard animals she had observed growing up in the country…but the idea had not thrilled her when she applied it to men and women. It had seemed ridiculous and physically uncomfortable.

But now, with this man staring at her, she thought she understood the passion that drove such acts, if not the actual physicality of it. That passion burned in her chest, made her breasts tingle, and between her legs an aching throb began. She could feel each breath draw down her throat.

His eyes would not let her go. They seemed to be drawing her soul out of her body, bringing her towards him across the room. He was so different! So…alive. His whole body radiated his emotions.

He is a dangerous man.

But the caution did not calm her at all. On the contrary, recognizing the uncivilized edge in him made her heart beat faster. She could feel herself sway towards him, her breasts pushing against the bodice of the dress. Her nipples rubbed with delicious pressure against her camisole.

He took a step towards her, and Natasha's breath caught again and her heart leapt.

Another group of people pushing in through the double-doored entranceway brushed up against him, tearing his gaze away from her. He was forced to deal with them, accept the fellow's well-meant apologies, and Natasha could feel his frustration, could see it in every line of his body.

Then he turned away, searching her out again—she knew he searched for her with utter certainty. A thrill raced through her body when his gaze caught hers once more, however, he did not come towards her. He smiled a little, and it was almost a grimace.

Her disappointment this time was a tangible thing. It swept through her like hot acid, leaving her trembling. As clearly as she had read his frustration, his impatience, and the shock her appearance had wrought upon him, she read now his regret.

The corners of his perfect, full lips lifted in a little smile. His hand rested against his breast and he gave a small bow, merely an inclination of his head.

I regret, that bow told her. *It cannot be.*

She could not muster even a smile in return. She felt like weeping. She swallowed hard, forcing back the tears, and managed to give a small nod of her own. She kept her shoulders and back very straight, determined not to let him see how his silent rejection had devastated her.

But he saw through it. His smile grew warmer, showing the edge of fine, white teeth, and the warmth touched his eyes, bathed her in his good regard. Then he turned his gaze away, returning to quartering the room.

She felt chilled, almost ill. The trembling had worsened. She stood very still, waiting for the sick moment to pass.

Did he look for his lover, a wife, a mistress, or a friend? A business associate perhaps? *Let it be the last*, she wished silently, but knew it could not be. Whoever he looked for had been the reason he could not speak to her—kiss her—and a simple business associate would not make such demands.

The quadrille ended and dancers began to drift from the floor. The man on the stairs took advantage of the clearing dance floor to hurry down the steps, heading towards the other end of the long ballroom, away from her.

Natasha tried to bring her hurried breathing under control, to calm her heart, which beat at her stays with an alarming, almost painful flutter.

Lord Shelburne, the host of the annual ball, stepped up onto the musicians' dais, and acknowledged the polite applause of the assembled people. A hotel butler hurried over to him, and handed him a long golden rope with a big tassel on the end. The rope soared up to the ceiling, where it was attached to the huge swan hanging over the heads of the dancers.

There were squeals of delight from debutantes, as they hurried to clear the floor, while all the young single men scrambled to stand beneath the swan. There was a lot of good-natured jostling and shoving to find the perfect position beneath.

Shelburne pulled hard on the rope and with a loud crack, the swan split apart, showering the men beneath with hundreds of nosegays made up of thornless red roses and sweet peas.

The guests oohed and ahhhed in delight, laughing and clapping as the men fought to pick up as many of the small bouquets as they could. Then the little squeals and giggles began as each man sought out a favored lady and offered her the nosegay. To accept the nosegay also signaled agreement to be escorted to supper by the gentleman.

Natasha released a heavy sigh. It was all quite ridiculous, really. Why had she ever found the custom exciting, even thrilling? It was an expensive gesture that meant nothing at all. Did the rich have nothing better to spend their money on? She pursed her lips together and shook her head slightly. If only the duke had put his money toward helping those less fortunate. No doubt what he had wasted on this extravagance could have helped an entire poverty-stricken village.

Then her breath caught in a painful mass in the base of her throat, for skirting the mass of young men in the middle of the dance floor was *him*. And he was coming towards her.

Chapter Three

He was carrying a single rose, letting it hang from his hand carelessly, with none of the formal delicacy the others used to present their bouquets. He stopped in front of her, and Natasha saw the debutantes beside her pause from their fluttering over the bouquets they had received to send her a sharp glance.

She didn't care. He was studying her, that same thoughtful expression. His eyes were silver, framed by long, thick lashes. He was so tall, she had to tilt her head to look up at him. As she was quite tall herself, there were not many men tall enough to make her lift her chin.

He was absolutely striking in his beauty. The most gorgeous man she'd ever seen. The breathlessness and the painful fluttering of her heart returned. She found she was completely without words, could not even dredge up the polite nothing-sentences she often mouthed at these affairs.

He held out the rose, letting it lie across his palm like an offering. "Sweet peas are not for the likes of you. But this one…this…is you." His voice was low. It caressed her mind, swooped through her body, made her toes tingle.

She picked up the rose by the head. "It still has thorns."

"Yes." His voice dropped even deeper. "The danger beneath great beauty."

She looked up at him again, unable to keep her gaze from his eyes for longer than absolutely necessary. He was drawing her to him again. Standing this close to her, his body seemed to be tugging her even closer, a silent compulsion.

"Who are you?" she whispered.

He shook his head a little. "A lost soul, alas, who has just these last few minutes wished it were otherwise."

"Is that why you refuse me?" The *need* to ask that question! It had uttered itself despite her desire not to abase herself with a demand for explanations.

There was a smothered giggle to her left, and Natasha grew abruptly aware of their audience—every matron, debutante and male companion within earshot was gaping at them, scandalized by the raw conversation.

Resentment burned in her, for she knew that this man would not linger in her life—his unfettered attitude hinted that this society had no hold on him, and he would soon be gone. These people twittering around her were destroying the few moments she would have with him.

For a moment she was tempted to turn to them, and tell them exactly what she thought of them all. It would be such a relief to speak the truth, and walk away, bringing him with her. But she could not. As much as she chafed under the restrictions of her life, they were all she had.

She wished she could explain it to him, yet knew she could not because of the people around them. She hated the dilemma.

Perhaps he understood—enough to dissemble a little, to play to the people watching them. He was, in a small way, protecting her reputation. He straightened himself, squared his shoulders and gave the small bow acceptable for someone who is unsure of the rank and titles of the person he was meeting.

"Seth Harrow at your service, my lady."

Seth Harrow. No title. A commoner. Oh, mother would not approve! The thought sent a little shiver of delight through her.

"Natasha Winridge," she replied, deliberately not adding her antecedents, which included her father's titles and estates, and those of her mother's. She extended her hand.

He took her gloved hand and lifted it to his lips, gently placing a kiss on her fingers. Heat and moisture touched her knuckles, and something deep in the core of her tightened, strummed pleasurably.

"You're new to London?"

"You are very astute, Miss Winridge. I have only just arrived in London." He released her hand. "My ship is at port, and even now my crew awaits me."

A tall, broad-shouldered, narrow-hipped sea captain with too-long dark hair, tanned skin and incredibly exotic light eyes that were framed by long, black lashes. The man's eyes were gray like a winter sky—so pale compared to his dark hair and skin.

She folded her trembling hands together. "Tell me, do you fare from England?" It was a deliberate probe for any and all information.

He shook his head, and her hopes were dashed. Damn, why could he not live here?

"Actually, I am heading home to Ireland."

Ireland. Then he was not English. Her father would have an apoplexy if he knew she was conversing with an actual Irishman.

"I would have thought, Harrow," came a third voice, "that you would call the antipodes home."

Natasha hid her frustration at the untimely interruption.

It was Sholto Piggot, carrying two glasses of champagne. He stepped up beside them. "Albany," he said to Harrow. "Is that not what you call that quaint little whaling town from where you hail?"

He offered Natasha the second glass, which she refused with a curt shake of her head, before looking back at Seth Harrow. "Australia?" she asked.

"Indeed, Mr. Harrow has spent at least the past decade in Australia," Piggot said. He smiled thinly. He was standing far closer to her than necessary, to the point where she felt an overwhelming desire to step away from him.

Seth's gaze shifted from her to Piggot and back again. As she had been able to read other emotions from him, this time she sensed a sudden wariness from him.

"Although why one would want to live there is quite beyond me," Sholto Piggot continued. "The colonies are full of convicts and savages."

Instinctively, Natasha changed the subject. "I thought I detected an accent," she told Seth. "I just couldn't place it. Were you born in Ireland?"

"Aye, I was," he said, his brogue thick. His gaze shifted to her throat, and she knew he had spotted the visible pulse throbbing there.

He turned slightly and she caught a glimpse of gold at his ear. Her pulse skittered.

"You wear an earring?" Shock pushed the indelicate question from her before she could censor her words. She smiled inwardly. Oh, her mother would have vapors!

Seth gave a small, wry grin. "It's a custom amongst seafarers," he said, almost apologetically.

"I thought it was a custom amongst pirates," Piggot said, with a laugh.

Seth shook his head. "For anyone who lives upon the open seas, it's customary to mark the first crossing of the equator this way."

Natasha shivered, with more than the tingling anticipation and excitement of his presence. This man really did live a life of utter freedom. He had crossed the equator, had seen the other side of the world. No wonder he seemed so ill at ease in this stifling little society he moved amongst tonight.

"You must find all this terribly boring then," Natasha said, waving her hand around the room.

"On the contrary." His gaze dropped to her lips.

And with that simple glance, all the hard, hot pleasure rushed back through her again, leaving her breathless and faint.

She grew aware of her breasts rising and falling with each constricted breath she took, and was astonished to realize that the flesh between her legs had grown moist, and seemed to swell and throb. Beneath her skirts, she moved her thighs restlessly.

Oh, how she wanted him to sweep her up into his arms, to plunder her with kisses, to run his hands over her!

Movement beyond his shoulder caught her eye, and she refocused. A tall man was standing there, staring at her, and for a moment she felt a rush of confusion.

It was Vaughn Wardell, Marquess of Fairleigh and Viscount Rothmere, the man who had crushed her heart, three years ago. She had always thought that meeting Vaughn again would be the hardest challenge she had yet faced in her twenty years, and that her pride would be sorely tested when that meeting occurred.

But now, with Seth Harrow in front of her, she merely felt an odd sense of disjointed consciousness. She frankly assessed Vaughn—his rugged good looks and the endearing, cavalier smile she had fallen in love with...had it been love, though?

For suddenly, she was glad to see both him and the achingly beautiful woman on his arm—Elisa Wardell, now his wife. She realized in that moment of recognition that neither of them suffered fools gladly.

She beckoned, with a delighted smile, and Vaughn's smile broadened, and even a brush of relief touched his expression. Perhaps they had dreaded meeting her again as much as she had agonized over the meeting.

It all seemed so trivial now. She almost laughed at the whispers around her. It seemed everyone was braced for a confrontation except her.

Vaughn and Elisa came towards her. Both Piggot and Seth turned to look behind them, alerted by her gesture and smile.

Vaughn had not changed in the few years, save for a few pronounced lines around his eyes that to her consternation, made him even more appealing. Despite a wicked father, Vaughn had been a man who knew how to laugh and enjoy life to its fullest.

She had heard rumors that he and Elisa were content to live a quiet life, far away from society. She wondered what had brought them to London.

Vaughn smiled genuinely. "Lady Natasha, you have grown into an exquisite beauty." He lifted her hand in his and brought it to his lips. "What a pleasure to see you after all these years."

Natasha trembled, feeling very much like the seventeen-year old girl who had been rejected. Then she looked Vaughn in the eye and all her fear fell away. He dared her even now to be strong, to hold her head up high, to be that girl who had stood in a room full of people while her betrothed had sworn his love to another woman. This was Vaughn—the man by whom she measured all other men.

And he was smiling warmly with reassurance and kindness.

"Lord Fairleigh—" she began.

"Vaughn," he said, his tone telling her that he would not accept any formality between them.

She laughed under her breath and grinned. "Very well, *Vaughn,* it is wonderful to see you as well." It was the absolute truth. She was deeply glad of his company at this moment, for it reminded her of the promise she had made herself three years ago, when Vaughn had publicly declared his feelings for Elisa. At that time she had sworn an oath to herself to never play the hypocrite again. Truth would be the only coin she would use. Now, with Vaughn standing before her, she was reminded once more of the courageous example he had given her that had led to that promise. "What brings you and Elisa to London?"

Elisa kissed Natasha on the cheek. "Raymond is attending Eton this year, and I can't bear to be apart from him. We're staying a while to help his transition to boarding school. It can be a frightening experience for young boys." And she smiled up at Vaughn, sharing a private moment.

Vaughn glanced at Piggot, and nodded. "Piggot." That was the full extent of his acknowledgement, and it told her that Vaughn didn't like Piggot, either. Vaughn was not one to hide his feelings.

Vaughn was turning to Seth. "Williams, isn't it? Oxford. 1822?"

Seth shook his head. "Sorry. Harrow, Seth Harrow." He held out his hand.

Vaughn took the offered hand, frowning. They stood eye to eye and he cocked his head a little. "Really?" Then he shook his head, like he was clearing his thoughts. "I apologize for my mistake. You bear a striking resemblance to an old friend. We both shared a miserable time, our first years at Eton."

Seth shrugged and spread his hands. "I'm a simple sea captain."

Vaughn nodded. "I see that," he said, pointing to Seth's earring.

Elisa touched Vaughn's arm. "You did promise me a waltz." Her voice was delightfully musical.

Vaughn glanced at the musicians settling back into their chairs on the dais, then offered Elisa his arm.

Elisa pressed a card into Natasha's hand. "Please call on us," she said. "I would be delighted to receive you."

Natasha slipped the card into her pocket. "I will," she promised. It was a promise she knew she would keep.

The two glided onto the dance floor.

Natasha looked at Seth. All good humor had left him.

Piggot seemed very quiet as well. "Will you both excuse me?" he asked. He didn't wait for their reply, but slipped away.

She looked up and found Seth watching her, his gaze gliding over her, from the diamonds in her hair, to the bows on her silk slippers, stopping only briefly at the low neckline of her gown. Why did she suddenly feel as though she stood naked in a room full of clothed people?

"What was Fairleigh to you?" he asked, his voice so low no one else could hear.

Natasha cleared her suddenly dry throat. "We were engaged once."

His dark brows lifted. "Ah. That would explain the change in your complexion."

Thankfully he did not give her that flash of sympathy she so despised. "Vaughn is a wonderful man. He treated me with nothing but kindness and respect."

He leaned forward, his lips grazing her ear. "His wife must be an inordinately astounding woman for him to have bypassed you."

His hot breath against her ear made the blood in her veins sizzle. "Thank you, Mr. Harrow, but you do not have to compliment me."

"That was truth, Lady Natasha. I wouldn't bother with complimenting one such as you."

"Why not?" she asked before she could stop herself.

"Because you hate the trappings of this world as much as I do. You have heard many compliments, but don't believe any of them."

She licked her lips. "How do you know that?"

He pointed to the rose in her hand. "I read your face. And I know these people..." He waved his hand around the room, including everyone there. "Your parents want you to marry, but you have no wish to be tied to a husband. You look as though you'd rather be anywhere else than at this ball, possibly even this country. You are looking for a place where you can be yourself."

She swallowed hard. How had he read her so plainly? How could he know her most secret thoughts, when not even her mother knew she yearned for so much more in life than to be a pretty ornament for a peer of the realm?

"You are right, Mr. Harrow. For many years I wanted only to make my parents happy in that regard, but no longer."

"What happened?"

There was an expression in his eyes, an interest there, that told her he would understand, would perhaps even empathize. "I met Vaughn and fell in love with him," she confessed.

"And you have not found a man who can replace him?" he asked, his voice matter-of-fact.

She shook her head. "No, that's not it at all. Vaughn—Lord Fairleigh—taught me how much more there was to life than my parents' ambitions for me. And no man can give me that..."

"Freedom?" he asked.

Her heart jumped. "Yes."

He watched her with those silver eyes, not missing even her smallest reaction.

Nervous, and embarrassed she'd been so blunt, her gaze shifted to his cravat, and then lower to his wide chest. It did not help her uneasiness. Seth Harrow had the body of a man used to long hours onboard a ship. Even now, fully clothed, she could imagine what he looked like bared to the waist. Hard muscle would contract beneath his olive skin with each movement. The corded sinew gave him a chiseled perfection the majority of the men she knew would never attain because of their pampered lifestyle, where eating and drinking were their only sport.

He reached up and brushed a wayward lock of hair from his face. She wished the gloves did not cover his long-fingered hands. He'd have masculine hands, no doubt callused and roughened from the hard work they had seen.

An image entered her mind, of long-fingered hands sliding around her bare waist, and she shivered.

"Is Piggot one of your suitors?" he asked, bringing her thoughts back to the present.

"I fear that he will be calling on me soon. My mother seems to favor him."

He lifted a dark brow. "Yet you do not?"

She pursed her lips. "I do not."

His gaze eyes flitted over the crowd, and Natasha felt his sudden disinterest like a slap to the face. How young and ridiculous she must seem to him, standing here complaining about her life.

"Who is it you search for?" she asked.

"An old friend," he confessed, an amused smile tugging at his lips. "Do you know Countess Innesford?"

Natasha nodded. "Yes, I do. She and my mother attended a soiree just last week."

That caught his attention. "Do you know if she has arrived?"

The countess, though only sixty, was not a woman who liked to dance. On the contrary, once she sat, she rarely moved, preferring to watch everyone else's affairs with an eagle eye. She had always seemed sad to Natasha, no doubt because her husband had been ill for quite some time.

Natasha looked for and spotted the countess sitting with a small group of older women talking amongst themselves.

"There she is. Shall I introduce you?"

"Please," Seth said, straightening his jacket and standing taller. He extended his arm, and Natasha took it, feeling the muscles beneath her fingers clench. Was he nervous? Who was the countess to him?

They stopped before Countess Innesford, who lifted her chin to examine Natasha.

Natasha's gaze lifted to Seth. He had gone completely still. She could feel him trembling. "Lady Innesford, I would like to introduce a friend of mine."

Lady Innesford smiled at Natasha, and turned to acknowledge Seth. Abruptly, her smile disappeared. She stood up, almost knocking over the chair in her haste, facing Seth. She had gone quite pale.

Natasha stared at the older woman. The countess was always composed. She had never seen her at a loss for words…until now.

"Seth Harrow, may I present Countess Innesford. Lady Innesford, this is Seth Harrow, Captain of the good ship…" She looked at Seth to supply the name of his ship.

"The *Artemis*." Seth stepped forward and lifted the countess' hand. He bowed low over it.

"Harrow?" the countess murmured. Then she nodded. "Mr. Harrow." She shook her head, as though to clear it, then abruptly pulled her hand from his.

Seth straightened up and stepped back. He was pale. "Please excuse me." He nodded to Countess Innesford. "My lady." Without another word he turned on his heel and left.

The countess watched his departure. "How do you know him, Natasha, dear?"

"I only just met him," Natasha replied. She hid her fury. How dare the countess treat Seth so horribly! "He is a sea captain, and an associate of Lord de Henscher."

"A commoner," the countess said with a sniff.

Natasha lifted her chin. "I admire him."

The countess smiled, though it didn't reach her eyes. "You know so very little of men, dearest Natasha. Stay away from Mr. Harrow. Men like him are dangerous. They promise you the world, then leave you with nothing." She sighed heavily, and her hand on her walking cane trembled. The countess had a reputation for being unflappable, yet a simple Irish sea captain had managed to completely fluster her.

But the countess swiftly recovered her composure, turning to skewer Natasha with one of her piercing glances. "I saw you speaking to Lord and Lady Fairleigh." The countess clasped her shaking hands together. "I am surprised you would give them the time of day considering what a fool they made of you—

barging into your party and announcing for all the world to hear that he would marry that whore. He is fortunate you are even civil."

Natasha forced a smile. "Lord and Lady Fairleigh are, and will always be, dear friends of mine, Lady Innesford."

The countess shook her head. "One day you will learn that there are people in this world that do not deserve forgiveness."

"Everyone deserves to be forgiven."

"Not everyone, dear." Her lips quirked. "When you have lived as long as I, you too, will understand this truth." And she turned her head to look back in the direction Seth had disappeared.

Chapter Four

Seth climbed the stairs blindly. He took them two at a time in his haste to leave the stuffy, overfilled ballroom. His heart hammered in his chest, whispering "Faster!" with each galloping beat.

He had to stay controlled. Now was not the time to let his damned temper loose. He had traveled too far and waited too long to beckon disaster to him—as he would surely do if he didn't rein in his mood and his tongue.

But he could not catch his breath to save his life, for ugly guilt kept battering at him. What had happened to his mother?

When he had been forced out of Ireland, fifteen years ago, she had been a vibrant woman in her fortieth year. In fifteen years she had aged twice that. Covered in unrelieved black from head to toe, her body had become frail. Her eyes had been as hard as ice, though, as she had stared at him as if he were no better than an insect.

Worse, he had seen a fleeting moment of recognition, then felt the instant rejection—all in one heartbeat. She had ripped her hand from his, as though she could not stand his touch, and that was the worst hurt.

His mother hated him. No—she *loathed* him

His stride lengthened, until he was pounding down the long, carpeted passageway, each heel striking a muffled blow against the pile. He reached the end of the dark, shadowed hallway, and knew he could not afford to return yet. He was not ready to face her again.

He opened the nearest door, and shut it firmly behind him and took a deep breath.

Silence, and blessed stillness. Dark shadows, relieved only by a solitary, forgotten oil lamp sitting on a dark mahogany desk in the far corner, where a scatter of papers, a heavy ashtray with the remains of a cigar and a brandy balloon with a puddle of gold liquid at the bottom sat, abandoned. A man's room.

It wasn't the *Artemis*. There was no small breeze ruffling his hair, no gentle, soothing rocking of deck boards beneath his feet. Seawater did not gurgle under the running bows, but it would serve as an escape for now.

He looked around, as the overwhelming pounding of his heart subsided, taking in the dark paneling, the tall bookcases, the settee and pair of leather wingback chairs. On a low sideboard behind the desk was a large silver tray, laid out with crystal decanters, lace doilies and a silver ice bucket.

Seth lifted the first carafe his hands fell upon, dumped the stopper, and drank deep. After the initial hard bite, the liquor warmed its way down to his knotted stomach. He saw again his mother's icy eyes, and felt the little jerk as she pulled her fingers from his, and gripped the narrow neck of the bottle harder, drawing another deep breath.

He had expected anger. In the last fifteen years he had played out in his mind every conceivable variation of his return to London, and he had known anger was inevitable. Mary Williams was pure Irish. It was from her he had acquired his black Irish temper. His personal acquaintance with the beast told him that when he finally faced his mother once more, anger was as sure to rise as the sun he watched each morning from the deck of the *Artemis*.

No, it was not the anger that dismayed him.

He took another long swig, closing his eyes to push away the memory of her cold gaze. She had stared at him as though he were a stranger.

* * * * *

Free at last of the attention of the countess, Natasha hurried after Seth. He had been far ahead of her, but she had seen him bounding up the stairs as if the hounds of hell were on his heels. At the top he'd turned right. Clearly, he did not intend to leave the ball, and while he remained in the building, she would find him, no matter what. Man he may be, and a confident sea captain, but somehow the countess had hurt him. The bleak expression in his eyes had been unmistakable.

She hurried across the ballroom floor as fast as the crush of people would allow her, and finally made the stairs. She picked up her skirts, and climbed up the center of the wide flight, avoiding the congestion at the handrails. She would have liked to have taken them two at a time, in the same manner as Seth, but knew she would not recover from such exertion while laced in so tightly. She made the top of the stairs, and clutched at her cinched-in corset, feeling her heart shudder against the stays with a fluttering beat that scared her.

She walked as quickly as her breath would allow her down the corridor. On the right it was open to the ballroom below, protected only by the same thick stone balustrade that adorned the stairs. There were people standing there, watching the dancers below, and gossiping amongst themselves. They took no notice of her passing.

The corridor turned sharply to the left, and along this length there were very few people, for the corridor merely led further into the building. There were narrower corridors leading off from it—service hallways, she assumed. She glanced down one as movement caught her eye, and found herself coming to a complete halt, her eyes widening.

The service hallway ended with a blank, unadorned door, but standing in front of the door were Vaughn and Elisa. They stood facing each other, their shoulders brushing the door, and they were both so absorbed in each other they failed to notice her standing at the other end of the corridor, her mouth opening in shock.

The pair was in each other's arms, and Natasha was instantly reminded of the naughty books she hid under her mattress. Vaughn bent over his beautiful wife, his mouth plundering hers. His tongue slid over her lips, tasting them, as his arms held her tightly against him.

Natasha stepped quietly to the corner of the corridor, so that she was all but hidden by the wall, and unashamedly watched, as her heart thundered and her whole body seemed to throb along with it.

Vaughn bore Elisa backwards until her back met the wall behind her, his hands about her waist. He gave her a wicked grin, kissed her firmly but swiftly on the mouth, before moving his lips over her throat, following the long, graceful curve down to her chest. His hands were busy behind her dress, and as he reached the slope of the top of her breasts with his mouth, the top of her dress sagged around her shoulders.

Elisa gave a small sigh that was almost a chuckle of laughter, her head rolling back against the wall and her eyes closing. She did not seem alarmed by Vaughn's actions.

When he tugged at the dress, to bare her breasts, she buried her fingers in his hair, and drew his head to them. Vaughn began to lick and stroke one of the pale colored nipples with his tongue, tugging on it with his teeth, and Elisa made a noise that was more primal than anything Natasha had ever heard, and her knuckles whitened as she clenched her hand in Vaughn's hair.

Understanding burst through Natasha. Elisa wanted that sort of attention. She welcomed it. She even deliberately sought the attention by not wearing a corset beneath her dress, making herself completely accessible for her husband.

Natasha turned away from the pair in the service hallway, leaving them their privacy, and leaned against the wall, letting her heart recover. Her books had never been this explicit. The "act", when they spoke of it, was described in frustratingly veiled references, and never had they portrayed the act as the earthy, mutually pleasurable activity Vaughn and Elisa had just revealed to her. The books had painted the love act to be a flowery, poetic marvel.

Seth. Her heart jumped again. Seth would be earthy. Seth would find it a mutually pleasurable activity. And with that thought, her whole body tightened and thrummed and an ache began between her legs. Seth.

She hurried after him, knowing that even though she intended to offer comfort, that Seth was the sort of man to demand more than simple comfort alone.

*****

Behind him, Seth heard the very soft sound of the door opening and closing. For a moment he froze, the decanter half-raised to his lips. With a mental curse, he lowered it to the tray, making the motion seem casual, unconscious. With his back turned, his hand was hidden, as he delved inside his jacket for the knife he normally kept in his boot.

For too long he had lived by his wits, and never forgot to keep his face to the door. He was astonished he had allowed this moment with his mother to disturb him to such a degree that he had failed to follow elementary precautions.

The next sound he heard was the unmistakable swish of lace and taffeta. He relaxed a little, and turned to face the woman, dropping his knife back into the pocket.

Natasha Winridge.

For a moment, his heart stopped. He found himself again tallying up the delicate, classic details about her that had struck him with such pleasure the first time he had seen them. There was the peeping toe of a satin-covered slipper beneath the lace edging of her petticoat. The lace edging was also on show, for she had lifted her satin skirts with one small hand, to clear the floor as she walked, and now she stood frozen just inside the door, her big dark blue eyes staring at him.

Then there was the trim waist—most certainly only a handspan around, for him. His fingers would meet at the dip over her spine he just knew was there. Her hips would be a sweeping curve from there, and he would be able to rest his hands on them, feel the heat of her soft flesh. From there he could slide his hands up her torso to the ripe, round breasts that rose from the low-cut ball gown. Fashions had clearly progressed while he had been away. Women in the colonies were still wearing the high-waisted frocks that fell from armpit to ankle. He had been astonished at the full-skirted gowns London considered to be essential now—the skirts were supported by layers of petticoats and starching. And the sleeves…

On Natasha, the drop sleeve device all the women were wearing seemed like a most delicious strategy to capture attention. The sleeves actually sat off her shoulders, and were so ridiculously puffed and ruffled that they looked in danger of sliding right down her arms, pulling the rest of the dress with them.

The provoking idea was more than enough to keep a man's attention riveted firmly on her creamy white shoulders and the bounty beneath. Seth could feel his body tighten in response, and his heart, which had been steadying, gave a little fluttering half beat, before hurrying on. Suddenly, he wished he had a glass of the port he had just been swigging, so he might knock it back and let the burning of the alcohol distract him from the low pull at his groin.

Then he noticed the expression in her eyes. They were soft, and full of sympathy. Fury touched him. He wanted no man's sympathy—especially not this beautiful, spoiled woman to whom the idea of being totally alone in the world, of being discarded and shunned, was inconceivable.

As she moved toward him, her silk skirts swishing with each step, he deliberately immersed his mind in crudities, as a way of punishing her for her ignorance.

He imagined those long legs wrapped around his waist as he thrust into her. God, but she was ripe for the plucking! His gaze settled for a moment on the swell of full breasts above her low-cut gown, the pale globes threatening to spill over. He groaned inwardly. What he would give to bury himself to the hilt and forget about this disastrous night! Perhaps he should take her to Ireland with him. She would be a very nice diversion.

Then every delicious thought scattered, and his mind stuttered to silence, for she circled her arms about his waist, laid her head against his shoulder, and…just held him. For a moment he couldn't even breathe. Everything about her enveloped him—her sweet perfume, her soft body, and the insistent push of her breasts against him.

How long had it been since a woman had tried to comfort him? Always they sought him out for sex, for mating, expecting nothing else in return but a sound fucking. But she was different. She held him out of compassion.

He closed his eyes and inhaled deeply of her scent—an exotic blend of floral and spices. Her hand moved up and down his back, soothing him, unconsciously causing a deep ache in his groin. It seemed all the blood in his body had raced to his cock, which throbbed against the buttons of his pants.

God help him, but he wanted her, this innocent young woman who knew nothing of his sordid past. It was no casual need that strummed through him, now. Her empathy had changed it, had reached deeper than the superficial bodily ache. Even as she cuddled closer, her cheek resting against his shoulder, his arms remained at his sides while warning bells sounded in his head.

This woman alone had sought him out in a dark room, while over five hundred people milled about downstairs. But what if someone walked in on them? The comforting embrace would be misinterpreted and scandal would rock the ton.

Yet he already knew Natasha would not care what others thought. He had seen it on her face the first instant he saw her. She found the excesses as tedious and grueling as he did. No, she would not be happy married to an effeminate shipping magnate or any other rigid peer of the realm. She wanted a man, a real man. She had said as much to him downstairs—not in those words, because she did not have the experience to recognize what made her so restless and dissatisfied. But he had recognized it, just as he had recognized her stubbornness, her determination to defy her entire world, if it would give her what she wanted.

She had understood his pain, even if she did not know the details, and now offered comfort, even though her mother and every other woman in her life must have instilled in her the dangers of being in a room alone with a man.

She was a woman of rare courage. If she knew the dangers, and her wide eyes when she first stepped into the room told him that she did, then she had deliberately flaunted conventions to take what she wanted.

His heart was starting to hurt as he put it together. She had spoken of Vaughn Wardell teaching her to value a true relationship, not an empty marriage. And now she had sought him out.

She wanted him, Seth Harrow. She wanted the pleasures he could bring her. Virgin she may be, but there had been awareness in her eyes, on the ballroom floor, that convinced him she understood the mating dance.

Finally, he allowed himself movement—a test of her intentions. His hands moved to circle her waist, and he smiled as his fingers touched each other behind her.

Her breath caught in her throat, a tiny hitch. She looked up at him, her long dark lashes shielding the desire he saw there.

Excitement thrummed through him. "Why do ye follow me, Natasha?" His voice was husky with longing.

He could feel her heart pumping wildly against his chest. She licked her lips, and her eyes dropped under his gaze. It was a telling sign. She knew, yes, but she could not bring herself to speak the words. Her courage had brought her only this far.

Pleasure thrilled through him. The combination of innocence and wantonness was overwhelming. He lifted a hand from her waist to the back of her soft, sweet shoulder, and tugged gently, so that her back arched away from him. He felt her hips beneath the starched petticoats, pressing against his swollen cock, and her breasts were thrust towards him.

He cupped one of them with his other hand. She gasped, stiffened, and he thought she would pull back. Instead, she looked up at him and her beautiful blue eyes narrowed a little. Then she relaxed, all within the space of a second.

Yes, she knew what she sought.

"I could see you were upset by the countess' behavior," she said, and her voice was low, controlled.

He brushed his thumb over her nipple, and her breath caught. Pink tinged her cheeks, but she did not pull away. He smiled as the bud tightened beneath the silk gown and rigid material of her corset.

"That feels positively wonderful," she breathed. There was a devilish smile on her full lips, and his excitement leapt to a higher plane, the surge of it battering at his mind and body.

He could not help himself. His mouth slanted over hers, his tongue stroking the seam of her lush lips, asking for entry. Tentatively, the lips opened and her tongue caressed his in a bold experiment, while her hands latched onto his shoulders.

He could drown himself utterly within her. He could sink into the sensual pleasures she offered, ignore every demand that hammered at his life, and drink of her until it all went away and she was all that remained.

He grasped her bottom through the petticoats, and pulled her tighter to him, rubbing his thick arousal against her belly. He heard her light gasp, and then her soft moan. It was a true wanton's exhalation, and it was the most erotic sound he had ever heard. Before he lost his restraint altogether, he ripped his mouth from hers. He was amazed to realize he was panting.

"Did ye mother never teach ye how dangerous it'd be in a room alone with a man?"

The side of her mouth lifted slightly, and her passion-filled eyes drifted closed for a moment. "I know what I want and it stands before me."

The knowledge in her expression acted like a goad. He slid his hand beneath the heavy skirts, searching for and quickly finding the slit in her drawers. He clenched his jaw against the groan of delight that seized him as he touched her there.

But she did not constrain herself. She fell against him with a low, womanly moan of pleasure, as he found her hot, wet center. He stroked her until she was panting. His thumb brushed over her clit, and her breath hitched.

There was such profound excitement in stroking a woman and knowing it was the first time she had ever experienced such pleasure. He did not know if he would have the strength to stop. Surely she would find this too overwhelming for her innocence, and tear herself away?

"Tell me to stop and I will," he demanded, his voice ragged.

Her chest heaved as she stared up at him. "Don't stop." Her voice cracked.

With a groan, he lowered his head and kissed her, his tongue dancing with hers as he slipped a finger inside her. Her honeyed walls gripped him tight. Heaven help him, she was a virgin. So hot, so tight…his cock throbbed. His whole body ached with the surges of pleasure rushing through it.

He lifted her, crossed the room and laid her down gently on the settee. Her gaze flitted over him, and settled frankly on his prominent erection. Her cheeks bloomed with color despite her daring.

It made him recall what he had forgotten in the last few moments—that she was the daughter of a lord, and innocent, to boot. She was destined to marry a man with title and wealth. That man would expect his wife to be a virgin when he came to her on her wedding night. The society she lived in would crucify him for sullying one of their daughters, but the punishment they reserved for her would be far, far worse. They may not physically beat her, but this society had other, powerful ways of making a woman's life miserable and empty.

She licked her full lips, before meeting his gaze once more. God, he needed release. He trembled with it.

He lifted one of her dainty feet, took off her shoe, and tossed it aside. The other quickly joined it. His fingers encircled her ankles, drawing upward over the soft silk of her stockings, baring her skin to his gaze. Her long, slender legs were creamy white and as soft as silk against his fingers.

How he would love to undress her, to take the time to unveil every inch of her pale skin. But the music floating up from downstairs reminded him where they were and that the absence of a young titled woman would soon be noted.

Time was crowding him. Though his instincts were telling him to walk her to the door and escort her back downstairs, he could not end it that way. He wanted to leave a small fragment of himself with her—an indelible mark on her soul.

He knew what he had to do.

* * * * *

Nastasha's heart hammered loudly as Seth looked down at her, his striking eyes shimmering with a promise she didn't fully understand. The sides of his mouth lifted in a sensual smile that sent excitement rippling along her spine.

She had already experienced so much that was thrillingly new. She knew she would spend many hours turning it over in her memory, studying it and recalling the rush of feelings and emotions he touched off in her. For now she simply accepted all that was happening, absorbing it.

He went to his knees beside the settee, and used his hands to spread her thighs. She was puzzled, but before she could articulate her question, he pulled her bottom close to the edge, and bent his head.

Her breath left her in a rush as his long, velvet-smooth tongue stroked her slit. She could not believe his daring, nor her own, but she could not stop him to save her life. Her fingers latched on to his shoulders, and she squeezed with each flick of his tongue.

Though her better judgment told her to run, she could not deny the pleasure he gave her. Her body hummed, pulsing with an energy she had never known. She glanced at the closed door, knowing they could be caught at any moment. All it would take is someone to open it, and she would be forever ruined. The scandal!

And though she knew the risk, she could not stop him. Instead, she glanced down at him, mesmerized by the sight of him pleasuring her. His fine silky hair brushed against the insides of her thighs. His long lashes cast shadows upon jutting cheekbones, and as though sensing her perusal, he looked up.

Her stomach tightened when she saw unmistakable desire in those silver depths. His tongue flicked over the tiny nub of flesh, making her shift her hips. She moaned and was amazed at the animal sound emerging from her, but Seth's only reaction was the sides of his mouth lifting just a little.

She closed her eyes as the tension within her body tightened. Then his hand covered her breast, his fingers caressing the nipple through the thick fabric of her gown...and she was lost.

Her breathing quickened and she was lifted higher and higher with each stroke of his tongue and his fingers, until she reached a pinnacle, the like of which she had never before known. Her body pulsed, her channel contracted as she rode it out, her fingers digging into his shoulders.

When her heart returned to a normal beat, she opened her eyes. Seth was still on his knees, and gently pulled her dress back into a decorous state. She could see his erection, swelling against the fabric of his pants.

Understanding flared in her. By rights, Seth should have his pleasure, too. She yearned to ease his ache, and knew that he would not dare take her here. They had risked too much already. Her channel still throbbed, with a deep ache, one she now knew could only be satisfied by his length filling her.

He leaned forward, kissed her hard. She tasted alcohol, and another flavor that she realized with a start was her own essence. "You must go now," he said against her lips, and then he stood, bringing her with him.

As she swayed, finding her balance, he retrieved her slippers and slid them onto her feet with gentle fingers. Natasha walked to the door on unsteady legs, finding it hard to believe that scant moments before she had been a naïve girl, with little knowledge of making love to a man. Now she was a woman, completely aware of the pleasure a man could give her. Her body ached for the ultimate completion that she knew only Seth could provide.

"I want to see you again," she blurted before she could stop herself. The thought of him sailing off to Ireland, after what had just happened, was too horrible to contemplate.

He grinned boyishly. "And you shall, but for now you must return or someone is sure to come looking for you."

She stared at him, taking in every detail of his handsome face, settling on his mouth that had just pleasured her. How she yearned to give him the pleasure that he had so skillfully given her. "Let them," she replied. "I don't care."

"You should." His answer was a whiplash. Then he sighed, and ran his hand through his hair, ruffling it in an agreeable way. "There's so much you don't understand, that you cannot know, that I dare not explain to ye. You must trust me in this. Now is not the time to recklessly abandon your life."

"But—"

He laid a finger across her mouth. "Trust me, lass." His gray eyes stared into hers, willing her to accept it.

Finally, she nodded. "I gave you my trust the moment I walked into this room, and you did not disappoint me. So I will trust you once again. Thank you, Seth Harrow."

Chapter Five

Seth found the brandy decanter and poured himself a thick, solid belt of the fine gold liquid. He drank, keeping his mind blank, then finished it off in one swallow. He still trembled.

He set the glass down on the mahogany table with a thud, and looked at the door Natasha had just passed through. What in God's name had he been thinking? He ran a hand through his hair. He could have ruined her in an instant. Destroyed her, and caused a scandal the likes of which London had not seen for decades.

After the six years he'd spent in MacQuarrie Harbour, he knew better than to let his passions rule his common sense. He'd slipped, and slipped badly, tonight. He could not afford to make such a mistake.

Yet how sweet she had tasted! He smiled as he recalled her soft moans, and the feel of her fingers digging into his shoulders. How he wanted to bury himself deep within her tight channel, to teach her all the ways to make love. He lifted his fingers to his nose, inhaling her musky scent. *Leave her alone, Seth*! his conscience taunted. He shook the memory away, as well as the desire.

He made his way back to the staircase, wanting nothing more than to escape into the night, back to the *Artemis*. Back to the familiar. He had seen his mother, and had his answer. Harry had been right—this place was an alien land for him, now. There was nothing more for him in London.

Except Natasha.

He frowned. He had promised to meet her again, and he would abide by the promise, but the meeting must be the last. He must sever the tie that had sprung up between them, as gently as he could. Perhaps he should ask Vaughn Wardell the trick of it, since he'd managed to maintain their friendship.

And you would be the second man to break her heart.

Guilt prodded him, and he tried to argue his way around it. She had found him. He had not encouraged her in the slightest. She had enticed him, but no excuse would push away the truth—that a connection had been born between them this night, and it would never go away.

As he descended the staircase to the ballroom floor, he barely noticed the stares of a group of young women. Their whispers and soft giggling might have amused him at any other time.

From the corner of his eye he saw Natasha. She stood with another, older woman, and Piggot. The strange man's hand rested possessively on her hip. Her cheeks were still pink. Although she was smiling pleasantly, her eyes were wary. She saw him, and his heart skipped a beat as her lips curved into soft smile that lit up her whole face.

One more night in London…to see her again.

"Why, Seth Harrow, seeing you standing there in your fine gentleman's clothing, I might be led to believe it was you who went slumming last night." The husky voice behind him was familiar, and the words confirmed the woman's identity. The whoring duchess he'd bedded last night was now standing behind him. Seth swore under his breath at the fates, but managed a smile as he turned to face her. He knew he could not bluff his way out of it. The duchess knew who he was, she would not have dared speak of such indelicate matters otherwise.

She was dressed in an expensive gown—green, of course. It was completely decorous, but still managed to display her ample chest to full effect.

There was a heat in her eyes Seth knew all too well. She licked her lips as her gaze roamed down his body, settling in the vicinity of his cock. The heat turned to an open hunger. Seth was amused at her bawdy public behavior. A well-behaved lady—especially a duchess—would normally never lower her eyes below a man's waist.

Judging by the open hunger in her eyes, she had forgiven him for tossing her out this morning. She leaned toward him, her chest brushing his arm. "Can I come aboard tonight, sailor?" Her lips grazed his ear.

Seth couldn't help glancing toward Natasha. There was a tiny chance she'd failed to see the exchange, and he couldn't resist the need to confirm it. Even if everyone else in this room was blind to the duchess' blatant overtures, Natasha would see, and he would spare her that hurt if he could.

Lady luck certainly was not with him tonight. Natasha watched him intently, her beautiful blue eyes narrowed a little.

This is your past sins come to take their due, Seth thought, with a mental sigh. With more force than he intended, he responded to the duchess' bald invitation. "Not tonight."

"Then, perhaps a turn about the gardens, hmmm?" She flicked her fan open, and leaned close to him, their faces hidden for an instant. "So you may finish what you started this morning."

"I did finish, m'lady."

She pouted, catching her lower lip with her teeth. "But not with me."

He shrugged. "I have other matters to attend to."

Her dark brows rushed together, and she snapped her fan shut. "You mean another woman."

"No, just business."

She relaxed again, her smile returning in force. "Tomorrow, then?"

"I am leaving town."

"So soon!" She winced at the volume of her exclamation, and glanced around to see who took note of her shrill cry. That told Seth that she still intended to be discreet. She was playing an outrageous game beneath the noses of everyone here, but she knew, as well as Seth did, that there were limits to what society would tolerate. Clearly, she had been playing this game for many years.

But now he had her measure.

He shook his head, refusing the walk in the gardens. "Sorry, duchess." He knew full well where such a stroll would lead, for he'd experienced the duchess' creativity the previous evening.

She did not even try to hide her frown. "Certainly you can spare a moment." She tapped his shoulder with her fan and motioned toward a set of double doors. "I intend to step out for a breath of fresh air. If you feel so inclined, follow me after a moment." She picked up her skirts and slipped onto the edges of the ballroom, working her way around the room towards the tall double doors.

Seth watched her go with a deep sense of relief. He had no intention of following her anywhere, now he knew she would not risk a scene to force the issue.

Instead, he made his way toward Natasha. He could see the uncertainty in her eyes. Her focus warned Piggot, who looked around, too. He met Seth's gaze with a thin smile, but Seth could feel his caution.

Natasha stepped around the thin man, and slipped her hand under Seth's elbow. The intimate little gesture would not be lost on anyone in the vicinity, and there were plenty of people peeping behind fans or else frankly staring at them.

"Come, let me introduce you to my mother," Natasha murmured. Then Seth realized why they had such an avid audience. Natasha's parents were actively encouraging her association with Piggot, who had been standing by her side. The tall woman completing the rest of Natasha's circle must be her mother. Their audience was probably hoping for a showdown of some sort.

Seth allowed Natasha to lead him to her mother, who was staring at him with that down-the-nose expression only the privileged could manage.

"Mother, may I introduce to you Seth Harrow, captain of the *Artemis*. And Mr. Harrow, this is my mother, Lady Munroe."

Seth bowed his head in the short nod one gave to a peer of the realm, even though technically, Caroline was only the wife of the peer. It was a way of flattering her. But when he straightened, her expression had not changed an inch. Her eyes coolly assessed him from toe to top, lingering for a moment on his earring.

"A sea captain? How…jolly," she intoned.

Despite his absolutely correct attire, and his court manners, he had failed to pass muster. A few short hours ago, he would have cheerfully shrugged off the rejection, and gone on his way, undeterred. Now, the woman's disdain burned in his gut and heart. He would have acceptance from these people for Natasha's sake!

And he found it ironic that if that black night in Ireland, fifteen years ago, had played out a little differently, then Lady Munroe and every other mother in the land would be doing the bowing, and shoving their eligible daughters at him with all the haste respectability allowed.

A portly man in his fifties, his dark hair going gray at the sides, joined the circle. His blue eyes were Natasha's eyes, and Seth stiffened, wariness flooding him. They'd called in the troops. This had to be Natasha's father, Lord Munroe himself.

The man thrust out his hand. "We've not been introduced. Munroe."

Seth took his hand, and gave the handshake just enough power to match Munroe's, and no more. He had no intention of proving his masculinity in that ancient ritual, it would put him at a disadvantage in Munroe's eyes.

"Harrow," Seth replied. "Captain of the *Artemis*."

"Tugboat?" Munroe hazarded.

Seth hid his grin at Munroe's puny effort to belittle him. He wouldn't rise to such pathetic bait. "Merchant," he responded.

Munroe narrowed his eyes, and Seth knew he was about to be interrogated—or filleted, if Munroe could find a way.

"What class of merchant?" Munroe demanded.

"She's a five hundred-ton East Indiaman class. Three-masted and ship-rigged." Seth did not bother hiding the pride in his voice.

"There's no *Artemis* that makes her home here."

"Out of Albany," Seth added.

Munroe turned red in the face and started spluttering. "If you're going to lie, young man, then get your bloody facts straight!"

"Henry!" Caroline cautioned. "Language, please! There are ladies present."

Munroe shoved his forefinger at Seth. "Albany's not a seaport. It's not even on the coast!"

"Albany, Australia, Daddy," Natasha put in. "Not New York."

"Western Australia," Seth amended, and smiled to disarm the tension.

Caroline gasped. "Good lord, where all the convicts are sent? Oh, my..." And she trailed off weakly, as if the concept alone was too much for her constitution. She grasped her husband's arm for support.

Piggot just grinned, enjoying the show.

"Albany is a free settlement." Seth kept his voice low and even. They were baiting him deliberately. He gritted his teeth.

Nastasha saw it too, for she frowned, and cast Seth a look of reassurance.

Do not lose your temper, he cautioned himself, for he could feel his ire rising despite the knowledge that Natasha's parents were simply protecting their daughter. That their combined efforts were striking home bothered him.

Munroe cleared his throat. Change of tactics, Seth realized and braced himself.

"You seem familiar," Munroe said, his brows furrowing as if he was trying to place him.

A chill touched him. Seth kept his smile in place as he cursed mentally. He should have anticipated this. Vaughn Wardell had recognized him, and Seth had his father's eyes and build. These people, Munroe in particular, would know his father.

Seth's only choice was to bluff it out. "I doubt we have crossed paths, Lord Munroe. I've been at sea for many years."

Munroe lifted a brow. "There's something about you, Mr…"

"Harrow," Seth supplied again.

"Good evening, Lord Munroe." Vaughn Wardell stepped up to the portly lord, holding out his hand. Elisa stood by his side, holding his other hand, and Seth saw her knuckles whiten. She was watching Munroe and his wife, and looked like she wished she was somewhere far away.

Munroe hesitated for a long moment, and even his wife straightened up her shoulders, like a mother hen preparing to strike.

Natasha took a half step forward. "Daddy, you remember Vaughn Wardell, do you not? I mean, do forgive me, Vaughn—I completely forgot. Daddy, this is the new Marquess of Fairleigh. Vaughn, I was sorry to hear of your father's passing. And Elisa, too. You must remember Elisa, Father." She held her hand out to Elisa, and when Elisa hesitantly took it, wrapped both her hands around the other woman's and smiled brightly. Then she looked up at her father with a winning smile.

Natasha had deliberately championed the pair, verbally stepping in front of them like a shield against her parent's wrath.

Seth put it together quickly. Natasha and Vaughn had been engaged. Vaughn had married Elisa. And now Natasha protected the pair from her parent's retribution. And he marveled once again at Natasha's determination to do what she thought was right, regardless of the weight of disapproval that might arise.

Munroe had no choice but to take Vaughn's hand, which Vaughn had continued to hold in midair. Vaughn nodded his greeting. "Munroe," he murmured, for Natasha had carefully mentioned his title to ensure her father greeted him as an equal. He nodded at Seth, including him in the circle. "Harrow," he added.

"You two know each other?" Munroe demanded.

Vaughn did not blink, nor did he look at Seth. "We met tonight," he told Munroe. "Harrow is owner of a merchant vessel out of Australia."

"Owner?" Munroe repeated, glancing at Seth. "You failed to mention you owned the ship."

"I failed to realize you needed the information," Seth said coolly. "Would you like to know the names of every ship in my fleet?"

"Fleet? You said you were a sea captain!"

"I am. I am captain of the *Artemis* because I like to keep my hand in. I employ other captains for my other ships."

Even Natasha's eyes had widened.

Vaughn grinned. "A success by anyone's standards," he declared.

But Munroe's expression only seemed bleaker. He shook his head, as if he were shaking off these revelations as mere irritants, and returned to his interrogation. "Did your father or a relation attend Cambridge?"

Seth fought to hide his reaction. Had Munroe put him together with his father? Again, he resorted to pure bluff. "Not that I'm aware of, Lord Munroe."

"I don't remember any Harrows at Cambridge, either," Vaughn said. And Seth realized then that Vaughn had, indeed, remembered him, and knew who he was, despite his earlier denial. Vaughn was silently supporting him.

Vaughn sent him a quick glance, and once again they were boyhood friends who abhorred their time in the purgatory called Public School, and the dusty old colleges of Cambridge. Seth relaxed a little. Most unexpectedly, he had found a friend and an ally.

Vaughn turned his attention to Munroe, and clapped him on the back. "Lord Munroe, Elisa and I would very much like you and your lady wife to join us at dinner one night this week."

Munroe looked at his wife. As the mistress of the household, it was her position to respond to social invitations. Caroline looked like she had swallowed sour milk, and Seth knew why. She could not refuse this invitation, now that Munroe had shaken Vaughn's hand and symbolically accepted him and his wife. "We would be delighted," Caroline said stiffly.

"Elisa, what would be the best day for you?" Vaughn asked his wife, who looked as pale as Caroline.

Seth caught Vaughn's glance at him. Vaughn gave his head a little jerk towards the stairs. His meaning was clear. Vaughn had created a distraction. Time to leave.

Seth glanced at Natasha. She watched him, biting her lip. Seth was very aware of people staring at them, taking note of every action and word. He restricted himself to a smile, and a bow, his hand over his heart, and slipped away, while Elisa and Caroline and the men discussed a suitable evening for what promised to be a most wretched dinner engagement.

He would have to find a way to thank Vaughn and the lovely Elisa, later.

* * * * *

Natasha watched as Seth walked away, until she saw that her father watched her intently. She immediately turned her attention back to the conversation. Vaughn asked her to name her favorite dishes, drawing her into the conversation.

"Corned hash," she answered, and waited for the expected outcry from her mother, over her love of the common man's meal. Also, as expected, her mother took over the discussion of the menu with Elisa, and by the end of the discussion, Natasha knew Elisa would end up with a menu that was all her mother's choosing, and would be helpless to do anything other than provide the meal.

She noticed, then, that Vaughn was staring at her. He'd been waiting for her attention to return to him again, for when he saw her look at him, he pointedly dropped his gaze to her waist.

She looked down. The odious Piggot's hand still lay on her skirt, and had probably stained the fragile silk with perspiration. She was grateful that, though he dared place a hand around her waist in a public place, he did not quite dare rest his hand on her torso. That would have been too much to bear.

She looked up at Vaughn again, and gave a rueful smile.

He grinned back, and one eye fluttered almost shut. A wink. She knew exactly what he was saying to her. *Stay strong, Natasha.*

She checked that her father's attention had returned to the conversation. He liked good food, and even though it was not considered manly, he would willingly involve himself in a conversation about meals if the opportunity presented itself. And indeed, he was frowning and arguing about the best wine to go with Duck a la'Orange, the new dish from the continent that was all the rage.

Natasha looked to the top of the stairs where Seth had disappeared. What if he left tonight for Ireland, and she never saw him again? She recalled the hot rush of overwhelming pleasure he had given her, and felt her cheeks burn at the memory. Even as they burned, she wondered how she might experience more moments like that. Was it that pinnacle of excitement that her books hinted at? She decided that as naughty as her books were purported to be, they weren't nearly as instructional as she'd thought them. There were too many practical aspects they failed to cover.

She needed a mentor, someone who would not faint with shock at such a subject. Someone who did not have the ear of her mother. But for now she must rely on her own instincts. And right now, her instincts were telling her to follow Seth. She could not let him part without a final word. Perhaps even a kiss like the one where his tongue had slipped inside her mouth. It was strange how such a kiss, described in her books, had struck her as most disgusting, but in reality it had been quite wonderful.

"Will you excuse me, please?" she murmured, hoping that no one would hear it, and slipped away from the group. Thankfully they were totally absorbed in a discussion of who laid the best table in the country, feasts of the past, and who had the best cook in London. "Claridge's, I tell you!" her father was insisting, as she left. As usual, he had entirely failed to take into account that a woman could never been seen dining in a public establishment.

Natasha hurried along the long side of the ballroom. There was a little-used door at the far end that gave access to a servant's hall. There was a passage from that hall that led directly to the front foyer of the building, where it emerged from behind the big tree ferns sitting in brass tubs next to the grand staircase. She glanced around for observers, and saw that at this end of the ballroom, at least, there were no major dramas being played out. It was too close to the orchestra for idle conversation. Everyone was either dancing or watching the dancing, swaying in time to the irresistible beat of a waltz.

She slipped into the passage and hurried along the dim path. It was blessedly cool and fresh, here, and the air bathed her heated face and shoulders as she moved. Her heart hammered loudly as she carefully edged the small foyer door open, and stepped out. She looked around for Seth.

He stood on the wide stone, awaiting a carriage. He looked very handsome in his well-cut suit, and he had the appearance of a complete gentlemen, and all evening he had behaved as one. But now, when he believed no one to be watching him, he stood with his arms crossed over his wide chest, and his legs apart.

That is how he looks on the deck of his ship, Natasha realized. The pose allowed her to mentally replace his finery with what she supposed a merchant captain would wear—breeches and high boots, and a billowing linen shirt. The earring would not look out of place at all. She resisted painting a cutlass at his hip, but in her mind, she knew a loaded pistol would not be far from his grasp.

Power radiated from every jaunty angle of his stance. *And this is the man who seduced you tonight.* She shivered in secret delight, and moved to the wide glass doors. The doorman tipped his cap and opened one of the heavy doors for her, and she stepped out into the refreshing night air.

Seth did not turn until she was but a few feet from him, and she was startled to see him frowning. Instantly, his frown was replaced by a smile that showed his very white teeth, and made his eyes twinkle.

"Did I…should I not have followed you? I only wished to say goodnight…"

He shook his head a little. "The frown was not for you, my sweet. And I would scarce begrudge you a farewell." But she saw his raking glance behind her. He was looking for eavesdroppers. Witnesses.

"You promised I'd see you again," she reminded him. She needed this reassurance, for his caution tripped off a rivulet of nameless fears. There was so much about this man that she did not know.

"That I did." But his frown had returned.

"What is it, Seth? Give me the truth you hesitate to voice. I would rather hear truth than a pretty lie. Did you simply dally with me tonight? Please tell me if it is so—I would rather hear that than compound my foolishness by trailing after you like a lovesick maiden."

His frown fled, and his gray eyes skewered her. "I think you know the truth already, if you'll but listen to your soul."

"I am too new at this," she pleaded.

"So am I," he returned, his voice low.

Her heart thudded hard. "Then I did not imagine…"

"No, you did not." His eyes held her captive. He took a step closer, so that his boots brushed her hem. "Natasha, end this now. Give the word, and I'll not return."

"I cannot." It was the truth.

"I'll ruin your life for you if I stay."

"If I am to tell you to go, would I not be the one to carry the blame?"

"You would take on the world for you and yours—I saw what you did for Vaughn and his wife in there. It takes a rare courage indeed, but Natasha…" He shook his head, almost as if he were in pain. "There are things about me…things you cannot possibly imagine."

She shivered. "You're scaring me."

"You should be scared! Send me away, Natasha. Now, before it's too late. Send me away, because, God help me, I've not the willpower to leave."

She laid her hand on his arm. "That is all the truth we need," she said quietly. "I will defy anyone, knowing that truth."

"For the love of sweet heaven—" he began.

"Natasha!"

Natasha jumped, hearing her father's firm summons, and let her hand fall from Seth's arm. She turned to find her father pushing the glass doors open, the doorman jumping out of his way. Her father's jaw was tense, his eyes glittering, as his gaze shifted from Seth to her and back. He was furious. "Return to the ballroom this instant."

"Father—"

"Obey me at once!" he roared.

She stood her ground, even though she trembled with fear. She had never in her life defied her father so openly. She tried to hide the tremble in her voice as she attempted another sally. "Father, you might at least—"

"Now!" And he raised his hand high.

Shocked slithered through her. Her father was about to strike her—and in public! He had never hit her in her entire life. He must be desperate beyond tolerance to resort to such an act. She braced herself. There was no way to avoid the blow.

As his big hand descended, it slapped into Seth's palm. Seth gripped her father's wrist, the knuckles turning white as he exerted force to halt it. "Lord Munroe, control yourself."

Her father wrenched his wrist out of Seth's grasp and turned on him with a noise that sounded almost like a growl. "I should have you arrested this instant. How dare you trifle with my daughter?"

There was a murmur behind her, and Natasha turned to see that her father's shouting had already drawn a crowd. People were oozing out through the doors, filling up the wide porch at the top of the steps to the street.

"I think you have misinterpreted the situation," Seth said quietly.

"I know what I see!" Munroe roared, his face turning red. "You think I don't know who you are, Williams? Did you think that this pap about ships and fleets and the colonies would fool me?"

"It's the truth," Seth said coolly. But his hands were curled into tight fists by his sides.

"You are the son of the Earl of Innesford. You're the scoundrel that killed two of your fellow Englishmen in that riot in Ireland fifteen years ago. Your real name is Williams. You've the look of your sire."

Natasha stared at Seth, willing him to deny it. But he made no sound, gave no sign of protest. His face had turned pale.

She could not let him take the assault unaided. "Father, this is madness. He is a sea captain, from Australia."

"Natasha, no," Seth said quietly.

Natasha stared at him, her heart pounding. Why did he tell her to stop? Because this was the truth? Oh god, was this the truth that he would not give her?

"Your father is right, young Natasha."

Natasha whirled to face the Countess of Innesford, who stepped from the crowd, pulling her shawl about her frail shoulders. "This is my son Seth Williams. I have not seen him since the riot in Ireland. To me he has been dead for fifteen years." She looked at Seth, and her expression was a replica of the haughty one she had given him in the ballroom earlier in the evening. "And he will continue to be dead to me."

She turned her back on him and walked away.

The small group that had formed now whispered loudly, passing on the nugget of information. Oh, they would be lapping this up!

Ice-cold fingers gripped Natasha's insides, and she began to shake. The countess' inexplicably rude behavior all made sense…if Seth really was her son. And Vaughn—Vaughn had recognized him, too, even though Seth had denied it. And her father…

Lord Munroe took a step closer to Seth. "Stay away from my daughter, Harrow. Williams. Whatever you style yourself these days matters naught. You are nothing but a thief and a murderer, and you are not welcome here."

"Seth, tell them they're wrong," she begged.

He looked at her, and she saw regret in his eyes. "I cannot, though I'd give my soul for it to be otherwise."

Natasha tried to absorb the information. Seth Harrow was the son of the Earl of Innesford. Bile rose in her throat. Dear God, she had very nearly given herself to a murderer.

She swayed, saw the ground rushing to meet her, and saw no more.

Chapter Six

Seth stared into the flames. The image of Natasha's white face wouldn't leave him be. He'd managed to catch her as she fell, and he could still feel her in his arms—her limp body and very white face.

He'd barely had time for a single stroke to her cheek before they'd unceremoniously hauled him away. Her family had crowded around her, then, shut him out. Even Munroe had scurried to his daughter's side, his fury forgotten.

That's when Vaughn had pulled him away, physically manhandling him into a waiting cab.

"Would you like another?" Vaughn filled Seth's glass with more of the fine brandy, not waiting for his answer. Last night his old friend had insisted Seth stay at his townhouse rather than return to the *Artemis*. Seth didn't know if he'd insisted in order to keep Seth from pulling anchors and stealing out of England, or if he feared Seth might try something more direct—like stealing into Natasha's bedroom.

Both ideas had tugged at him with equal compulsion, and the need to do something—anything—had flayed at him until he felt he would go mad. Perhaps Vaughn had sensed his desperation, too, for he had also insisted on staying up until the wee hours of the night, playing chess, and drinking a very fine drop of Madeira. After the Madeira, they'd turned to brandy, and after too many brandies, Seth found himself being guided to a comfortable guest room.

He spent the remainder of the night sweating beneath the cool sheets, trying to rid himself of the memory of Natasha's white face in his arms, and still the surge of panic and fury it invoked.

Now he sipped the brandy, tiredly trying to find a course of action that might take away the horror he'd seen in her face just before she'd fainted.

"You know she'll understand, once you explain." Vaughn stoppered the decanter, and sat in the wing chair drawn up to the fire next to the hard bench Seth had chosen. He couldn't sit still, anyway, and a hard bench was more suitable for writhing upon.

"Explain what? That none of what she heard last night was a lie? That her family is right? I'm a criminal…a murderer, in the eyes of the law?"

Vaughn leaned forward, warming the brandy glass in his two hands. In the firelight his eyes glittered like hard ice, giving a glimpse of the strength of character behind the handsome features. "You only met her last night, yes?"

"Yes." Seth looked away. "You can call me a fool. I won't hold it against you."

"Oh, I don't think it's foolish. It's very Irish, and just like you. It might surprise you to know that I understand because I experienced the same thing."

"You?" Seth was shocked enough to look back at him, and saw Vaughn's small smile. "You were the sensible one, the strategist, you were always the one telling me to stop thinking with my heart."

Vaughn's smile broadened. "It's still good advice, but it's of little defense against *amour*." He tossed back the remainder of brandy in his glass, and put it back on the side table. "You have no intention of letting her go, do you?"

Seth clenched his jaw, and fought back the fury over his helplessness one last time. "No," he said stiffly.

"Then you need a plan to get her back. Do you have one?"

"No." He pushed his hands through his hair, amazed to find they were shaking. "How the hell do I take on a whole country? A whole political system? I have a rusty rapier and a brace of dueling pistols. They, on the other hand, will band together and call in every debt and favor owed them across the country, in order to bring me to heel."

Vaughn grinned. "I'm the strategist, remember? You've been away from England too long, Seth. You've forgotten how to beat these people at their own game."

"I never had the chance to learn," Seth amended.

Vaughn sobered. "How old were you when they arrested you?"

"Nineteen."

Vaughn considered that for a moment. "And I thought I was the one who had been imprisoned. I cannot imagine what it was like for you." He eyed Seth with a cool, calculating look that Seth recognized from their school days. Vaughn was hatching a plan. "And did you, in fact, commit murder?"

Seth jumped. "Does it matter?"

"If I am to help you, it does."

"You must consider me capable of the act, if you must ask that."

Vaughn grinned. "Capable, yes. I know of old that black Irish temper of yours. For the right cause, for the right reason, yes, I think you could kill a man. But never for your own sake, not for gain. You would kill for the sake of those you love."

Seth could feel his cheeks burn. "You've changed," he said bluntly. "You speak of strong emotions with ease."

A shadow crossed Vaughn's face. "I nearly lost Elisa once. It's not a lesson I need to learn twice. And you won't deflect me, Seth. I must know the truth of your conviction. Did you commit this murder of which they accused you?"

Seth took a deep breath. "No," he said, on the exhale. It came out gustily.

"What happened? I heard a little of the affair, filtered through too many mouths at school. They said you were a Fenian, and arrested for sedition as well as murder."

"They had it half right," Seth admitted. "Sedition was one of the charges. One of many. They found any charge they could, and added it to the roll."

"Why? What happened?"

"After that first year at Cambridge, I returned home to Ireland." Seth grimaced. "To the estate at Harrow. I remember how much you resented that I got to go home, while you must spend your days at the college. You should not have envied me, Vaughn, for it was a miserable homecoming. Liam and my friends from the village had changed."

"I remember you often spoke of Liam. His family was in the village, and his mother worked upon the estate, and his father in the mine."

Seth nodded. "Yes, that was Liam. But when I returned that summer, things were very different. His mother had slipped and hurt her back and was unable to work at the estate. And they had laid off men at the mine, as production slowed down, and his father was without work. His sister, Siobhan, was barely fifteen, but already in service, and what little she earned supported the entire family, for Liam could not find work that a dozen other older, experienced men desperately needed, and usually got."

Seth cast his mind back to those hot summer days that had been the end of his boyhood. Liam, who had been a staunch friend throughout their childhood, had become bitter and sullen. He spoke often of England as an enemy, and the ills the English domination brought upon his family, his village, the whole country.

Seth had only to look around to see that much of what Liam said was true. There was little food—two bad seasons had destroyed most of the crops, and whole families were subsisting on potatoes and what they could poach in the forests…or steal. But poaching and stealing carried their own penalties. The English army, ordered to keep the peace at all costs, would ensure anyone caught stealing was sent to trial, and even the most minor charge carried heavy penalties. Most of the Irish sent to trial were sentenced to transportation to Australia.

Almost daily, Seth took food from the cook's pantry, and gave it to Liam's mother, who was too desperate to refuse the gift. Seth didn't tell Liam, who would sooner starve his entire family than accept such charity.

The plight of the people, and Liam's growing hatred for the English put Seth in a difficult position, for though he sympathized with their trouble, he was half-English himself. His father was the English overlord, the Earl of Innesford. Marcus Williams spent so much time in England attending parliament, however, that he was virtually blind to the troubles of his earldom.

Seth spent the summer watching villagers die of hunger, while his rage over his own helplessness grew. One night, Liam asked him to come along to a meeting, and he had accepted.

"Fenians?" Vaughn asked sharply. "Surely you knew he had to be involved with them?"

"Oh yes, I knew. It was one more secret both of us knew, but neither of us would speak of. Just as Liam knew I supplied his mother with food from my own pantry."

"Then why did you go?"

"Because Liam was my friend. And I thought, perhaps, that somehow, I might be able to help."

"You were helping already."

"I wasn't making a difference." Seth shrugged. "And I ached to find a way to solve it for them, to make it better. My father would not…or could not. To this day, I still don't know which."

"Ah…" Vaughn nodded.

The meeting had been well-attended, yet it had barely begun when English troops burst in upon them. The Irish had scattered and run, their survival instincts well-honed under the English yoke. Seth had been caught by surprise, and although he, too, tried to flee, he found himself amongst the handful of armed Irish who held the rear while their friends escaped into the night. The troops had overwhelmed them in both numbers and arms, and the rearguard had been rounded up, Seth amongst them.

Vaughn frowned into his drink. "Why would they arrest a son of an English lord, particularly one with such power in parliament?"

"I didn't tell them who I was."

Vaughn lifted his brows, clearly startled. "Why on earth not?"

Seth shrugged. "I had spent months hearing how the English oppressed the Irish, and applied a harsher, unforgiving law that kept them downtrodden and meek. If I had told them who I was, my father would have made sure the charges were dropped, and I was set free. It would have confirmed everything they said about the English. I wanted to show them that it wasn't true."

"Did you not realize what that would mean?"

Seth shook his head. "I truly believed that I would merely be reprimanded. I had not been part of the armed group who killed those troopers. It was my first meeting, and everyone at that meeting knew it. I didn't think it would ever get so bad."

"So...you really didn't believe the Fenians when they said the law for the Irish was harsher?"

Seth gave a hollow laugh. "Well, I learned for myself. My protests and my claims of innocence fell on deaf ears. I was herded into and out of cells and courthouses and then sentenced to seven years transportation to Port MacQuarrie—the harshest penal settlement in the new colonies. They didn't care that I would not identify myself—and nor would any of the Fenians who were arrested with me, although they all knew who I was. So the English filed my name as Seth Harrow, as that was where I had been arrested."

"Surely your father tried to minimize the sentence?"

"By the time he learned where I was, sentence had already been handed down." Seth shook his head. "I was too filled with fury. The Fenians were right—I had lived through three months of English justice. I would not let my father, the Englishman, lift a finger to help me. I would not acknowledge him, and I refused to let him see me. I was half-English, but in my heart, I was as fully Irish as Liam."

"Did Liam not come to your defense?"

"They would have thrown him aboard the same prison hulk as me."

"A prison hulk?"

"The ship that was to take us to Australia. It sat in the port in Dublin for nearly a year, until it had cargo and prisoners enough to make a profitable run to the colonies. By the time we made landfall at Port MacQuarrie, I was the wild man they thought they had sentenced. Two hundred prisoners set sail from Dublin. Only one hundred and thirteen of us reached Port MacQuarrie, and none of us arrived unscathed—we'd survived fever, hunger and oppression from the ship's guards, who had been paid when they left Dublin, and had no reason to care that we lived or died. It was worse for the women, who were forced to submit to the attentions of the guards, but the younger men were not spared, either."

Vaughn glanced sharply from under his brow. "You?"

"None of us arrived unscathed," Seth repeated gently.

Vaughn cleared his throat, and then rose to pour himself another brandy. The fire crackled loudly in the silence, and a log split with a pop and a shower of sparks.

Seth sighed. "For fifteen years, I have thought of nothing but returning to Ireland a free man, and helping my friends where and how I could. I didn't give a damn that I had been branded a criminal. In Australia, that's a brand most of us can call our own. It makes no difference. A man is judged by his actions, there." He ran a hand through his hair. "But now…"

Vaughn turned to face him once more. "If you are to take on these people at their own game, then you must play by their rules."

"Granted," Seth agreed.

"I took them on once, Seth, and I won…but by the skin of my teeth, and Elisa's past was a mere maiden's blush compared to the past that dogs your heels." He swirled the liquid in his glass.

Seth saw the path ahead that Vaughn had just drawn. "The only way to have what I want is to take back my place as the son of the Earl of Innesford. To do that, I must clear my name of this past that dogs me, as you say. That means I must prove my innocence, not just to my mother, but to Natasha and her family…to everyone."

Vaughn grinned. "Welcome home, Englishman."

*****

Natasha wanted nothing more than to return to the muffling warmth of her bed, where the world could be forgotten, but her mother would not hear of it. The change in her mother's attitude was startling, for Caroline had spent the previous day hovering by her bedside, insisting she rest and recover from her terrible ordeal. Caroline had shooed away all the servants, too, and waited on her daughter herself.

Now Natasha was required to attend a visitor. With her maid's help, she had dressed and styled her hair, and her astute maid also informed her of the visitor's identity—her Aunt Susannah, a woman who thrived on gossip and the self-importance it gave her.

Dressed in a gown that had gone out of style years ago, Aunt Susannah sat across the dining table from Natasha's mother. Sisters only two years apart in age, they were more like twins, for their coloring and features were nearly identical. The only difference was their social status. Susannah had married for love, a continental baron who had died over a decade ago. His death had left her in debt and at the mercy of her wealthy sister, who did not let Susannah forget her generosity for a minute.

As Natasha entered the dining room for morning tea, Aunt Susannah was occupied watching a young footman pour her tea. She was taking a rather keen interest in his backside. The young man's face was as red as his hair, and Natasha smiled inwardly. She'd heard whispers about her aunt's appetite for younger men, and while most of her friends thought it merely a scandalous fairy tale, Natasha knew, now, that it might well be true. She didn't think she could be shocked by anything this world presented her, anymore.

And with the indirect reminder of Seth, all her humor fled. She took the seat the butler held out for her.

"He killed the man in cold blood, I hear," Caroline said, slathering cream onto a scone.

Natasha knew of whom her mother spoke. The hot wave of nausea swept through her again, making her temples prickle, and her heart thud with a sickly booming. It had been this way since the ball, the reminder of Seth Harrow…Williams…and the kind of man he was made her physically ill. And she would return to the question that now haunted her—how could she have been so wrong about him?

Aunt Susannah waited until the footman disappeared behind the kitchen door to respond. "Indeed, that is what I hear. An English soldier!" She shivered with delight.

Natasha put down the spoon she had just picked up, deliberately letting it clatter on the saucer with an unmusical note. "You can not believe everything you hear, Aunt Susannah."

Susannah's lips thinned. "My dear girl, he spent the past fifteen years in a prison colony in Australia. One of the worst in the entire world." She reached for her tea and took a sip, no doubt for dramatic effect. Susannah had spent years honing her story telling to a fine art—the better to hold the attention of people who would otherwise dismiss her out of hand. "He is an animal. A man with no conscience. I am simply amazed they released him at all." She held out her hand to Caroline. "And my dear...he sports an earring as well, I hear."

"I saw it on him at the ball. It was quite vulgar," Caroline said with a shudder.

It wasn't anything of the sort, Natasha thought. It had been a simple, small gold ring—nothing like what pirates were supposed to wear. "It's customary for sailors to wear an earring to mark their crossing of the equator," she provided.

Susannah put her cup down quickly, staring at Caroline, Natasha's comment completely ignored. "You spoke with him? Directly? Oh, dear sister, do tell me everything! What did he look like? Was he simply vile to look upon?"

"Oh, really!" Natasha exclaimed, disgusted with her aunt's vicarious curiosity. "The law believes that once a man has been released from gaol, he has paid for his crimes, and is ready to return to society and take up a useful place." And Natasha was amazed at her own hypocrisy. For she had been as dismayed by Seth's past as anyone else—perhaps more so. But this outright salivation over the details of his crime and his person, as if he were a specimen under a bell jar, irritated her. Why couldn't they leave the man alone? He had not asked anything of them, and they were turning him into the latest cause célèbre.

Her mother gave her a gentle, concerned smile. "We know how he trifled with your affections, my dear. You are hardly in a position to call judgment upon him."

"He did not trifle with my affections!" Natasha cried. And the wild voice inside her crowed loudly, *Liar! Liar!*

Again, her mother favored her with a patient, understanding smile. "He won your sympathy. He was intimate with you. How else would you know why he wears an earring?"

"Because I read books, Mother. Perhaps you should try it?"

"Oh dear..." Susannah said in a die-away voice, her hand at her throat.

"She's been through such an ordeal," Caroline explained to her sister.

Fury pricked her at her mother's blindness. Unexpectedly, a memory of Seth's eyes entered her thoughts. She saw again the deep hurt in them when his mother had snatched her hand from his. Would a hardened criminal feel any hurt at all over such a rejection? Would he have even bothered to seek his mother out? For plainly, that had been his only reason for attending the ball—to find his mother. Yet he had not declared himself her son. Why not?

Because he had no intention of claiming back his heritage. He was going back to Ireland. He stopped in London to check on her, and then remove himself from her life once more.

While Natasha considered this new perspective on Seth's actions the night of the ball, her mother leaned towards Susannah, and dropped her voice. "He dared to give my daughter a rose. A rose!! The arrogance of the man!"

Natasha was startled. How had her mother known about that rose? She had been nowhere near the dance floor at the time. Then she sighed. The gossips had been hard at work the last day or so.

Aunt Susannah gasped, setting her tea down so it rattled on the saucer, and turned to stare at Natasha with a horrified expression.

Under her mother's and aunt's regard, Natasha felt her cheeks flush hot. She lifted her chin a fraction. "He did indeed give me a rose, but only as a gesture of kindness."

Her mother sniffed. "A man like him does not know the first thing about kindness. He made me uncomfortable from the moment I met him, and I did not like how much attention he paid you, my dear."

Aunt Susannah sighed loudly. "Natasha, you have so much to learn when it comes to men."

"Mr. Harrow was nothing but a gentleman at all times," Natasha said coolly. How horrified these women would be if they knew what really transpired between herself and Seth Harrow. Her cheeks burned remembering the intimate kiss they shared, the way he'd stroked her womanly folds with his tongue, the way her body had pulsed and throbbed…and how his thick erection had strained against the buttons of his pants. He could have taken her night before last, and she would not have stopped him.

And then the thought struck her with all the force of an express coach. *I still want him to take me.*

Natasha blinked, and realized she was holding her teacup halfway to her lips, as she stared blindly at the velvet swags adorning the archway between the dining room and the big formal front drawing room. She put the cup down carefully on its saucer, while she processed this new revelation. It was true—she burned for him…even after hearing the horrific news of his past. It didn't matter a whit what they said about him, she still ached to feel his thick manhood slide into her, and his soft, blurred brogue in her ear. She wanted him. She wanted to be in his arms.

She didn't care what his past had been. Not now. It had been a shock to hear it, but now she had absorbed the news. She realized she had two facts to support her decision. First, Seth had been kind, gentle, and empathetic. The look in his eyes when he'd begged her to make him leave—she knew with every fiber of her being that the fear in his eyes had been genuine. Secondly, whatever his crimes had been, he had paid for them. Aunt Susannah had summed it up perfectly— Fifteen years in the worst penal colony in the world.

"A gentleman would never kill another man, my dear," Aunt Susannah said, heaping three spoonfuls of sugar into her tea, and thereby proving by at least two spoonfuls that she was not a lady, either. "And he is not Mr. Harrow. He lied to all of us, and you most of all."

Natasha set her fork down on her untouched plate. Something Vaughn had said to her once slipped back into her mind, along with his melodious tenor voice. "This society is too quick to condemn and too lazy to question. If someone had just asked Elisa to explain herself, she would have been saved eight years of misery, and her son, too."

Natasha touched her napkins to her lips. "Perhaps Mr. Harrow had cause for what he did."

Her mother's disgusted sigh filled the high-ceilinged room. "For the love of God, Natasha, what cause would any person have to kill another?" Both her aunt and mother stared at her as though she had grown another head.

"And it's Mr. Williams, too," Susannah added piously.

Natasha addressed her mother first. "I am not excusing the act. I just wonder what actually happened. Perhaps there is more to the story than we know. Has anyone bothered asking Mr. Harrow what happened?"

Her mother's eyes widened.

Natasha turned to her aunt. "And I will continue to call him Mr. Harrow, until he gives me leave to call him otherwise. You failed to note, amongst all your sensational tidbits, Aunt Susannah, that Mr. Harrow did not come waltzing back into London to reclaim his heritage and commit a rash of crimes and scandals. Send a message to the harbormaster and ask him to confirm his listed departures. I think you will find that Mr. Harrow intended to leave yesterday, for Ireland. He was in London merely to ensure his mother fared well, and that was all. It was my father who quite rudely, and without consent, revealed Mr. Harrow's former name at the top of his voice."

Both women were staring at her now, their mouths open. And indeed they might. Natasha had never spoken to either of them in this fashion before this day. She was swiftly adding a long list of novel behaviors to her tally.

Her aunt was the first to recover from her shock. She shook her head. "The man spent fifteen years of his life in prison, Natasha. You cannot gainsay that fact."

"And why did he deny who he was? He is an evil man, plain and simple. Even his own mother could not hide her shame at the ball," Caroline added.

"Oh, the poor dear," Aunt Susannah said, cutting her ham into bite-size pieces. "As if it is not enough that her husband has taken ill. Now she has the return of her murderous son to contend with. We really must visit her soon, Caroline."

Natasha bit the inside of her lip. How badly she wanted to defend Seth. But how could she, when she did not know the truth for herself? And once again, memories of the way his soft lips had felt against her own, his long-fingered hands on her…and in her, and the way he had pleasured her with his mouth. The blood heated her veins, swooping low into her belly, causing a throbbing ache between her thighs.

"No doubt he has returned because his father is near death," her mother said, taking a bite of her scone. "He stands to inherit all that wealth, as well as his father's titles."

Aunt Susannah lifted a painted brow. "Indeed, he is an only child."

Had they heard nothing of what she had said? Fury touched her. To be so ignored was humiliating. Neither of the older women believed she held a single useful thought in her head. They were talking to each other as if she were not there, and anything she said was discounted immediately as the verbal meandering of a child.

She gripped her napkins under the table, wringing it in both hands, and heard the hemstitches tear.

Jenkins, the butler, entered, which effectively halted the conversation. Jenkins carried the silver door tray, with a single cream-colored calling card sitting precisely in the middle. He held the tray out to Caroline, who read it and glanced at her sister. "Oh dear. It's that Elisa woman. The new Marquess of Fairleigh's wife," she said, as though she and Elisa had not been friends when the younger woman had moved north and lived at Fairleigh Hall, the land adjoining Natasha's parents' home.

"Wardell's son?" Susannah asked, her curiosity pricked. "Didn't she..." Then she glanced sideways at Natasha, suddenly remembering her presence. "Well, er..." She reached for her teacup.

Caroline handed the card back to Jenkins. "Tell her I would be delighted to receive her, Jenkins."

"Yes, m'lady." He strode away, not giving a hint of reaction to what he had just heard.

Caroline placed her hand against the teapot. "We'll need a fresh pot." She rose and pulled the velvet bell pull, just as the dining room door opened again.

Elisa stepped into the room, looking beautiful in a soft yellow gown that complimented her wheat-shaded curls. Two bright spots of color touched her high cheekbones, and she started a little when she saw Susannah on the other side of the table. She turned to Caroline. "My apologies, Lady Munroe. I would not have dreamed of interrupting had I known you were entertaining company."

"Not at all," Natasha's mother answered politely. "You know my sister, Susannah, Baroness Beaufort, of course?"

"Baroness," Elisa said, with a tiny nod of her head. Married to a Marquess, Elisa now outranked both women in the room. But she seemed nervous, and Natasha knew that Elisa was finding her return to society a trial. Vaughn may have won her respectability back, but even though society had nominally accepted her, there were dozens of ways of putting her back in her place, and her mother and Susannah knew all of them. Caroline had never forgiven Elisa for taking Vaughn from his destined place beside her daughter. Elisa had a right to be wary.

"Indeed, my dear," Susannah added, "Your arrival is well-timed. We were just exchanging the latest delicious gossip."

"Oh..." Elisa said, clearly startled. It had been gossip that had destroyed her life in the first place—vicious rumors that had circulated unchecked and unchallenged, all behind her back. She bit her lip.

Caroline motioned for the footman to pull out a chair for their guest, which forced Elisa to sit down. The footman poured her a cup of tea, and once he stepped back, Elisa straightened her back, and lifted her chin. "Unfortunately, Lady Munroe, I cannot linger to hear what I'm sure is absolutely divine scandal. I have an appointment with my seamstress within the hour, and she is in such high demand, I dare not miss the appointment, or I will not have my gown for the Harvest Ball next month."

Caroline lifted her brow. "Oh, and who would your seamstress be?"

"Madame de Torville, of Saville Row."

Susannah's cup hit her saucer and clattered, until she put both hands out to save it, and lifted it upright again. "Madamee de Torville accepts your appointments?" she asked, her voice rising.

Natasha hid her grin. Madame Solange de Torville was the most highly sought seamstress and designer in all of London. Accordingly, she picked her clientele with a sharp eye for the most influential of *the ton*…and those she believed were up-and-coming. To have Madame de Torville accept your appointment was an indication that you were a personage of importance in the London set. Anyone could visit Paris and have a Worth dress made, but only the very elite wore a gown designed by Madame de Torville.

Elisa bit her lip. "I'm sorry…did I distress you? It was most unintentional."

Caroline looked as startled as Susannah, but she smoothed her hair back and cleared her throat. "Not at all. Well, we must not keep you from your vital appointment…"

"You are most kind, and I will keep you from your affairs no longer." Elisa rose to her feet. "I merely dropped by to ask Natasha if she would care to call on Vaughn and me this afternoon, for tea." And she smiled at Natasha.

Natasha smiled back, relieved and touched by the invitation. "Why, thank you—"

"She will not consider it," Caroline said firmly.

"Mother!" Outraged, Natasha bounced to her feet. The chair behind her tumbled onto its back with a muffled thud.

Elisa's eyes widened, and her face turned pale.

Caroline gave her a stiff smile. "It's quite inappropriate for my daughter to call upon a man to whom she was once engaged."

"Vaughn and Elisa are my friends!"

Caroline glanced at her, then back at Elisa. "You must forgive my daughter's hysterical outburst, Lady Wardell. She has had a most distressing time lately—subjected to unwanted attention from a murderous criminal."

Natasha stomped her foot. She was wearing day boots, and the heels were quite sturdy. The boot rapped against the floorboards beneath her feet with a satisfying bang that jarred all the way to her hip. Everyone looked at her.

"Elisa, I would ask you to leave before my mother extends you any more rudeness disguised as good sense. I will call upon you later."

Elisa looked from mother to daughter and back. "Perhaps I should," she murmured, pulling on her gloves. "Thank you for tea, Lady Munroe, Baroness Beaufort." She gave them both a nod and sailed from the room, her chin square and her shoulders straight. She didn't look back as she stepped out the door.

"How dare you!" Caroline cried, circling the table to reach Natasha.

"I dare, because you were insufferably rude to my friend!"

Caroline stopped with her skirts pushing against Natasha's. "She's a whore that stole the man that should have married you! I will not have you associating with people of their kind."

"That's a fine piece of hypocrisy, coming from you, Mother. Our family is hardly a proud example of chastity and forgiveness."

Caroline's eyes widened. "You dare speak of such matters!"

"It's high time someone did! Vaughn Wardell is the only one who has dared speak of it, and that was three years ago! Were you ever going to explain to me about my mysterious half-brother? Did you even mean to tell me his name? Or did Vaughn betray a secret you had no intention of revealing? I'm curious, Mother. Did Father find it awkward having our dirty linen aired in public like that? It's a pity he didn't keep that lesson in mind when he pilloried Seth Harrow!"

Caroline slapped her. Her hand cracked across Natasha's cheek, and sent her staggering a step or two backwards. Susannah cried out, but Natasha gritted her teeth and remained silent. She touched her numb cheek. Her eye was watering freely.

"Go to your room." Caroline's voice was shaking. "I will send the maid to lock the door behind you."

"Oh dear, oh dear…" Susannah dabbed her forehead with her napkin.

"I am going to see my perfectly respectable friends," Natasha said as calmly as she could. She stared her mother in the eye. "Or would you prefer that I spend my time with that hardened criminal, Seth Harrow, and give you a real scandal to waste your time discussing?"

Caroline's face paled. "I will not tolerate this impudence! I am your mother! You will do as I say! And you will never, ever, speak that man's name in this house again! Do you hear me?"

Natasha stared at her mother, awed at the genuine fury she radiated. Caroline never shouted—it wasn't ladylike. But now she sounded like a common fishwife. The veins in her forehead were pulsing visibly.

"I hear you," Natasha told her. "I will be at Lord and Lady Fairleigh's townhouse for the afternoon." She walked out of the room, trying to imitate the gracious glide Elisa had used, but her knees shook too much.

Chapter Seven

Vaughn and Elisa's townhouse sat on the finest street in luxurious Mayfair, a glorious brick home with wrought iron fencing and a gold knocker in the shape of cupid. Very appropriate for the couple who lived there, Natasha thought, as she knocked three times on the black lacquered door. She looked around as she waited for an answer, for she rarely visited Mayfair and the lovely old shade trees always caught her attention.

Hyde Park was within walking distance, and even from the front steps of the townhouse she could hear the clatter of carriages and laughter as Londoners spent the afternoon on The Row, taking advantage of the cool, sunny day.

She took a breath as deep as her stays would allow, and let it out. She was still shaking. All the way to Vaughn's townhouse, she had replayed in her mind the argument in the dining room. Her parents' retribution for her highhandedness would be severe, indeed.

The door swung open and Vaughn appeared, and to Natasha's great dismay her heart skipped a beat. How handsome he was! His green eyes sparkled with genuine warmth, reminding her of a time when he'd been the focus of her world.

"Good lord, I was expecting your butler!"

"I knew it would be you at the door. Natasha, I'm so glad to see you." He lifted her hand to his mouth and pressed his lips against her fingers. "You look lovely."

"Thank you. You look quite handsome yourself."

He grinned devilishly, then his grin faded quite suddenly. With gentle fingers, he lifted her chin and turned her face so he could see the cheek under the brim of her bonnet.

"It's nothing," she said quickly, pulling his hand away.

"It's a swollen nothing, then." He firmly turned her cheek again, so he could examine it. "It needs a cold compress. Come inside, Natasha, and Elisa will take care of it." He tugged her gently across the threshold, tucked her hand in the crook of his arm, and walked her down the marble hallway and into a drawing room.

The long, narrow room had walls that had been papered in a floral with pinks, deep mauves, while beneath the chair rail, the wall was a deep forest green, which blended beautifully with the cherry wood furniture. It was not a fashionable color choice, but it was delightfully welcoming, and quite different from anything Natasha had seen in the public rooms of the ton. A fire crackled in the hearth, warming the room.

Natasha removed her bonnet, gloves and wrap, and gave them to the butler who had silently appeared at her side.

"Please sit down." Vaughn offered her a high-backed chair near the fire. As she seated herself, Elisa glided into the room. She wore the same yellow dress, but this time her smile was warm and friendly. "There you are. I am so glad you did not change your mind. Oh my goodness! Natasha, your cheek!" She raised her hand to her mouth. "Oh, my dear, you didn't receive that on account of my invitation—please say you did not?"

"No," Natasha responded calmly. "I received it because I choose to spend time with genuine friends, regardless of what other people might think of them."

Tears welled in Elisa's eyes, but she gave Natasha a hug and a smile. "I'll attend that for you immediately. Sit down, please. Oh, Gilroy!"

The butler slipped into the room immediately, carrying a tray that held a pan and a snowy white pile of linen. "I anticipated the need, my lady."

"Bless you, Gilroy." Elisa took the tray, and dipped one of the cloths into the pan. Natasha heard ice tinkle.

"My mother always applies liniment to such injuries," she said.

Elisa smiled. "Vaughn learned this trick from professional pugilists, when he was quite young. It works so well, 'tis a wonder all London doesn't use it." She folded the damp cloth, and applied it gently to Natasha's cheek. The chill bit into her flesh, but did relieve the ache. "Hold it there for a minute, until it warms, then we'll put on another cloth."

"Thank you."

Vaughn sat on the settee opposite Natasha's chair. "I admire your courage, Natasha, but you must choose your battles more carefully. It's all right for me, a man, to go his own way, but for you, a maiden under the protection of her family, and entirely dependent upon them, it is a much more difficult task to choose your own fate."

Natasha nodded. "And I do begin to understand this more clearly with each passing day, but Vaughn, if you heard what she said about...well..." She realized that to continue would mean repeating her mother's words, and she had no intention of doing that.

Vaughn laughed, and Elisa smiled a little.

"Let me guess," Vaughn said. "Elisa is a whore, I should have married you, and we're both reprehensible and a disgrace to proper society."

Natasha couldn't help her blush. She could feel the heat of her cheek beneath the palm of her hand. "How did you know?"

Vaughn laughed even harder. "We've both heard those sentiments...more than once." His laughter faded, and he leaned towards her. "Natasha, you should not defend us. You don't have the power to do that. I know your helplessness to choose your life frustrates you, but you must work within the limitations of your world if you are to find the way out of it."

"Is there a way out for someone like me?" Natasha asked, feeling a burning at the back of her eyes that heralded tears, for Vaughn had placed his finger precisely upon the despair that had been growing in her for nearly a year.

"Perhaps," he said, but there was a gleam in his eye that she knew of old, and even though he said no more, Natasha was reassured. She felt herself relax.

"I hope you will point me toward the portal when it appears, Vaughn—you've had more practice at this than I."

"Of course I will. Both of us will keep a watchful guard for you."

Elisa took the cloth from Natasha, replaced it with another chilled pad, and squeezed Natasha's shoulder. "You must consider us as very special friends, Natasha. With us, you are always welcome, whatever the day or hour. In this house, you are free to speak your mind, and say exactly what you feel. None of it will be repeated outside these walls, and no one will chastise you or think oddly of you for what you say. You must always remember that we understand."

Natasha gave a smile, and felt it tremble. "Truly, I am so glad you stopped by and extended the invitation."

Elisa and Vaughn shared a smile, and Natasha felt a pang of envy. What would it be like to be in love as these two obviously were? She wondered if she would ever find out. A life alone seemed infinitely more attractive than being the wife of a man like Sholto Piggot. She shuddered at the image of sharing a marriage bed with the man.

If only she possessed the strength of character Vaughn and Elisa had! They'd married despite the rumors and scandal it caused.

"We want you to be one of the first to hear our news, too," Elisa said, turning back to Natasha.

Nastasha looked from Vaughn to Elisa. Both wore wide smiles.

"A child?" Natasha asked, and struggled to bring her voice above a whisper. The bearing and birthing of children was something only matrons' spoke of, usually behind fans and closed doors. Men and maidens never discussed it. A woman gravid with child rarely appeared in public, and if circumstances forced her to do so, no one would acknowledge her condition until the happy event had taken place. Then the entire world would be conventionally surprised by the news.

Elisa blushed prettily.

Vaughn grinned. "We are both delighted, as is Raymond. He's always wanted a little sister."

Elisa shook her head. "Vaughn insists it shall be a girl."

Vaughn shrugged and kissed his wife's cheek. "I will be happy whatever the child may be. But I want a little girl who shares her mother's fair beauty."

Elisa rolled her eyes as she sat next to him on the settee.

"Hello, Natasha," said a low voice with a brogue blurring it.

The damp cloth dropped from Natasha's suddenly nerveless fingers. Even as she turned to look behind her chair, her heart lurched, and seemed to stop for an aching, dizzy moment. Once, when she had been much smaller, her father had picked her up and thrown her up into the air. He had failed to warn her of what he intended to do, and as she flailed about in midair, her heart had seized, and her stomach had rolled in a way that was both sickening and exciting at once. That feeling slammed into her now, produced by the same potent combination—extreme danger and thrilling surprise.

Seth stood at the other door, his hand resting against the handle, as if he hovered between entering and leaving. And perhaps he did. He watched her as the mouse watches the cat, waiting to see what the predator intended to do.

He wore pants and a shirt without collar or cuffs. The white linen was thin and soft from many washings, and lay open at the neck. The flesh of his throat rose from the gap, tanned a deep brown that was a startling contrast against the cloth.

Her pulse skittered alarmingly. In the light of day he showed a different face from the urbane gentleman in evening wear. He had a shadow of a beard and his hair was rumpled as though he'd just woken. But none of it hid the tension in his shoulders, or the tiredness around his eyes. Seth Harrow had not had an easy time of it since the ball.

All Natasha's indignation at being surprised by his presence faded as she studied him. While all of London had been dissecting Seth's past and the scandal that her father had unveiled at the ball, she had selfishly been toting up how he had affected her life. She had never once asked herself how Seth felt about what had happened.

Well, she had just glimpsed a small part of the answer. "Hello, Seth." She was dismayed to hear her voice tremble.

The hand on the door quickly lifted, palm up. "Ye dinna have to be afraid of me."

She shook her head. "You misunderstand. You surprised me. I did not think I would ever see you again."

He came toward her slowly, warily. Even his stride seemed sensual, and the animal-like quality reminded her of her womanhood. The black cloth clung to muscled thighs and an impressive bulge at the apex. Last night she had seen it in its glory—huge, and clearly defined in his pants.

She swallowed hard and looked away, to see that Elisa was watching her closely.

"It's glad I am to see you here." He took her hand in his warm one and lifted it to his lips. The feel of his soft lips against her fingers burned. There was a heat in his silver eyes she recognized from the night of the ball. He was staring into her eyes, and she felt trapped under his gaze, unable to look away. Her heart was thundering against her bodice with an unsteady flutter, and the same tremble that had shaken her voice now transmitted its way through her fingers. He must surely see it!

The rush of feelings and thoughts overwhelmed her. She did not know how to begin to sort them out. For over a day she had been listening to her aunt and mother and her father's tirades on how dangerous this man standing before her really was, how he would ruin her life, how he had ruined the lives of so many people before her. Yet his touch and the expression in his light eyes seemed to give lie to all of it. Should she trust her own judgment? Or believe everyone else in her life?

She needed time to consider, and with Seth standing so close, she could not think at all. She wrenched her gaze away from Seth, and found Vaughn's sober face. Her own must have been telling, for he came forward, and rested his hand on Seth's shoulder.

The Irishman let her hand drop, and spun away, as if he, too, forced himself to it. He turned, looking for a chair, then finally stood at the end of the mantelshelf, and propped his head against his elbow, against the shelf.

He's too uncomfortable to sit, Natasha realized, and that brought her a measure of ease. She was not alone in her nervousness. But what was Seth nervous about? She looked at Vaughn, who had clearly orchestrated this meeting.

"Natasha. Lady Munroe, may I introduce to you Seth Williams, son and heir of Marcus Williams, Earl of Innesford."

Natasha glanced at Seth. He was standing very still, as if he waited for her reaction. "Surely, you must know that this is not a surprise to me, Seth. Even if you had not made me believe it the night of the ball, I could scarce ignore your mother's claim, nor the twittering of every gossip and scandalmonger in London."

Vaughn continued. "You should know, Natasha, that Seth and I have known each other since we were children."

"Yet night before last you asked him if he was Seth Williams, and he denied it." She looked at Seth. "You introduced yourself as Seth Harrow. You lied to all of us."

He pushed his hand through his hair, the long fingers raking through the waves. She realized, then, why it looked so rumpled. This was not the first time he'd vented his nervousness in that way. "Natasha, for fifteen years I have been Seth Harrow. Williams was a name I left behind in Ireland—forever, I thought. Your father has changed that now. If he had not spoken, then no one in London would have known of my connection to the Earl of Innesford."

"But now you claim the name. Why?"

Seth visibly hesitated. She saw him swallow before he spoke, his voice low. "Because of you."

"Because of me? But why?" There was a roaring in her ears, and her legs were suddenly too weak. Even as she demanded the explanation, she saw the shape of it—the incredible, sweet shape of it. He wanted her. Not as a dalliance, or an interlude. He wanted her in a way that society would accept.

Abruptly, she fell back into the high-backed chair, all the strength in her legs draining.

"Vaughn, she's gone white!" she heard Elisa cry.

Natasha saw Seth was about to lunge towards her and held out her hand. "I'm all right," she said quickly. "Please...don't. Not right now."

Seth gripped the edge of the shelf, his knuckles turning white, but he remained where he was. He glanced at Vaughn, and Natasha recognized the plea in his expression.

Vaughn brought his hands together. "Let me tell you Seth's story, Natasha. Then you can decide what you want to do. Will you let me do that?"

"Of course. I need to know. But first, Elisa...please, may I have some tea? Or water, perhaps?"

Elisa rose and reached for the bell pull, and when Gilroy magically appeared, asked him to serve tea.

Vaughn told her, then, the incredible story of Seth's life—their shared history at Eton School, and then Cambridge for a year, before Seth returned to Ireland for one last fateful summer, fifteen years ago. She listened with total concentration as Vaughn laid out the night he was arrested, and the next year and a half as he was tried, sentenced, transported, to finally arrive in Port MacQuarrie.

"They say it's the worst penal colony in the world," Natasha remarked.

"They have the right of it," Seth replied, the first comment he had made. Vaughn shot him a look, then, and Natasha realized that Vaughn had made Seth agree to let him tell the tale. Perhaps because Vaughn was a more impartial storyteller than Seth may have been, or perhaps because Vaughn knew her a little better, and knew what she could tolerate. For Natasha recognized from the awful details Vaughn supplied that there was more he did not speak aloud. One day, she decided, she would have those details from Seth himself. And she would not judge him by them.

But for now she listened and thought of Seth as a young man of nineteen, confused and alone in the world, sent to a foreign land to work off a crime he'd never committed. "Seven years. It's so long…" Fifteen years ago, she had been a mere six years old, with ringlets, short skirts, a soiled pinafore and scuffed boots. Her kitten had been her greatest possession, and now so much time had passed she could barely remember the kitten's name or even what had become of it. From the time she had been six, until the year she turned fourteen, Seth had been a convict doing hard labor for his crimes. Quickly, like wine from a decanter, a stream of significant events and memories from those years poured through her memory. The birthdays, the parties, the family dinners. Holidays in the country, and her first tour of Europe at thirteen. Arguments with her parents about appropriate dresses for a girl her age. Balls—so many balls and grand soirees! The excitement of the start of the season and the highlights of the year's social calendar. All those memories, all those watershed moments. And throughout all those years, Seth had lived his desperately mean little life in the worst prison in the world.

She closed her eyes for a moment, unable to shake the horrible image. "How terrible it must have been for you."

"There were some that were considered unskilled, and they were assigned to laboring camps," Seth said, his voice low. "Day in and day out, they did naught but break rocks and build walls. They lived out of tents year-round, and Van Dieman's Land has weather every inch as bitter as a cold winter in Innesford." He frowned. "Those poor sorry lads died like fleas, but there was always a new supply of convicts for England kept sending more and more."

Seth shook his head. "I was one of the lucky ones. I found myself assigned as a servant to an Englishman who was trying to set up a trading business out of Port MacQuarrie. He had himself a grand little whaler that he used as a merchanter. He'd run supplies down from Sydney town, and sometimes England itself, when the going was fair. And for six years I worked with John Foley. He was a proud man, but honorable, 'nd he alone was the only Englishman I could stand to be in the same room with. The man was without his letters, though. He needed someone to read and write and deal with his correspondence. He must've looked upon me as a God-given blessing—a convict that'd do his paperwork, yet wouldn't cost him a penny beyond food and shelter. Then, when he died, well..." Seth rubbed the back of his neck. "He gave me the business."

Natasha stared at him. "Gave it to you? A convict?"

Vaughn shook his head. "Seth is leaving out a most vital part of his story, so I will tell it."

"The ladies haven't the need to hear the lurid details," Seth said quickly.

"This lady has already heard them from Vaughn," Elisa replied firmly. "Vaughn is right, Seth. She must know all of it—as much as you can tell. And this part in particular."

Seth took a deep breath. Natasha could see his chest rise beneath the shirt, and bit her lip to fight the sudden urge to pull the shirt from his pants and run her hands beneath the linen, to spread her fingers over the flesh she just knew would be hot, pliant and silky. Then he pushed his hand through his hair again, and nodded to Vaughn.

Vaughn put his fingers together, and touched his lips with them, composing the start of his narrative. Natasha saw Elisa was watching Vaughn's fingers, her eyes narrowed a little, and her breath coming quickly.

Feeling like she was eavesdropping, or intruding upon a moment Elisa had intended to be quite private, Natasha returned her attention squarely to Vaughn's face again, and sipped her cooling tea.

"For transportees, perhaps the worst part of their sentence is the journey to Australia. They're herded upon ships, and crammed into holds too small to contain them all, and for eight, ten weeks or more they must survive storms, corrupt guards, and inadequate food. These ships are paid to transport the convicts, and the more they carry, the higher their fee. There is no penalty and little investigation if a ship arrives in Australia with fewer convicts than when they left port, so they have no reason to care for their prisoners' welfare.

"In the sixth year of Seth's service to John Foley, his master decided that transporting convicts seemed like a profitable venture. Seth tried to explain to him the truth of it that to profit at all would mean treating fellow human beings with less regard than the Herefordshire bulls he regularly shipped from England. But Foley could only see the profit, he'd spoken at length to other transportation ship owners and they had painted a rosy picture for him. Foley took Seth with him on his first voyage, using an old whaler he'd just acquired and equipped for human transportation."

Natasha was startled. "How could you go with him?" she asked Seth. "How could you stand to watch their suffering?"

"I went because I couldna' stay away. If I was there I could watch over them, be sure they were treated as well as it was in my power to arrange."

"I see." Natasha looked at Vaughn, waiting for him to continue.

"The contracts for transportation were difficult to get, for there were plenty of merchants willing to turn a profit at the government's expense. But there was a new opportunity looming. Foley knew that if he could get his ship to England, he could win a contract to transport convicts to the new prison colony starting up in Fremantle, in Western Australia. The one journey would be so profitable, he could re-convert his ship back to the whaler it is designed to be, and either sell the ship or work the whale trade down in Albany. Crews were easy to find down there, for Albany was a free town, well established, and the whale trade was thriving.

"He took Seth with him, because Seth was a steady hand on board, and had learned much about handling boats over the six years he'd been his servant. And as Seth just told you, he went to keep an eye on the convicts.

"On the return voyage from England, in 1829, there was a terrible storm at sea. Seth risked his life to help the transportees in the prison deck up onto the top deck, where they could survive the storm without drowning in rising bilge waters. He also saved Foley's life by lashing him to the mast, and then he single-handedly steered the boat through the raging seas until they reached calmer waters." Vaughn grimaced. "Seth made light of this, but I happen to know a little about ships, and I can tell you that one man trying to handle a ship through high seas would be a next-to-impossible task. It would take physical strength, and endurance beyond imagination. What happened next doesn't surprise me in the slightest."

Elisa sat forward, her eyes shining with anticipation.

"After the storm, they toted up the damage, and souls lost to them. Many of the crew, you see, had been washed overboard, or were injured, and couldn't work the sails. Foley didn't know enough about handling a ship, for he was a businessman first. Seth convinced the transportees to work with him to keep the boat afloat and sea-worthy, so that they could all make it to port alive. And so they did.

"When the ship arrived in Fremantle, Foley petitioned to the Governor of New South Wales, who was the nearest representative for the crown, for Seth's unconditional pardon. Six weeks later, an answer was received. The convicts who had helped Seth had their sentences reduced by half. And Seth was a free man.

"For the next year, Seth worked for Foley, and saved his meager salary. He intended to buy himself one of the castoff whalers that were used for transporting most of the convicts. The whaling industry was still growing there, although there was sharp competition from American whaling vessels. In 1832, Foley died. He'd made Seth his sole heir, and Seth was suddenly the owner of a fleet, with a small fortune to his name, and a thriving merchant business that was not subject to the vagaries of whale spotting and American competition."

Natasha shook her head a little, and looked at Seth. "And you did not feel that was something I should know?" she asked.

He rubbed the back of his neck again. "I'm not proud of my part in the affair. I should've talked Foley out of the venture in the first place, and not scurried around trying to patch things together with spit and prayer after."

"And the men, women and children who had their sentences reduced would still be in prison, if you had."

"Aye, well, there's that," Seth agreed sheepishly.

Natasha put her forgotten cup and saucer aside. The tea was quite cold now. "That was, what, five years ago? You stayed in Australia, Seth, yet you said you wanted nothing more than to return to Ireland to help your friends."

"True enough," Seth agreed easily, and Natasha could see that he had relaxed. The worst of the telling was done, then. And what a tale! If only all of London could hear it, then perhaps they might change their minds over this most desperate and dangerous criminal.

"Why did you stay?"

"I had six ships, and their crews to look after. Many of the crews had families settled in Albany, and they all looked to me for wages to feed their kin. I couldn't up and leave them stranded. As healthy as the trade was, there was little enough cash for a journey to Ireland that held not a single promise of profit. Foley took nearly six years to build the funds he needed to finance his first journey to England. I took nearly as long as that, myself. I spent the years building the business up. I was always counting the pennies, and adding up the margins, watching the surplus grow. I transported goods and people—paying customers, ye mind—between Albany, Port MacQuarrie, Sydney, Fremantle, anywhere I could turn a good profit. And it'd be an astonishing year if someone didn't offer me their whaling boat at a price that brought a blush to my face."

"You kept buying more boats?" Natasha asked. "I thought you were trying to raise cash?" She'd had ten formal years of education at the hands of indifferent tutors, but mathematics and economics had been her strongest subjects. She knew that buying a ship—investing back into the business—would drain whatever cash Seth had put aside.

And again, Seth rubbed the back of his neck. "These others thought they would bring whalers out to Albany and turn themselves a handsome profit, but it was an overcrowded business they found when they got there. They'd last maybe a year, their cash pouring from their hands like bilge from a leaky boat, and then find themselves in a jam they couldna' figure their way out of…until they heard Seth Harrow would buy their boat for cash. So they'd come to me, hat in hand and humble, and…well."

"The ships all had crews who looked to the owner for their wages," Vaughn explained simply.

Natasha bit her lip to hide her smile, and looked back at Seth. "You couldn't let them starve, could you?" she asked, keeping her tone reasonable.

"Of course I couldn't, lass! There's too much of the starving to go around as it is." Seth almost glared at her, his indignation making her bite the inside of her cheek even harder. Then he added softly, "I've seen too many babes wailing for the pain in their empty stomachs, too many children staring at me with wide, puzzled eyes, wondering what sort of world it was that could keep food from them and let them die unremarked. I'll not sit still and allow babes to go unfed while there's breath in my body. Not again. Not ever."

Natasha's humor fled. "I'm sorry." She couldn't think of what else she could say that would take that angry glint from his eyes.

He pushed his hand through his hair again, and took a deep breath.

Vaughn shifted in his chair, and took over the tale once more. "Seth finally scratched together the cash he needed in 1837. Last year. He set sail the day after Christmas. The night of the ball—the night you met him, Natasha, was his first night on English soil in fifteen years. There were two reasons he bothered to visit this country. And I think you can probably guess both of them."

"To see your mother," Natasha said instantly, glancing at Seth for his small, confirming nod. "And…food. For your friends in Ireland. Liam, and the others."

"Well done," Vaughn said softly.

"I only ever intended to linger long enough to fill the holds with food, then set sail immediately for Cork," Seth added. "Once I'd made Ireland, I thought I'd be able to convince many of them to come away back to Australia with me, if I made a good accounting of my life there. And in truth, it's a far better life than most of them face under the English yoke. I would steal in and out of London, and none'd be the wiser, but…" He grimaced and shrugged. "I'd not made allowances for this black bloody temper of mine, nor…" He looked at her then, straight into her eyes. "Nor did I plan for you."

Natasha shivered, and her heart picked up its pace, but she fought to think things through despite the heady implication behind his words. For despite them, she was still wary. She'd had her coming out season when she was sixteen, and within the first six weeks of that season, she had realized with an abrupt shock that she was considered a rare beauty, one that men would willingly fight over. It garnered her attention she did not want. Her appearance drove men to desperate measures to possess her, and she had long ago learned how to deflect even the most ardent of them. Only Vaughn had appeared indifferent to her looks. Perhaps that was why she had been drawn to him.

But now she tried to contain her runaway heart, and consider Seth's words coolly. "You could still go to Ireland," she pointed out. "There's nothing holding you here in England. You could steal out of the county in your ship and go help your friends. No one will stop you."

"No one but you," Seth added, and her heart stopped, and her stomach rolled over in a lazy way that made her tremble.

Vaughn stood up. "Elisa, a walk to Hyde Park would be just the thing."

"Yes, you're quite right," Elisa agreed, putting her teacup aside.

"No, please don't go on my account," Natasha said quickly.

Vaughn shook his head. "We will give you two some privacy. Take it, Natasha, for you won't find such an offer anywhere else in London. You and Seth must talk, and you can only talk freely if we are not here. Gilroy will be within calling distance, if you feel the need, but I'm confident you will not. Not with Seth."

Natasha bit her lip, uncertain. Fear was looming large again. Even though she knew the truth about Seth, she still did not really know him. He was asking her for a decision that would change the course of his life and affect the lives of hundreds of people who looked to him for their daily living, based purely on a story—a fireside tale.

Vaughn must have seen something of her fear in her face, for he smiled kindly. "Before I go, I will tell you something that may help you think about this." Gilroy held out his coat, and he slipped his arms into it, and then held up a finger for emphasis. "None of what Seth and I have told you has been proven. There isn't a single fragment of evidence, for I have yet to see even this boat of his that he claims to have tied up at the East End."

"It's a ship, ye great lout. If that's your way of helping the lass, I'd ask ye kindly to save your breath," Seth growled.

Vaughn glanced at his friend with a smile, as he buttoned up his coat. "It reads better if it's all laid out," he said simply. "Remember. Strategy, Seth."

Seth scowled and crossed his arms.

Vaughn continued, undeterred. "What you should know, Natasha, is that the conviction for which he claims he is innocent fits in with his character. He's passionate, Irish to the core, despite being half-English, and fiercely loyal. Seth is one of the most honorable, loyal men I have ever known. It's those two qualities that make me believe his story."

Elisa settled her shawl around her shoulders. "What he says is quite true, Natasha. Vaughn is so sure of Seth that he has spent the last day contacting all his people—especially those in Ireland—with the sole intention of helping Seth find the proof he needs. And Vaughn is better at this than any man that I know, for he found my son when no one else could…or would."

She smiled and rested her hand on Natasha's arm.

Then Vaughn and Natasha left for Hyde Park, Gilroy following them from the room.

She was alone with Seth.

Chapter Eight

Seth was staring at her, his silver eyes dark like a coming storm. Natasha realized she was trembling, and moved to sit on the end of the settee, which was as far from the fireplace and Seth as the room allowed.

"It's…quite a life you've had, Seth," she ventured, for he seemed to be in no rush to fill the silence that had bloomed.

"Ye don't believe me, do you?" he asked, his voice low.

"I need time to…absorb it," she pleaded. "For two days I have heard nothing but terrible stories about your conviction as a murderer, and how you have ruined so many people's lives. And no one, not even you, disputed that you had, indeed, been transported to Australia for murder. Now I find that there's a whole facet to the story that wasn't visible before."

He moved towards her. "Surely you suspected I'd have my own story to tell?"

"Yes," she whispered.

He sank onto the sofa beside her, and rested his elbow on the chair's arm, running his fingers along the plush red material. His hands were large, the fingers long-tapered, and calloused. Silence fell again, broken only by the crackling of logs on the fire. She could feel him watch her, his silver gaze burning into her. She could feel a blush race up her cheeks. Dismayed, she tried to compensate for the telling reaction. She caught his gaze and held it. "Why do you stare at me so?"

The sides of his mouth lifted in a lazy smile. "I think you are more beautiful without all the makeup and frills." His gaze shifted over her face, reminding her that she wore no rouge, or any ornament in her hair. The dress she wore was equally plain.

She touched her hair self-consciously. "I left the house and did not even pause to glance in the mirror…I was so mad."

He lifted the hand that lay on the back of the sofa, and very gently, with just his fingertip, touched her cheek. "They hit you?" he asked. Tiny flecks seemed to swirl in his eyes, as if the storm drew closer.

"I was horrible to my mother."

"Did she deserve it?"

"Well…perhaps. She was being a hypocrite."

Seth sat back suddenly, and his eyes darkened even more. It was like watching the sky to guess the mood of the coming weather. She could read his anger in his eyes. "About me," he said flatly.

Should she tell him the truth? He had honored her with the truth of his past—and had held almost nothing back. "Yes," she admitted finally. Reluctantly.

He abruptly stood, and turned, as if he sought a direction to move. His hands curled into fists.

Natasha scrambled to her feet and grasped his arm. "Seth, it is only what all of London says about you." His arm under her fingers was iron hard with muscle. "If you spend your fury upon my family, then you must spend it upon the whole city. The whole country. They can only judge by what they see, and all you have shown them is a man convicted of murder, who tore his family apart."

He whirled suddenly to face her. "Is that what you think? That I want to wring their necks for what they think of me?"

She hesitated, dropped her hand from his arm. "Is it not what angers you?"

"For the love of…" He wrapped his arm about her waist and drew her to him, and Natasha did not try to pull away even though her heart hammered loud enough to wake the dead. He pulled slowly, as if he did not want to startle her, until she was held tight against him, and she could feel the heat of his body against hers. She found herself gazing into his eyes, held by the swirling emotion there. His fingers touched her cheekbone again, gently. "My anger is not for what they say of me, my sweet Natasha. It's for the pain I have delivered upon you. I would do all I can to rid myself of this wretched past of mine—all but put you in danger."

"This was no doing of yours."

"Would you have defied your family if the criminal they disparaged had not been me?" he asked, his voice low.

Natasha swallowed. His nearness was making her thoughts blur. She could not think beyond the need to have him run his hand all over her. Her breasts ached for his touch.

He shook her a little, to emphasize his words. "I asked this of you once before, but now you have had the full story, you should get to choose again. Send me away, Natasha. Tell me to go, and I will."

"Will you ever hurt me, Seth Harrow?"

"Not I, but there are things in my life, people—"

She placed her fingers against his lips, and thrilled at the touch of the soft flesh against hers. "But you will not ever hurt me, in spirit or in body?"

He took a deep breath. "I would kill and be a murderer for true than allow any harm be done to you."

"Then that is all that matters, isn't it? The rest is for later."

His mouth slanted over hers in a kiss that was surprisingly gentle. One hand braced the back of her head, the other cupped her jaw. His tongue eased her lips open, and he groaned low in his throat when she allowed him entry. He tasted like mint, sweet and cool, and she heard herself moan, could do nothing to stop it.

The fingers at her jaw slipped down her neck, over the pulse beating wildly, down further to the swell of her breasts. She caught her breath in surprise at the touch, which was at once familiar and strange. Seth paused, lifting his head up to check her face.

Her stomach tightened as she read the desire in the silver depths. The raw need. His eyes asked a silent question. She smiled and kissed him for her answer, and his lips were hot against hers.

God help her, but she did not want him to stop. She found she was arching her back, almost offering herself to him. She wanted his hand over her breast to touch the breast properly, without impeding cloth or corsetry, but she didn't know how to speak the wish aloud even though it throbbed in her veins in thick demand.

His lips lifted from hers, and his hand from her breast. She stifled her protest when she realized that he was addressing the buttons on the front of her day dress. Her heart leapt high.

He stared into her eyes. "Tell me to stop," he whispered.

She slid her hand beneath his and loosened the button below the one he tackled, then nimbly slipped the rest undone, well below her waist. The dress sagged open, revealing the satin covering of her corset and the camisole beneath.

Seth's fingers hovered over the swell of her breasts above the lace edges of the camisole. He seemed afraid to touch her flesh, although his gaze was riveted upon her décolletage. Understanding flared in her. He was as unsure of seducing a maiden, as the maiden was unsure of how to make it happen.

She tugged at the bow holding the camisole closed, unraveling it. The camisole spread open, and with an impatient jerk, she pulled the sleeves of her dress and the straps of the camisole down both shoulders. Her breasts were not quite fully exposed, but they were as easily accessible as the wearing of a corset would allow.

In her mind, she saw Vaughn's hands on Elisa's breasts, her dress sinking around her shoulders…

She took Seth's hand and placed it against the flesh of her breasts, and gasped at the touch of his hot flesh. Even through the thin cotton of the camisole, her nipples reacted to the touch, tightening up into hard buds.

Seth groaned, and his grip around her waist tightened, bringing her hips hard against him once more. His hand swept over the flesh of her shoulders, the thumb stroking with a gentle caress. Then, with considerably more expertise than she, he pushed the camisole down, revealing all of her breasts except for the underside, which was supported by the corset.

Natasha caught her breath. No man had ever seen her breasts before this moment. She was aware of the trembling sweeping through her, even as the moist flesh between her legs throbbed.

Seth kissed her shoulder, actually licked the skin, sending a quiver through her, and his lips began to kiss and smooth their way down to the upper swell of her breast. Natasha found she was holding her breath, knowing that he was about to take her nipple into his mouth. She wondered what it would feel like…

When his lips finally closed over her distended, sensitive nipple, she threw her head back with a hard moaning gasp. The pleasure! It leapt a hundred times higher, as his teeth—yes, his teeth actually tugged on it, and his tongue laved the nipple and the flesh around it. She thought she would die if he stopped…or if he did not stop. Her world, her life, narrowed down to focus on that delicious sensation that sent spiraling, climbing waves of excitement through her.

She felt the tickle of his hair against her shoulders, neck…and her hand. She realized her hand had buried itself in his hair, and was encouraging him with a restless arching of her fingers. Her other hand was at his shoulder, holding him against her. Such wantonness!

But then his mouth caught her other nipple, and her thoughts were lost in the maelstrom of deafening pleasure swooshing through her. She was hot and cold at once, racked with shivers of delight. Her clothes were an impediment—she longed to be rid of them.

She felt soft support at her back, and realized that Seth had laid her upon the settee. She was pleased rather than alarmed. Now he had two hands to provide pleasure. Her thighs fell restlessly apart beneath her skirts, and she wished she had the audacity to pull her skirts aside, to give him complete access to the hot, wet juncture of her thighs. The flesh there felt thick and swollen, and it throbbed with a beat that matched her heart. With each little frisson of delight that his mouth imparted to her breasts, the pleasure was echoed there. The place where his tongue had stroked now responded with silvery spasms.

Perhaps...perhaps she might experience once again that explosion of the senses she had felt before.

But Seth was pulling away, lifting her hands from him.

"No!" Her voice was husky, weak. "No, don't stop. Please."

"Hush, lass. Hush." His hand on her wrist was gentle, but firm. "We must stop now, while I have will enough to leave ye be." He was returning her camisole to rights, covering her breasts, and fastening the buttons of her dress as he spoke. His eyes were half-closed, but beneath the lowered lids she could see that the irises were wide and dark, consuming the silver gray.

"But..." She could say no more, for humiliation seemed to be swallowing her. Hot, hard tears were gathering into an indigestible lump in the back of her throat, and burned her eyes.

Seth glanced at her face, and then looked back. His hands stilled. "Don't look at me like that," he pleaded.

"You don't want me, after all," she said, forcing the words past the restriction in her throat. It hurt to speak them.

His brows rushed together. "Ye don't understand, Natasha. It's because I want ye that I must not take ye."

"No, I don't understand," she said, and then the tears spilled. She sat on the sofa, feeling a helpless mortification as they slid down her cheeks.

Seth wiped them with his thumb and sat back. "You're the most confounding woman, Natasha. A maiden like you...does your virtue mean nothing to you?"

"I resent it," she said truthfully. "To keep it means I cannot experience..." She could feel herself blushing furiously—her face glowed hot. "I cannot experience that which you gave me…at the ball." She dropped her gaze to her lap, unable to look into his eyes as she finished.

"Ah—" He sounded almost relieved, which made her lift her chin, surprised, to look at him again. He was smiling a little, a knowing gleam in his eyes. "If that's all it is, then your virtue is no barrier." His thumb stroked her cheek again, although her tears had almost dried. "Who would have suspected the wanton that lies beneath these elegant silks and ruffles?"

"You did," Natasha said flatly.

His hand fell away, and his eyes grew darker. "Yes," he agreed.

"But the pleasure you speak of…it is not all of the matter, is it?"

"No." His eyes were even stormier now. She was drowning in their turbulent gaze. "But until our union is accepted by all of London, that is all it must be. Do you understand, Natasha?"

She swallowed. "Yes." She understood clearly. The final act, the hazy, barely understood concept of a man taking a woman…it was the one she craved above all else, but would not have. Not now. Not until Seth had taken on all of London…and won.

*****

"So, what do you think of Seth?" Elisa asked Natasha, a knowing smile on her lips.

It was the day after Seth had gently refused to seduce her. Much had happened in the twenty-four hours that had passed since then. Natasha had returned home in Vaughn's carriage, bracing herself for the confrontation with her parents, but when she had arrived home, her father merely nodded his greeting at her before sinking back behind the broadsheet he was reading. Natasha stared at the masthead of the newspaper, puzzled. He must have known what had happened, for he had not risen to his feet and kissed her temple, as he tended to do upon returning home. But neither was he standing at the fireplace, whiskey glass in hand, waiting for her, as he always did when she had transgressed his demands in some way.

And her mother was nowhere to be seen.

Finally, she turned away from him, intending to go to her bedroom.

"Natasha."

Her father's voice halted her, a pace from the door. She faced him once more. He lowered the paper enough to look at her over the top of it. His expression was bleak.

"You're a grown woman, and even though you are a woman, you have an excellent mind. Because I know that you are capable of making good decisions, I will not gainsay those decisions, so long as they do not affect your duties to your family or to me."

She nodded. Her duty to the family had been long preached to her—to find and marry a peer of the realm, and bear him a suitable heir. "I understand, Father."

"I have explained this to your mother."

No wonder her mother was nowhere to be seen! To be told her daughter was free to think and make her own decisions… Her mother must have expired on the spot. "Thank you," she said, inadequately. She waved towards the door. "I must change for dinner."

"A moment." He cleared his throat, and the paper lowered a little more. "You should know, Natasha, that even though Wardell is accepted by polite society and his reputation is impeccable, there are whispers. You know a little of his history, and his wife's. Be wary of being seen too much in their sympathy, daughter."

Then, in a blazing rush, she understood that her father and mother had no idea that Vaughn and Elisa were harboring Seth in their house. If they even suspected this fact, they would surely lock her in her bedroom for the rest of her life.

She took a deep breath. "Thank you for your confidence, Father." And she hurried from the room before her burning face gave lie to her demeanor. Her sleep had been restless and broken as she felt the true burden of her conscience. She found only one small seed of comfort, she was making the best decision she could with information she had that no one other than Vaughn and Elisa shared. She trusted Seth, and must stand by him.

Her mother did not appear downstairs until noon the next day, and she was silent and pale, picking at her lunch. When Natasha rose from the table and called for her shawl and bonnet, her mother showed the first sign of real animation that day.

"Where are you going?" she demanded.

"I am visiting Elisa again this afternoon. She is holding a formal afternoon tea."

Her mother blanched even whiter, and the veins in her forehead stood out. "But…" Then she caught herself. "Will there be anyone else in attendance. Anyone we know?"

"Lady Danforth, I believe. And Sophia, Baroness Luciano." These ladies were solid pillars of society, their reputations unimpeachable. Natasha relented a little, for her mother was very pale. She added gently, "I will take care to make sure my reputation is not sullied, Mother. Father spoke to me last night."

Caroline bit her lip and stirred her tea furiously. "Very well then," she muttered. But she had not said goodbye.

After Elisa's elegant and most proper tea party, the ladies Danforth and Luciano had departed for their respective city mansions and townhouses, to prepare for a small soiree they both were attending that evening. Elisa had suggested that Natasha accompany her on a stroll through the Park, and Natasha had tried to refuse, for she was seething with frustration. Seth had not made an appearance all afternoon. Neither had Vaughn, but Seth's absence was as tangible as a sore tooth, and she barely managed polite conversation with the ladies at the tea party, and she tried to put off Elisa's request for a walk in the park with the same lack of grace.

But Elisa had insisted with a gentle firmness that Natasha found difficult to refuse. Now, at four o'clock, she found herself walking along one of the many graveled paths in Hyde Park, this one less traveled than the others. Elisa had seemed preoccupied, and Natasha wondered if it was the babe she bore that took her attention, but could not bring herself to ask such an indelicate question.

Then Elisa had asked her own indelicate question about Seth.

"How do I feel about him?" Natasha repeated, giving herself time to collect an answer together. Her feelings were not straightforward at all, and she barely knew what words to use, or even how to voice them aloud. "I think he is very handsome," she ventured, inadequately.

"Is that all?"

Natasha lifted her brow at her friend's bluntness. "Well, I confess I am attracted to him."

Elisa stopped walking and turned to face her. "Attracted? That sounds so very…mild."

Natasha felt her cheeks heat. "What is it that you want to know? You want me to use shocking words?"

"I want nothing but the truth." Elisa's voice was mellow, but there was a core of relentlessness there that told Natasha Elisa would have her way in this—that truth was the only coinage with which Elisa would deal. Elisa looked up at her, for she was somewhat shorter than Natasha, and smiled a little, her eyes sparkling in the fading sunlight. "So, tell me how you feel about Seth?"

"He scares me," Natasha blurted, then hurried to amend the indictment. "But he also makes me feel…" How could she speak of concepts, which she barely could hold in her own mind? "Oh, I do not have the words for this!" She rested her hand against her midriff. "It's all in here, a hot stew of dilemmas. My own feelings fight against each other, even as they fight against my family, against Seth himself."

Elisa laid her hand on Natasha's arm. "Be calm, Natasha. Be calm. Tell me. Why do you fight Seth?"

And suddenly, just like that, the words were there. Natasha explained it all, as Elisa slipped her hand under Natasha's arm and coaxed her into walking again. As they walked, Natasha would seize upon a fragment of feelings within her, and convey it, and then another would present itself, then another. And piece-by-piece, with simple words, she revealed it all.

Elisa was silent for a while once Natasha finished speaking. She gave a little laugh. "To think I once believed you to be a fragile, fragrant rose, empty-headed beyond the single-minded ambition to find a husband. I had no idea…"

"I was once all of those things, Elisa. Vaughn changed it. He showed me—both of you showed me—the value of truth. Oh, not just spoken truth, but the hard truth."

"The truth that sits deep inside you and resents even your own probing?" Elisa finished.

"Yes." Natasha felt relief. Elisa understood this, too.

"Then you believe Seth. Believe his story, his innocence."

"I believe his story, yes. I believe he is not a murderer or a criminal. But he is not an innocent, Elisa. There is…" She struggled to put her finger upon her fear. "There is a fury in him, a well of anger. I believe that he is capable of all which they charged. And I think that is what most people see, that anger, and because of it, they are forced to believe the charges."

"His has not been an easy life." Elisa squeezed her arm a little. "But he would not harm you. You know that, don't you?"

Natasha's breasts were still tender from where Seth had touched her, his fingers and mouth playing with her overly sensitive nipples. Her stomach clenched at the memory. "I know." Her voice was a husky shell, and Elisa cocked an eyebrow at her, her smile wicked.

"That is how I feel with Vaughn."

Natasha smiled. "Yes, I remember that feeling with Vaughn. I hope you do not mind me saying so?"

"We are friends, Natasha. We can discuss anything, even my husband."

"But it's not the same as it is with Seth. With Seth, it's…stronger. Harder to resist. Oh, Elisa, I make a fool of myself in his presence! I feel so ignorant!" Her eyes pricked with tears, and she dashed them away.

"Ignorance is a natural part of maidenhood, Natasha, dear. Seth must understand that, surely?"

"But he will not teach me. He says…he says he will not—not until…"

Elisa pursed her lips, and her eyes danced. "Oh dear, I can see the shape of your dilemma clearly now," she said, with a little laugh.

"But I cannot!" Natasha cried, and looked around quickly to see who had heard her protest. Doves fluttered at the base of the nearest tree, but there wasn't anyone else within earshot. This was a most secluded path.

"Of course you can't!" Elisa replied firmly.

"Then, for heaven's sake, Elisa, please…tell me how to give a man pleasure. How can I make him…want to take me?"

Elisa grinned. "Where should I start?"

Natasha bit her lip and looked over her shoulder, just to make sure they were still alone. "Touching him down there," she whispered.

"Men are very sensitive to touch, just as we are, but they show it in a more obvious way. You can scarcely go wrong when touching a man's shaft."

"Shaft?" Natasha asked, liking the sound of it.

"Yes, shaft…or cock, or manhood. You can use a myriad of names for his sex," Elisa said with a coy smile. "Caress his member with the tips of your fingers from root to tip, then wrap your fingers around his length, moving your hand up and down in a gentle stroke. Not too fast, but not too slow either."

"How do I know if it is too fast?"

Elisa laughed, a wonderful tinkling sound that made Natasha giggle. "He will tell you, usually by stilling your hand. Do not take offense, just know that you are doing it right."

Knowing she was being incredibly bold, Natasha lowered her voice even more. "He pleasured me the other night."

Elisa stopped in mid-stride, and grabbed hold of Natasha's wrist. "What do you mean?"

"I am still virgin," Natasha assured her. "I think I am, anyway. He did not use...his uh—manhood."

Elisa released a sigh. "Thank God. You must be careful, Natasha. There are consequences to such an act that none can gainsay. An unwanted child, dear lord...it would be the ruin of your life and Seth's. But there are ways of avoiding such things."

Natasha's eyes widened. "There are?" She was shocked.

"But then, there is no need to worry about such matters for now. If Seth will not consummate the act, you are quite safe."

"He used his mouth in a myriad of ways." Natasha could not help the smile that came.

Elisa laughed loudly. "And you would like to know how to do the same to him?"

"Yes."

"Well, one must be careful when it comes to giving oral pleasure."

"Is that what it's called? Why must one be careful?"

"Use your teeth with restraint. You do not want to hurt him. And be mindful to touch all of him, not just his cock, for it is all sensitive."

"There is more to him than just...just his—" Natasha's cheeks burned remembering Seth's erection, hidden behind his trousers. She wondered what it would look like, bared to her gaze. "Would he think me less of a lady for doing such things?"

Elisa snorted. "Dear girl, he will adore you. Trust me."

"I always thought it would be different. Not as pleasurable as I'd heard."

"As young women we are told that giving yourself to a man is a duty, but believe me when I say there is pure pleasure in making love. Not just the act itself, but all the splendid things that go along with it. They are an entertainment all on their own."

Natasha considered this. "You make it sound like it is far better not to…do that."

"On occasions, yes," Elisa said firmly.

"But I want all of it!" She lowered her voice. "I burn with it. I'm not sure what it is all about, or how one goes about it, but I can feel it, down there. I ache, and feel empty. I want…" She held her gloved hands to her burning cheeks, and closed her eyes. "I want him in me," she whispered.

"In time, Natasha. In time. For now, you should enjoy whatever Seth offers. And that is quite a considerable thing on its own. Besides—" Elisa suddenly laughed, low and with a wicked note. "Oh dear, should I?" she said to herself.

"Elisa?" Natasha asked, puzzled.

Elisa pursed her lips, as if she was holding back laughter. She even brought her fingertips to her mouth, pressing hard. Then she nodded, deciding. She grasped Natasha's elbow, and pushed her into walking again. "Natasha, dearest, you must listen to me carefully, and trust me. I will teach you how to have your revenge upon Seth. It will be a pleasurable revenge, but Seth will pay for his refusal to give you everything you want."

And Elisa proceeded to explain in blunt, shocking details, the form and shape of Natasha's revenge. Natasha listened, trying to put aside her shock so that she might absorb all the details. Elisa was thorough and frank, and Natasha found her body growing warm, the cleft between her legs growing slippery with moisture, and her nipples prickling hard with excitement just considering the course she might take. She bit her bottom lip. "And no one will know?" she whispered. "No one will suspect? My reputation will be safe?"

Elisa gave a merry peal of laughter. "Oh, my dear, there is so much one can dare, if only one takes a few elementary precautions. For you and me, for all women, appearance is everything..."

Totally captivated by the subject, Natasha failed to hear the crunching of approaching carriage wheels until the vehicle was almost upon the both of them. They moved aside enough to allow the carriage to pass them, and Natasha glanced over her shoulder to ensure the carriage had seen them.

It was a plain black coach, without adornment or shield upon the door. The coachman was dressed in black from head to toe, and his high collar was pulled up over the lower half of his features, which was odd, for it was a cool day, but hardly crisp.

The carriage slowed as it passed them, and Elisa pulled her skirts out of the way of the wheels, for it was crowding them to the edge of the path. Natasha saw the carriage door open, but Elisa was not looking up.

Alarmed prickled through Natasha, but it was already too late. Another man, also wearing a heavy black coat with an upturned collar, and his hat low on his forehead, leaned out of the open doorway, one hand gripping the doorpost. With a swing of his arm, he scooped Elisa up by the waist.

She shrieked and began to struggle even as he pulled her inside the carriage, which was pulling ahead. Natasha stood, stunned at the sudden disaster. Her mind was blank and questioning. Then she heard the carriage door thump shut, and it broke her paralysis.

"Elisa! Oh my lord, Elisa!" Natasha cried, running after the carriage.

The coachman whipped the horses with a growled curse, and the carriage rocked on its springs as it tore along the gravel path, turned around the bend ahead and disappeared.

Think, think! Natasha told herself. The questions would have to be answered later. For now, she must act fast. She let her shawl fall to the ground, scooped up her skirts in both arms, careless that she might be displaying both ankles and calves, and ran off the path, directly through the trees and plantings. She headed towards The Row, where there was sure to be more traffic. When she burst out upon the wide, busy path, she made a quick decision. An open carriage was bearing towards her, and she ran out into the road, and stopped right in the path of the carriage. She dropped her skirts, and held out her hands. "Stop! Stop, stop!" she screamed.

The coachman's eyes widened. He hauled on the handbrake, and then threw all his weight into pulling back the horses. Natasha stood her ground even as the horses drew closer. Nothing could make her more afraid than she was already. The women in the carriage behind the driver were screaming, their hands over their mouths, clutching each other. Natasha thought she knew the older one, but the woman's name would not come to her.

The horses came to a halt a bare pace from her, and climbed into the air, their hooves flailing. She could feel their hot breath blowing over her, and she grabbed one of the halters as the horses' hooves touched ground again, and stepped around its head so she could see the coachman.

"Bloody 'ell, my lady, I could've done you in!" the coachman bawled. His face was red and sweat rolled down his cheeks.

"Shut up and listen!" Natasha shouted back and the ladies gasped in pure shock. She strode around the horses, making for the coachman's steps. "My friend, Lady Fairleigh, has just been kidnapped."

"Wot the bloody 'ell are you blathering about?" the coachman demanded as she lifted her skirts enough to get her boot onto the step, and then hauled herself up onto the driver's seat.

"Move over," she demanded. "I'm going after her."

"Now, look 'ere!"

"Oh dear!" one of the women murmured.

Natasha straightened up to her full height, and called upon every skerrick of training regarding her station in life that her mother had ever imparted. She held out her hand, and poured as much upper-class haughtiness into her tone as she could. "I demand you give me the reins at once."

The coachman, also trained from boyhood to the complexities of class, fell into a confused silence, looking from Natasha to his two charges.

"Immediately!" Natasha insisted.

It was enough. He handed over the reins and whip and Natasha settled herself onto the seat. She had only ever handled a coach and pair once in her life, but she didn't care. Speed was all she required from this pair. She snapped the whip. "Go, lads!" she cried. The horses lurched forward.

Chapter Nine

When Elisa realized that there were two men in the carriage, and that they were both much stronger than her, she ceased her struggling. She was very much afraid, but knew that she must keep her head now, and watch for an opportunity to escape.

"What do you want with me?" She was relieved her voice did not tremble. It even sounded a little angry. Good.

The man opposite her had hidden his features behind a kerchief tied about his face, and had also drawn his hat down low on his forehead. He leaned towards her, and she realized with a cold chill that he held a knife in his hand. The knife slid towards her and she shrank back, until she was up against the shoulder of the man who had pulled her into the carriage. The knife kept coming closer, until it rested against her throat.

My babe! The thought was a despairing one. She would not plead with them. She would not let them know that she would do anything to ensure the safety of the child within her.

The knife slid from her throat, down to the swell of her breasts. She closed her eyes. Was this a matter of rape? Very well, then. She would endure it. She would live beyond it, and so would her child. Her heart wrenched for her husband. Vaughn would have the hardest time of this…

The knife sliced her dress open, and the lace fell away, to reveal her corset and the silk of her camisole. Bile rose in her throat.

"She's a fine bit o'lady," the one holding the knife said. His voice was low, with a hungry note to it.

The man holding her recognized the hunger. "'Urry up, will you? The longer we stay 'ere, the quicker they'll be after us."

The knifeman flipped the knife in his hand with an expert, casual flick of his wrist, so that he was holding the handle like a pen. Gently, he scraped the blade over the silk stretched across her breasts, bumping against the nipples beneath. The blade was so sharp, it severed the silk and her nipple pushed through the slit. "Well, look at that!" the knife man exclaimed with a hoarse voice.

Elisa moaned sickly. She could feel a wave of nausea and dizziness pushing at her, threatening to overwhelm her, but knew she must keep her wits. She struggled, forcing herself to action.

"Ooooh, and she writhes just like a whore, too," the man crooned.

"Yer a sick bastard," the other muttered. "Let's get on with what we were paid for. 'E'll not thank us for meddling with 'er."

The reminder seemed to cool the knifeman's ardor. He swore under his breath and reached into his pocket. Elisa saw something pale yellow in his hand. The other man reached around her and unhooked half of her corset. She began to struggle harder, as the knifeman shoved his hand inside her corset. His big hand squeezed her breast painfully.

At all costs she must not faint. She swallowed against the rise of sickness.

Then his hand was removed. The knifeman sat back, and kicked open the carriage door with a curse. She saw the flash of trees and bushes swishing past the carriage.

Even as Elisa tried to fathom why he would do that, the man holding her was pushing her up, onto her feet. No, not onto her feet, but through the door.

She screamed as she flew through the air. There was a yew tree right before her, and she threw up her arms to protect her face just as she impacted against its hard, thick bole.

The blackness overwhelmed her at last.

*****

Seth paced before the fire, chilled to the bone despite the warmth of the room. Every now and again, he glanced at Natasha, and marveled at her stillness.

She stood near the big window staring out into the night. Each time he looked at her his heart stirred again, and he would remember how she had brought Elisa home.

He and Vaughn had been in Vaughn's study when they'd heard a woman screaming, out on the street. They'd hurried to the windows, in time to see the astonishing sight of Natasha driving a carriage and pair. Her hair had come loose and hung in a long dark waterfall down her back, ruffled by the passing air. Her face had been set with an expression Seth would never forget. It was at once fearful and angry, yet determined. She'd had to stand to step on the footbrake with enough force to bring the frothing, driven horses to a stop. They'd halted, shivering, their eyes rolling, while Natasha screamed for Vaughn.

Up and down the street, people were coming to a halt, sensing drama, and wanting to watch. Vaughn touched Seth's arm. "Stay here. It's broad daylight and too many are watching the house now."

Seth swallowed dryly, and nodded, even though he wanted to dash out with Vaughn and find out what could possibly bring Natasha to such a public display.

As soon as Natasha saw Vaughn, she pointed into the carriage, and called something to him—Seth could not hear the words, for she had meant them for Vaughn alone. Inside the open carriage was what could only have been the real coachman, and two women, all huddled together on the backseat. Vaughn turned to the front seat, and dipped down. When he straightened, Elisa was in his arms.

Seth clenched the curtain. Elisa was white as a ghost, and lay in a faint in his arms. Her dress…something had ripped her dress open to the waist.

Natasha threw the reins to the driver, and climbed from the carriage and for one priceless moment, Seth saw her trim ankle, wrapped in neat blue leather, and a long, slender calf in white silk stocking, before her dress fell back to the ground. She led Vaughn to the door, and Seth could hear her talking all the way.

Seth hurried to the front door, and was in time to see Vaughn shoulder his way into the house, before Gilroy could push the door aside. Gilroy gripped the door, held it steady, and Natasha took the lamp from him. "The bedroom," she told Vaughn, who was heading towards the study. He glanced at her.

"The bedroom," she repeated firmly. "A doctor must be fetched to see to her."

Vaughn seemed to hesitate a little.

"Vaughn, she's bleeding from there, from the woman's place," Natasha said, and Seth realized that she neither stuttered nor blushed at speaking of such things before a butler, maid, and two men.

Vaughn's face drained of color, but he nodded, and turned to the stairs, taking them two at a time despite his burden. Natasha climbed right behind him, her skirts bundled up in one arm, the other holding the lamp high to show Vaughn the way. Her loose dark hair rippled all the way past her waist, to swing about her hips.

Seth pushed on Gilroy's shoulder. "Ye best get the doctor right quick," he said softly.

Gilroy nodded, staring up the stairs at his master and mistress with concern. "I'd best do that," he agreed, and stepped out the open doorway. He was wearing neither coat nor collar, for he had taken a rare afternoon away from his duty of running Vaughn's household, but he had clearly forgotten his lack of proper attire—an event that was just as remarkable as any other this surprising day had held.

Natasha had stayed with Vaughn and Elisa until the doctor arrived, and for some time after that, while Seth had begun to pace in front of the fireplace. Gilroy had reappeared to stoke the fire, his tie back in place, and striped jacket buttoned firmly. After he had rebuilt the fire, he poured Seth a whiskey, unasked, and held the glass out on his tray.

"I cannot tell the young Lady Winridge that I have sent word to her family that she is here and safe. Perhaps you could let her know when she emerges from Miss Elisa's chamber?"

Seth nodded, and Gilroy bowed and left. Seth knocked back the whiskey in one swallow and resumed his pacing. Finally, there had been a creak of the stairs, a quiet murmuring, and the sound of the front door opening and closing. Natasha stepped into the room, looking tired and sad.

"The doctor just left?" Seth asked.

She nodded in answer. He wanted to pull her into his arms, but hesitated. There was an air about her tonight that told him she would not stand for such things right now. Perhaps when he learned what had happened to Elisa, he would understand why.

Natasha moved to the window and looked out into the night. "Elisa…lost the baby," she said, keeping her back to him.

Seth nodded. The news was not unexpected after Natasha's revelation in the front hall, but he felt a grim sadness anyway. Vaughn would feel this loss keenly.

"What happened, lass?" he asked softly.

"If you don't mind, Seth, I'd rather just tell it one time…when Vaughn comes back." Her tone was remote. Ethereal. And still she kept her back to him.

That was when Seth began his pacing again.

Later, when the fire had begun to die again, Vaughn came into the room. He looked exhausted, and his eyes were haunted. He went straight to Natasha, and hugged her. Hard. His eyes closed as he rested his cheek against the top of her head, and Natasha clung to him just as firmly. Seth quelled the tiny voice of protest inside him. Vaughn's hold was nothing but a friend clinging to another. Finally, Vaughn let her go, and kissed her cheek. "How can I thank you?" he asked, and his voice was a croak.

Natasha looked back at him steadily. "By loving her, and getting her with child again as quickly as possible."

Seth felt another little shock. Something had changed in Natasha this long afternoon. She was facing and dealing with the world like a man—no compromise, no apology, and no embarrassment. And suddenly his fear rose another notch or two. It was strangling him. He'd ached to know what had happened to Elisa. Now, as the cold fingers rippled down his spine, he would do anything not to hear what Natasha was about to say, for he knew with every superstitious bone in his body that somehow, this matter was his fault.

Vaughn sighed in response to Natasha's frank answer, and sat down. But he did not sink into the wing chair. He sat on the edge of it, his arms resting on his knees. "Tell me," he said to Natasha.

She sat on the sofa opposite him, and she, too, sat on the edge, and leaned on her forearms. Unlike Vaughn, she kept her knees together under her stained, creased and torn dress. In a steady monotone, bereft of emotion, Natasha related the tale of Elisa's abduction, and her pursuit in the carriage. Although she gave few details about how she managed to overcome a coach and driver and drive it herself, Seth still marveled at this incredible feat. But Natasha's narrative continued on, how she had raced along the lonely, narrow path in the park, and how they'd found Elisa, a crumpled heap at the base of one of the old yew trees at the southeast corner of the park. They'd only found her because her white dress had glowed softly in the gloaming.

The two women had been alarmed at the way Elisa's dress had been slashed open, but Natasha had been more concerned about Elisa's health. Blood on Elisa's underskirt had confirmed her fears. While the driver blustered about Natasha scaring and shocking his mistresses, Natasha had thrown the horse blanket over Elisa, clambered back up to the driver's seat, and turned the carriage around to race for Vaughn's home, the nearest haven she could think of.

A log fell apart with a hiss of sparks, as Natasha finished her tale. On cue, Gilroy appeared, and stoked the fire again. Natasha sat back, watching him, and Seth knew she had more to say that she dared not speak aloud in front of Gilroy. It chilled him. The full meaning of this day would become clear when she spoke again, he knew.

Finally, Gilroy shut the parlor door. Vaughn looked at Natasha. "What is it?" he asked.

She pulled a folded sheet of parchment from her sleeve and handed it to him. "They stuffed this inside Elisa's dress. I took it before anyone else saw it."

Vaughn unfolded and read the small sheet, and his lips thinned. He glanced at Seth.

"What does it say?" Seth asked tiredly.

Vaughn held it out to him, and Seth took it with a trembling hand. He took a deep breath, and read it.

Stop the investigation, or else.

"God in his heavens," Seth muttered, his voice hoarse. "I feel sick..."

Vaughn reached up and tugged at his forearm. "Sit down before you fall down, man."

Seth sagged onto the sofa. The trembling in his hand had spread throughout his body. "I feel a chill to beat the depths of a Harrow winter..."

A glass was pressed into his hands. He looked up. Vaughn had risen and poured him a whiskey. Seth clutched the glass with both hands, and drank. The glass chattered against his teeth.

"It's all because of me, don't ye see?" he told them both. "My past, my lousy bloody past. The only reason Elisa lies upon that bed up there now is because of me. I should've just...stayed away. I should've been content with my lot these past fifteen years. Sailed off to Ireland and lived a simple existence. But instead...oh god, instead..." He gulped down the last of the whiskey, and gritted his jaw as his stomach rolled in protest. He clutched at his temple, where the steady thumping had turned into runaway horses galloping through the halls of his mind, the beat reverberating through his head, each beat a flare of pain. "I should leave this place."

Natasha looked over at him. Her eyes were enormous in her pale face. "Why?"

"D'ye not see that if I stay, I'll only bring more trouble down upon yer heads?"

"Natasha is quite right. How will leaving help?" Vaughn asked.

"If I'm not here—"

Vaughn shook his head. "This is not your fault, Seth. I will not have you thinking it is."

"Yes, it bloody is!" Seth stood too, facing him. "Don't go giving me any of the blarney about fate and all that rubbish, because the only reason—the only reason this happened was because I talked you into investigating that black bloody night in Harrow, fifteen years ago. D'ye not know how much I wish that night hadn't happened? How much I wish I'd stayed nice and cozy in my bed that night? D'ye not understand how much I regret the last fifteen years, how much I—" He couldn't help himself. He glanced at Natasha. "How much I wish I could still lay claim to the title that's rightfully mine? I swore I'd do anything to change all that, but I did not mean this. Never this."

"But it's done now," Vaughn said softly. "And while your Irish charm might work on the ladies, don't ever think you talked me into doing this. I did it of my own free will." Vaughn took the empty glass from Seth's nerveless hands, crossed the room and poured three drinks. He gave one to Natasha. "It's neat whiskey," he warned. "But it will steady you." He handed Seth his glass back.

Behind him, Natasha tipped back her glass, swallowing the shot in one mouthful. She put the glass aside with the same gentleness she might return a teacup to its saucer, and sat back.

Vaughn sipped his own drink thoughtfully. "In fact, this note is an encouraging sign, Seth."

"And how could that be?" The pounding in his head seemed to be taking away his ability to think, to even speak steadily.

"We must be digging for information in the right places, or they would not have reacted this way. This is simply meant to scare us away from investigating further, and to scare you into running away. They're expecting you to run back to Ireland or perhaps even Australia."

"But who are they?" Natasha asked.

"I don't know. But I intended to find out," Vaughn answered.

"Vaughn, ye cannot—" Seth began.

Vaughn held up his hand, demanding silence.

Seth swallowed his protest. He remembered the ruthless expression on Vaughn's face from their days at Eton, but he'd never seen it so clear and hard before.

"They want us to walk away, our tails between our legs," Vaughn repeated. "So, we'll do the opposite. We will step up the investigation. I have twenty-five men at my disposal. I'll have them sniffing in every corner of England and Ireland before sunrise."

"Are you sure, man?" Seth asked, feeling a burgeoning blossom of hope stir in his heart.

Vaughn met his gaze. His eyes glittered, not with the black, passionate fury that Seth suffered, but a cold, implacable anger. "They've pushed the wrong man."

*****

Natasha and Seth walked in the small garden behind Vaughn and Elisa's townhouse. It was deep night, but still relatively early. Gilroy had sent a man to prepare Vaughn's carriage to take her home. Soon, the carriage would be at the front door.

Vaughn had returned upstairs to be by Elisa's side when she awoke.

Seth spoke out of the darkness, breaking the silence that had drawn around them like the night air. "You said that you loved Vaughn once. Do you still?"

Shocked by the intimate question, Natasha met Seth's intent gaze. She realized, too, that he'd spoken without the brogue—his words had been as stilted and correct as any English lord's. In the dark of the night lit by a small moon, his eyes glowed with a warmth that heated the blood in her veins. He was such a beautiful man, in both spirit and body, this man who had endured so much for a crime he did not commit. The agony he had visibly suffered when he'd believed that Elisa's misfortune was his fault had softened her heart.

To return his kindness, she answered his question truthfully and without prevarication. "I love him as a friend. He will always be my dearest friend, and so will Elisa."

"But you do not desire him?" Again, the proper grammar, the rounded, educated English.

"No."

He watched her, his eyes narrowed a little, gauging her expression. She wondered what he looked for, and how he had worked his way into her heart in so short a time. The sides of his mouth lifted a little and he nodded. "So tell me how ye came to be engaged to the lad." Abruptly, his brogue had returned, almost as if he'd relaxed, or let down his guard.

"Vaughn's father and my parents are…were, friends, of sorts. His estate in the north adjoins our own, but I did not meet Vaughn until I was eighteen. I heard he'd been sent away from Fairleigh Hall when his mother died, when he was very young.

It shocked us all when Vaughn came home after so many years. We had dinner with Lord Fairleigh, Vaughn and Elisa, and Vaughn charmed my father over, and then my mother."

"But not you?"

She laughed under her breath. "Of course he charmed me. How could he not? So young and handsome, and gallant. But it wasn't only his looks and charm that I fell in love with. It was the way he talked to me, like no other man before or since. He asked me a lot of questions and would listen to my answers. Properly. I was not accustomed to that. Not at all. For the first time in my life, someone cared what I thought about."

"But he fell in love with Elisa."

Natasha shrugged. "Yes, he fell in love with Elisa."

"Did he break your heart?"

Surprised at his intimate question, Natasha lifted a brow. "Yes, he did, but he didn't do it on purpose. One can't help whom one falls in love with. I know he would not have deliberately hurt me, and if he could have spared me the embarrassment he would have." She paused, then reached for the deeper truth. The harder truth. "I respect him for his courage, Seth. He faced the entire ton, and spoke of his love for Elisa, and that he intended to marry her. He told them all to go to hell."

The slightest hint of smile played at Seth's lips. "As Vaughn tells it, it was your bravery that saved the day for them."

"Really? He said that?" To be thought well of by Vaughn and the man before her gave her a warm glow of happiness.

He was staring at her. In the light from the lamps on the verandah, she could just see his face. Her mouth went dry. She knew that look—the dark, heavy-lidded expression. His gaze shifted to her lips and she licked them, suddenly self-conscious. Her heart began to beat more swiftly.

"You are so beautiful, do ye know that?"

She spread her torn skirt ruefully, and touched her hair. She'd not had time to do anything but pull the front hair up into a crude knot at the back of her head. The rest of her hair hung loose. She would have to fix that before she returned home, and spare herself endless questions from her parents. "Even torn and dirty?" she jested.

"They're badges of courage, lass."

"Are they? I was simply trying to help Elisa because Vaughn could not."

"You did what must be done, and didn't turn from the hard task. I'll remember it all my days." Seth's voice was low, with a timbre that vibrated up and down her spine.

She took a deep breath, searching for the courage he declared she owned, and curled her hand around his neck. "Kiss me, Seth," she murmured, glad of the night that hid her warming cheeks.

Seth looked startled, then smiled, his white teeth flashing in the dark. "Anything for my lady," he murmured, and swept her into his arms. But she lifted her head the slightest bit and met his lips with her own. She kissed him gently, tentatively, and felt his fractional pause. Was he shocked? Pleased? She remembered what Elisa had told her, and encouraged, she continued to explore. She traced the seam of his lips with her tongue, feeling their softness, urging him to open them, and he did.

"Taking a warrior's reward, my lady?" he murmured against her lips. He smelled of sandalwood and musk, a pleasant scent, and she could taste a trace of whiskey on his lips and breath. All of it was overwhelmed by his heat and size, which dominated her thoughts, and made her feel weak and very feminine.

"Hush," she told him. She brought his mouth back to hers with her hand on his head, and pressed herself against him. She liked the feel of him against her, along the length of her body. She closed her eyes and savored the scent of him, the warmth of him, the taste of him. She probed with her tongue, sliding it over his lips, and was enchanted with the sensation. She let her hand slide down his back, lower, to his tight buttocks. She slipped her hand beneath the coat he wore, and laid it firmly over the mound of muscle, spreading her fingers to explore the shape and feel of it.

Seth jerked his head up, to look at her, and even in the dim moonlight she could see a little of his shock. "M'lady, your courage still burns, I see."

She smiled a little at him, and pulled him tight against her with the hand on his buttock. "You speak truly, Seth." And her heart gave a great leap as she realized that she could feel him pushing against her—his thick cock. It was a hard lump against her hips that she could feel even through three layers of dress and petticoats. She couldn't help it, she moved her hips a little, to explore the shape of it.

Seth gave a great groan, and his hands tightened around her waist. "What is it ye intend, Natasha? To drive me mad?"

Yes, exactly that, she thought, with a wicked mental chuckle. Confidence blossomed in her, along with a hot swirl of excitement. Elisa was right, she could have her revenge. She slanted her head a little and gave Seth a lazy smile. "I merely wanted to kiss you."

She heard a cough behind her, from the verandah. "My lady, the carriage awaits," Gilroy added.

"Thank you, Gilroy—I'll be in at once," she called over her shoulder. She rose up on her toes to kiss Seth one last time, and this time, she let her hand slide around his hip to brush lightly across the bulge at the front of his trousers. Even that light touch imparted a sensation of hot, rigid flesh, and an answering quiver swept through her.

Seth sucked in his breath in a gasp.

A thrill ran through her at the sound. "Good night, Seth," she bid him, and ran lightly for the verandah where Gilroy stood with one of Elisa's bonnets and a shawl and gloves for Natasha to wear home. As Gilroy dropped the shawl around her shoulders, Natasha looked back. Seth stood still in the moonlight, his hands on his hips, watching her. From her perspective, she could see nothing but dark shadows over his face, but she knew his eyes were narrowed, even as his body pulsed with the shock and tiny touch of pleasure she had given him.

She hid her smile and moved into the house.

*****

Vaughn sat at Elisa's side, holding her hand as she slept.

There was a hot, hard mass of pain sitting in the middle of his chest, and he didn't know how to rid himself of it. The longer he sat, the harder and larger the mass grew. He could feel it building inside him, and he knew that if it continued to build, there would come a moment when he could no longer hold it inside. It would spew from him, in scalding words and violence. He almost welcomed that moment—it would bring a small measure of relief from this acid ache.

How badly Elisa had wanted this child! They had all welcomed it—even Raymond had come to him and confessed his delight.

He brushed back a pale curl from her face, and she stirred. She opened her eyes, blinking a few times as she focused on him. The pain in her blue eyes made his heart lurch. If only he could take away the hurt. "I am sorry, my love," he said, and kissed her gently.

Tears welled in her eyes and spilled down her cheeks. Heedless of the doctor's advice that she not be moved, he slid onto the bed, pulled her into his arms, and let her weep. He brushed a hand along her spine, as each quiet sob added to the mass in his chest. "I will find who did this, Elisa. I swear I will find them."

She looked up then, her eyes red-rimmed. "But what about the note? They will kill you if you try."

The pain in his chest cracked and split open, sending sharp shards through him. This was the heart of the matter. "Elisa, we must do this. You and I…we have faced monsters before this day, and together, we found a way past them. Those monsters tried to dictate the course of our lives. They held you outcast, and kept your son from you. They tried to keep us apart. But we won through, and my love, I would not exchange these last years with you even for the sake of my life. They are far too precious to me."

"No, you mustn't say such things! Vaughn, what would I do without you? Please, take it back. My life without you would not be worth living."

"Shhh…" He held her tight until she calmed a little. "Would you give up these last threeyears, Elisa, just for a guaranteed future with me in it?"

"To not have them at all?" She shook her head, and her wet cheek rubbed against his shirt. "No, I could not give them up," she said at last.

"Neither could I, my love. And that is why we must not give way to this new monster. Whoever it is, they are trying to tell us how to live our lives. And if we give in, Elisa, if we do what they say, we will be diminished, our lives will have lost a little of the freedom we have fought so hard to win for ourselves."

"If you pursue this, Vaughn, they might kill you. Or me. Any of us."

He lifted her chin so he could see her eyes. "Yes, they might," he said, as evenly as he could. "I believe they are quite serious in their intentions."

She stared into his eyes for a long, silent moment, and then gave a gigantic sniff, and wiped her tears from her face. "You are quite right. You showed me how good life could be when I fought to live it for myself. I could not go back to the fear-filled, empty life I had before, so I will support you in this. You must pursue them, Vaughn," she said, her own voice firm. "You would not be the man I fell in love with if you did not."

Chapter Ten

"Although, if I'd be of a mind to be frank," Seth said, holding his brandy balloon up so the firelight flickered through the golden liquid, "I'd be asking meself why they decided to pick on you and yours. It is me they want run out of the country, after all."

"I'm more of a threat to them, right now," Vaughn answered. His fingertips were together, the untouched brandy by his side. Unlike Seth, he was quite sober. "You don't have the means I have to reach deep into Ireland and furrow through their history. If they had succeeded in removing me from the game board, you would have become much easier to deal with."

"Means?" Seth said, affronted. He threw his legs off the arm of the chair and swiveled to glare at Vaughn. "I've got three thousand English bloody pounds in my cabin. Cold, hard cash. Sterling, mind ye."

Vaughn smiled a little. "And by god, we'll use it," he assured him. "But you don't know a single person of influence in this entire land who would care to lift a hand to help you."

Seth swallowed the last of the brandy and grimaced. "Except you."

"Exactly," Vaughn finished quietly.

Seth rubbed his hands through his hair, and sighed. "So they come at ye wife. Fine and honorable, they are."

"Another point we agree upon." Vaughn dropped his hands. "But now we know they will come at us through others, indirectly. We know they give no quarter, Seth, so we know what we're dealing with, and can take precautions. Do you want another brandy?"

"I've 'ad more than enough," Seth said, and rubbed the heels of his hands over his eyes. It was very late. "Is there not something we can do beyond wait for your men to report?"

"No."

"I'm likely to go blind with all this waiting," Seth warned.

"You never were very good at it." Vaughn grinned.

Seth found himself smiling back. Even though Seth was the elder, it always seemed to him that Vaughn had a wisdom that tapped centuries of experience, and the cool head to go along with it.

The image of Natasha standing by the window, cool and calm, while he had paced the fireplace, flickered through his mind as it had done repeatedly all night. And along with it came the sensation of her small hand against his cock. The deliberate brush. And his body tightened and throbbed in response, just as it had all night, every time he thought about it. "It's not only you and Elisa that this tragedy has touched," Seth ventured.

Vaughn speared him with a calculating glance. "Natasha? Yes…she seems to have found her feet, at last."

"When I beheld her beauty, at the ball, I wouldn't have guessed in a thousand years the warrior maiden that lay beneath."

Vaughn smiled a little. "Most people underestimate Natasha. Including her parents." His smile faded. "And Natasha herself."

"Not anymore," Seth finished. And again, he felt the brush of her hand against him, and the knowing look in her eyes as she had smiled up at him.

Vaughn laughed suddenly, and then dropped his head back on the chair. "You two are a pair, indeed. I wonder who will rule your house?"

"Don't be bloody silly, man. I'd be the master of my own house!"

"Of course you would," Vaughn said smoothly. He stood up, stretching. "It's time to find a pillow," he declared. "You'll stay the night, of course?"

"Oh, Harry can watch the ship well enough, but I should be returning anyway." Seth rose to his feet, and stretched mightily, too. "Either that, or I use the servants' entrance tomorrow morning, when I leave. I'm beginning to think I should be more cautious."

The sound of shattering glass made him whirl towards the window, his heart galloping. As he turned, something slammed into his shoulder with a force that made him stagger backwards. At the same time, Vaughn gave a great shout and ran for the door of the parlor. As Seth reached for his shoulder, he heard the front door open, and Vaughn's steps on the porch outside.

A stone the size of his fist lay at his feet. Curiously, it was wrapped in twine. As he rubbed his shoulder, he turned it over with his foot, and saw the twine held a folded note to the rock.

His heart thudded hard. He looked up at the broken window, and the empty path on the street beyond. The projectile had been aimed deliberately.

The front door shut quietly and Vaughn returned. He shook his head. "Gone," he said shortly.

Seth picked up the rock. Tiredness and all traces of the brandy had left his system. He pulled the note from under the twine and unfolded it.

"Evidence that they weren't content with warning only me," Vaughn said, examining the broken window. He turned to face Seth. "They're warning you away, too?"

"In a manner of speaking." Seth tried to shrug off the deep puzzlement and dismay the note had provoked, and read it aloud. "'Talk to your father. Ask him to explain the price of sticking your nose where it's not wanted. Then leave England…or else.'"

*****

Seth rose to open the carriage door, and looked back. "You're not coming in?" he said.

Vaughn had not moved from the bench. His hands rested on the silver-topped cane he'd brought with him. Seth had assumed it was a mere affectation, until Vaughn had handed it to him to feel its weight and balance. The lead-lined cane was a lethal instrument. "Perfectly balanced for a blow to the back of the head," Vaughn had assured him coolly.

His friend looked at him, now, with the same cool, assessing look and shook his head. "This must be between you and your father, Seth," he said quietly. "Your father is clearly part of this business, but he is your father, and you must face him alone."

Seth sank back onto the opposite seat, and looked out the window at the large Georgian mansion with its pillars and marble stairs, and the parkland and wrought iron fencing surrounding it. Here in the middle of London, it was an almost embarrassingly large private residence, where land was in such demand. But this pocket of parkland had belonged to his family for nearly three hundred years, well before London had reached out to surround it. Seth had once loved the graceful white building. Now he looked at it with dismay.

"He cannot harm you any more than he has already," Vaughn said quietly.

Seth clenched his fists. "Albany seems far more fair to my eyes right now."

"Remember why you do this."

Natasha. Elisa's babe. Liam. His mother. And every transportee ever sent to the colonies. Seth nodded. "Don't wait for me," he told Vaughn. "I'll get a cab back."

Vaughn touched his hat brim. "Take care."

Seth adjusted his cravat one last time, and lurched out of the carriage before he could change his mind. He strode to the steps, startling doves and sending them aloft, while behind him, the coach driver clicked the horses into motion, and the wheels of the coach crunched over the gravel as it passed out of the driveway and into the cobbled street.

At the doors, Seth rapped sharply, and resettled his hat upon his head. He was wearing the very best broadcloth suit a man could buy on Saville Row, his shirt was silk, and his boots of finest hand-polished leather. But he refused to part with his earring, and as he stood before the door, waiting for the butler to answer the summons, he felt that the earring was the only real part of Seth Harrow on display. Who did he really think would be fooled by the finery and the rounded vowels?

Certainly not his father.

The butler was almost bent double with age, and he peered up at Seth, blinking in the harsh morning light. "Can I help you, sir?"

"Is Lord Innesford in, this morning? I'd like to speak to him." The precise grammar came to Seth automatically. It was triggered by the clothes, and the memories the aging butler brought flooding back to him.

"I'm afraid Lord Innesford can't be disturbed, especially without an appointment," Humphries replied. His voice quavered, but his dignity was intact. The butler was properly indignant that someone dared disturb his master without the courtesy of arranging the affair ahead of time.

"Come, Humphries," Seth said gently. "Surely he'd make time for his son?"

Humphries blinked. "Surely you make a crude jest, sir? Lord Innesford's' son has been dead these fifteen years gone."

Despite being braced for such difficulties, Seth still felt his heart pick up speed and the prickling of discomfort like a hot rash across his skin. *Keep ye temper, boyo*! he reminded himself. "Humphries, surely you recognize me? I know it's been fifteen years, but I refuse to believe you've forgotten that much about me."

Humphries stared at him, and there was nothing in his expression to reveal his thoughts. That poker face had served his father for thirty years, and was serving him still. "I am sorry, sir, but his lordship is not in." He began to close the door.

Seth slapped his hand against the wood, holding it open. "Ask him," he said softly. "Tell him who I am, and ask him. I at least deserve that much civility."

Humphries considered this. "I will see if his lordship is in," he said, with formal stiffness.

He made to shut the door again, but Seth pushed it open, and stepped inside. "I'll wait in here," he said, taking off his gloves and hat, and dumping them on the hall table beneath the ornate gilded mirror on the wall. Beyond the foyer he could see the marble and wrought iron steps climbing to the upper floors, with their priceless Oriental carpets. The carpets had been brought back to England by his grandfather, who had traveled to Constantinople to see to his business interests there. Those Oriental interests wound back in time to the second crusade, where another ancestor had fought and died valiantly on the fields before the walls of Jerusalem, slain by the infidel who now traded carpets with his family instead of insults.

At the top of the stairs, the big grandfather clock softly chimed the quarter hour, emphasizing how quiet the house had grown. Seth remembered it as a bustling place, with servants hurrying to and fro.

So much had changed, even here.

Humphries descended the stairs at a sedate pace, his white gloves at his sides. Even at his advanced age, he would not lower his dignity by grasping the stair rail. Seth moved out of the foyer, to stand at the bottom of the steps. He knew Humphries would not be hurried, nor would he consent to calling out his information from halfway down the stairs. Seth gritted his teeth and waited until the man stood next to him.

"Lord Innesford is not in, young sir."

His temples began to pound. "Did you tell him his son was here to see him?"

"I did." Humphries turned and held his hand out toward the front door. "If you'll step this way, sir…" The butler's other hand was hovering behind Seth's back, ready to coax him physically if necessary. But Humphries had also aged fifteen years while Seth had been gone, and his days of force-marching unwelcome guests out the door were over.

Seth spun out of Humphries' reach, and raced up the stairs. He instinctively turned to the left at the top. In all the years he had lived here, he'd most often found his father in the big corner study, where morning sunlight flooded in through the banks of windows, and a fire crackled in the fireplace. His father had always sat behind an ornate empire desk, said to have come from the royal palace in Vienna. Even as a child, Seth understood that the desk gave his father power and authority he did not always feel—especially when dealing with his recalcitrant son, who had plagued his days.

As he strode along the hallway towards the big door, Seth realized that his whole childhood had been a long series of scrapes and difficulties, each punctuated by a mortifying interview with his father. Only after he had met Vaughn at Eton, and learned how to move around authority rather than meet it head-on with both fists, had the endless series of interviews and interrogations diminished.

In a way, his conviction and transportation had capped off his childhood, and closed that period of his life irrevocably.

He pushed open the door to the study, stepped into the brightly lit room, and shut the door firmly behind him, locking it with the key that sat in the lock. The room smelt unpleasantly of stale camphor and an odor that made Seth think of wet, rotting leaves.

"Is that you, Humphries? Has he gone?" It was his father's voice, but weak, trembling. And it came not from the massive desk, but from the high-backed wing chair that stood before the fireplace.

Seth's heart was racing hard now, and it had little to do with the climb up the flight of stairs. "No, he hasn't gone, Father," he said. He moved to the fireplace and stepped around it to face his father, and fought hard to keep his expression even.

His father was an invalid.

The door handle was rattled loudly. "Sir!" came Humphries' voice from the other side. "You cannot disturb the Earl!"

Marcus Williams lay propped in the wing chair. He had once been a robust, red-cheeked man with a full set of whiskers and all his teeth. He had always eaten and drunk heartily, although not to excess, and rode the hounds whenever he could. He had stood taller than Seth at eighteen, and had twice the bulk. Now he was shrunken, frail, huddled beneath a checkered blanket. His face was an alarming shade of gray. But his eyes were bright enough as they looked up at Seth. "Tell him I'm already disturbed," he said, his voice a painful wheeze. Speaking sent him into a paroxysm of coughing that shook his whole body, and stole his breath for an endless minute while Seth watched, alarmed.

Then it subsided, and his father fell back into the chair, his eyes closing, and his mouth slack.

There was a muffled metallic thud from the doorway, and Seth looked up. The key had been pushed out of the lock from the other side of the door, to fall onto a newspaper slipped under the door. As he watched, the newspaper was drawn back under the door, taking the key with it.

Seth crouched in front of his father. "Sir, they will be through the door in a few seconds, and only you can stop them from throwing me out of this house. I need only a few moments of your time, then I will remove myself from your life once more. That is all I ask of you as my father, and nothing more."

"Why should I give you that much?" his father husked, his eyes opening a fraction.

The door was being rattled and Seth heard the key being fitted into the lock on the other side. He spoke quickly. "Because, Father, last night a woman I know—the wife of a friend—was injured and her babe lost. The agency responsible for that loss tells me I should ask you why I must leave England and cease asking questions about what happened in Ireland fifteen years ago."

Astonishingly, his father's face paled even more. It made the flesh seem as thin as parchment. All the bones in his head seemed to push against it, stretching it taut. He groaned, and his eyes rolled.

The door burst open, and two hefty young footmen sprinted over to grab each of Seth's arms, hauling him back onto his feet. "You, sir, are leaving," one of them promised.

Humphries was close behind them. "Get him out!" he declared, waving his finger at Seth, his voice quavering.

Seth looked down at his father. "Father!"

His father sighed. "Leave him," he whispered.

"My lord!" the footman protested. "He burst in 'ere without so much as a by-your-leave."

Marcus Williams waved his hand weakly. "Leave him," he repeated, in a firmer voice. "He is my son, he deserves that much."

The hands on Seth's arms loosened, but did not lift away completely.

"Are you certain, my lord?" Humphries asked. Seth saw that he carried a pistol. Such was Seth's reputation as a hardened criminal that Humphries felt arms were a suitable defense.

"No, I'm not certain," Marcus Williams said with a sigh. "But it is what I wish. See to it, Humphries."

"Yes, my lord." Humphries bowed, and jerked his head to the two footmen, who reluctantly backed away. They left the room.

Seth caught the butler's eye, and stepped around the chair to speak to him. He lowered his voice. "How long has he been like this?"

"His lordship has been indisposed for some years now," Humphries said stiffly.

"He has been this frail for years?"

"No, sir. He was much stronger than this, even though he could not ride the hunt, or even sit upon a horse." Humphries glanced at the back of the wing chair. "His condition turned suddenly to the worse a few days ago." He wrung his hands. "I have not been able to get him to eat." Honest worry showed on the old man's face. He had been taking care of his master's affairs his entire life.

Seth put a hand on the man's shoulder, to give him a measure of comfort. But Humphries glanced at Seth's hand, then straightened up as much as his stoop would allow, and dropped his own hands to his side. The butler was back in control. "He suffered an attack on Tuesday morning. I found him here, on the floor…"

Tuesday. The day after the ball. The day when all of London fair rocked with the news of Seth's reappearance on the ton.

Seth did not ask the obvious question, for he already knew. His father had suffered his attack when he learned his disgraced, convict son had returned to London.

"Thank you, Humphries," Seth said, and turned back to his father. He pulled up the matching wing chair and rested against the edge of the seat, so that he was eye-to-eye with his father. He heard Humphries shut the door. Alone, at last, with his father. He pulled from his pocket the crumpled note that had been tied to the rock, and held it out to him. "This was sent to me last night, after Elisa—Lady Fairleigh—was attacked. Do you want me to read it to you?"

His father lifted a bony hand covered in liver spots, and waved the note away. "I believe you, boy." His eyes closed, as if he was in pain.

Seth returned the note to his pocket, staring at his father. There was something awry here that he did not understand. He had expected far more resistance than Marcus Williams had shown so far…it had almost been too easy to gain an audience with him. "Then tell me what the note means. You know, don't you?"

In answer, his father turned his face into the shielding wing of the chair. It was the movement of a man racked in shame, or guilt.

"You must tell me. Elisa was hurt yesterday because of me—because of what happened in Ireland."

"Because of the crimes you committed?" His father kept his face averted, but Seth could see that he held himself taut, waiting for Seth's answer. Something important hinged upon what he said next.

Seth sighed, and pushed his hand through his hair. He could feel the shadow of his past around his head like a storm cloud. He still did not understand what role his father played in this matter, but he didn't like the way everyone surrounding him was being drawn into the cyclone, whether he wished it or not. He took a deep breath and marshaled his words carefully, knowing he would only get one chance at answering this question. "Sir, you were never one to tolerate excuses or justifications, so I'll not abuse your patience with long-winded tales—it takes far too long to explain fifteen years."

His father, astonishingly, winced.

Seth could feel his own heartbeat picking up speed, hurrying along too fast, too hard, feeding off the tension emanating from his father. He tried to relax. "You must, for now, take my word that what I'm about to say is utter truth. I do not have proof—yet. And if the people behind this note get their way, I will never have that proof. So you must trust me for now.

I did not do the things I was accused of—the sedition, murder, all of the charges, bar one, were falsehoods. The only crime I committed that night in Ireland was feeling compassion for my friend Liam and his family, and attending his meeting because he so badly wanted me to prove that I cared."

His father exhaled slowly. "I know. I've always known." And shockingly, his face crumpled and two big tears slid down the paper-thin, dry cheeks.

Seth clutched the arm of the chair, staring at his father, trying to absorb his answer. "How could you know?" he whispered, as his father raised both frail, shaking hands to his face to hide his tears. "How long have you known? Fifteen years?" His fingers dug into the brocade, as anger built in him. "Father, Elisa was abducted and then tossed from a moving carriage. She lost the child she carried because of me. If you know what this is about, if you know anything of this at all, you must tell me. I need to know the truth. I must know who the enemy is."

His father's hands stayed over his face, and he was silent, but Seth saw that his shoulders shook.

Seth got to his feet, unable to sit still any longer. "My lord, you must explain yourself. I have spent seven years a convict, fifteen years far from anyone I cared for, and all the while you knew I was innocent. You let them do this to me. I was nineteen years old. I was your son!!"

His father's shoulders bowed even more. "Oh god…" he wailed into his hands.

"For that I demand the truth, and your pride and dignity be damned! Tell me who the enemy is!"

Finally, Marcus Williams dropped his hands to his lap. They lay palm up, the flesh glistening wetly. He kept his gaze upon them. "I don't know," he whispered. "I don't know who they are. I've never known. Do you not believe that if I had known, if I'd had any hint at all, that I would not have pursued it to the ends of the earth, to stop this thing, this terrible fate from falling on you? I tried to visit you in Dublin, at the gaol. I would have tried to explain this…somehow. But you would not see me." And finally, he looked up at Seth with red-rimmed eyes.

Guilt extinguished some of Seth's fury. "I was angry," he said stiffly.

"With me?" his father asked, wounded.

"With the bloody English!" Seth shouted. "God, Father, how could ye not have known what was happening there? Were you deaf and blind both? They were starving. Children, whole families, with barely a bushel of grain to eke out winter. You could have made such a grand difference to their lives, if you'd showed even the slightest bit of attention!"

His father wiped at his eyes. "You sound like your mother."

It was an accusation—an old one that Seth remembered from long ago, but this time he chose to take comfort in it, instead. "Aye, I sound Irish," he agreed. "'Tis a wonder you find that so offensive. Mother is Irish. I'm half-Irish, but ye don't like that reminder, d'ye?" Seth curled his lip. "Tell me what you know of this enemy. What have you to do with my conviction?"

Marcus Williams sighed. "Everything, although I'm sure you'll take no comfort in that, either. You weren't taking an interest in my affairs, even though they would one day be yours. You probably don't remember that a few months before your arrest, the most ambitious Irish trade bill I'd even proposed was being debated in both the House of Commons and the House of Lords?"

Seth shook his head. "How would I know that? I was at Cambridge."

His father gave a small smile. "Studying law, as I recall."

Seth tried to shrug off the touch of guilt. "I don't remember the bill," he said, a little more sharply than he intended.

"Oh, no one remembers the bill." His father smiled sourly. "I withdrew it from consideration, the day after your conviction."

Shocked touched Seth with fresh, cold fingers. "They made you? Because of me?"

"No, Seth. Your conviction was my punishment for not withdrawing the bill the first time they demanded I do so."

Seth sank back onto the chair he'd deserted. "That's…that is…" He shook his head. "And you told no one? Not even Mother?"

"They insisted I tell no one. Or, they said, your mother would face a future as interesting as the one they had arranged for you."

Seth stared at his father, realizing that for fifteen years, Marcus Williams had carried this untold secret inside him. It was little wonder the man had suffered ill health for most of those years. And his collapse on the day he learned his son had returned to London…

Marcus Williams opened the eyes he had shut in pain. "The enemy clearly has Irish interests, or else why try to void a bill that would affect Ireland?" He coughed a little, and caught a quick, wheezing breath before he began to cough again in earnest, the spasms racking his body. He dug into his pocket and produced a snowy white linen kerchief that he held up to his mouth. When the fit had passed, he fell back against the chair, drained.

The kerchief was spotted with blood.

Seth swallowed, his throat dry and raspy. "What else?" he coaxed.

He took a moment to answer. "There is nothing else," he husked. "Like you, I was sent messages that were impossible to follow back to their source. They told me to withdraw the bill, and I thought myself above it all—I was doing what my conscience demanded, and a higher God would protect me." He sighed, and his eyes closed. "I was wrong."

Seth looked at the spotted handkerchief, at his father's emancipated body. It was as if this knowledge had been steadily eating at him all these years. His father had already paid for his guilt. Seth stood up. "I will let you rest."

Marcus Williams opened one eye. "Remember this, Seth. The enemy will defeat you by attacking the ones you love."

Seth nodded. They'd tried to subdue Vaughn by using Elisa as their leverage—if nothing else, that incident convinced him that the people that had coerced his father were the same people who now were trying to stop Seth.

Natasha.

The name whispered in his mind, and it was as if his heart had seized. Pain clutched at his chest, and his breath whistled from him in shock. He was moving towards the door before his mind could engage again. If they attacked those they believed to be your loved ones, what would they do to Natasha? The pair of them had stood in that garden last night, arms about each other…how could they fail to have missed that?

By the time he reached the top of the stairs, he was running. He took the steps three at a time, his hand sliding down the cold, iron balustrade, 'til he reached the bottom, and could fling himself over the rail. He pushed open the front door and was out of the house before the footman could even stir from his perch in the little room off the foyer.

Outside, the air was crisp and still. Seth hurried into the street, looking for a cab. He hailed the first one he saw, and climbed inside. The driver leaned down to hear Seth's directions, and Seth rattled off Vaughn's address.

As the horses began to clop, Seth banged on the roof. "No, wait!" he cried.

He stared about the street, at the boys hanging off the wrought iron fencing, staring at him, at the woman selling flowers from her cart, at the people huddled together on the other side of the road from his father's house. At the shopkeeper sweeping his footpath. There were too many people. Too many eyes watching him.

He felt sweat break out on his temples. "Just drive around. Go to the park," he told the driver.

"Right, guv," the driver agreed and touched the horses with his whip again. It was of no matter to him where he went—he would be compensated anyway.

Seth tried to relax back onto the bench, to look like he was not suddenly conscious of everyone who glanced at him. His heart was thudding at a pace that would surely drive him into the grave if it kept up for too long—each beat hurt, as if the heart was throwing itself against his chest.

The enemy—whoever they were—must be watching him. They must be watching, for they had known every move Vaughn and he had made so far. They'd known where Seth was to throw the rock that passed the note along, they'd known Elisa and Natasha were in the park…it could mean the enemy was someone he knew, or someone that moved around so naturally in this world that they were overlooked.

He could not drive back to Vaughn's and bring the enemy to the doorstep. Until he knew who that someone was, he had to assume he had no privacy, and no secrets, that he would be followed and his every move examined for weaknesses and vulnerabilities. For the lever that would push him out of England.

They attack the ones you love.

Chapter Eleven

Natasha sat with her feet and knees together, her hands folded demurely in her lap, and her perfectly straight spine eight inches from the back of the chair. A small, meaningless smile adorned her lips. She wore a modestly cut evening gown, and her hair was dressed conservatively. She wore the barest skerrick of rouge and powder and appeared to be the very model of maidenly decorum.

Beneath the placid exterior was a maelstrom of hot yearning for rebellion, vengeance, and carnal desires.

It was just over a day since she had returned home in Vaughn's carriage, her hair and clothes in utter disarray. Her timing had been unfortunate, for she had stepped into the house to find the drawing room full of titled guests, and all of them gaped at her appearance, eagerly taking note of every shameful detail.

Her mother, dressed in blue satin and lace, with the family's heirloom diamonds dripping from her neck and ears, stepped around a bevy of her guests and hurried over to take Natasha's arm in a painful pinch. "You dare appear here in that condition!" she muttered, hurrying Natasha towards the stairs.

"Mother, I did attempt to simply go upstairs. I had no idea you were entertaining tonight. You certainly didn't inform me."

"You have indicated that you are not interested in the affairs of this family." Caroline's voice was an acid hiss as she marched Natasha up the stairs. "Your father insisted we abide by your wishes as long as you did not shame us. I told him you would not honor your side of the agreement, and I was right, by god. Two days…and you have already made us a laughingstock!"

"Mother, what on earth—"

But Caroline was not listening. "Cavorting about Hyde Park, showing your ankles, and screaming like a fishwife…have you no sense of propriety? No pride?" She threw open Natasha's bedroom door. "How could you?" she demanded, turning Natasha to face her.

Natasha shook her head a little. "I don't understand. If you've heard about what happened in the park today, then you must know I was merely trying to help Elisa—Lady Fairleigh."

"By bellowing at the top of your lungs in a public place, and baring your legs? Worse, you demeaned yourself by taking over a task better suited to the working class, when there was already a driver there." Caroline's face was red, her lips white. "Do you know the humiliation you have made me suffer tonight? They're laughing at us!"

Natasha stepped away from her mother, toward the window. "But…I was merely helping…"

"You completely abandoned every lesson, every principle I have ever taught you. You have shamed your father. He can barely hold his head up, down there, and we must endure this excruciating dinner, knowing that they came to stare at us…at you!"

Natasha sank onto her bed. "Let me understand you properly, Mother. You are saying that the correct action today would have been to do nothing? To let Elisa's abductors take her to god knows where?"

"Calling for help is not beneath the dignity of a lady," Caroline said, squaring her shoulders. "But the public display you put on—oh, I shall never live it down!"

"I see," Natasha said, hiding her outrage. She kept her fists tightly closed, let her fingernails dig into her palms and welcomed the pain—it was something to focus upon. She recalled the astonishing lesson Elisa had imparted that very afternoon. For a lady, appearance is everything.

She took a deep breath. She wasn't sure she could do this, but she would try—for Elisa's sake. "I am most terribly sorry I've disappointed and shamed you and Father, Mama. It was not my intention. I forgot my station—I thought only of the danger in which Lady Fairleigh had been placed. How can I make amends?" The words left a sour taste in her mouth, but her mother's startled expression, the softening of her features to the warm, tender parent Natasha remembered from her childhood suddenly seemed worth it.

"I appreciate your contrition," Caroline said stiffly. "But such a transgression cannot go unpunished. You will remain in your room until such a time as I see fit. And I'm sure your father will also have words to share with you."

"Yes, Mother." Natasha gritted her teeth to hold herself silent. She could not afford to inflame the situation now that her mother had calmed.

Caroline walked over to the mirror above the fireplace mantle and checked her hair. "I must return to the drawing room, so that dinner may be called. If a sufficient amount remains once the serving is done, I will ask one of the maids to bring you a supper plate."

"Thank you, Mother."

Caroline grimaced at herself in the mirror. "I declare I do not know how I will survive this evening. They are the most catty..." She took a deep breath, smoothed the satin over her abdomen, and picked up her train. She spared a glance at her daughter. "You might spend your confinement profitably," she suggested. "Think upon the expectations your birthright brings. You must learn to deport yourself in a manner that fits your station."

"Yes, Mother."

But Caroline did not acknowledge her response. The door shut and the lock turned, leaving Natasha alone in her room.

She remained there until five o'clock the next day, and saw no one except the maid who brought her food. She spent the time not in reflection of her duties in life, but upon the exciting contemplation of her next meeting with Seth. What would he do? Say? What could she do? She brought out her secret novels, and read revealing, stimulating passages. She wondered, as she always did, about the practical aspects the books left hazy. Elisa had helped somewhat, but soon she would know just what they had left out. Very soon.

Just after the carriage clock on the mantel chimed five, Caroline appeared, with two maids in tow. "You must prepare for dinner. We are attending Lord Dulsenay's dinner party tonight."

"We?" Natasha asked.

"Your father will accompany both of us. You are expected."

Caroline must have accepted on her daughter's behalf. Natasha gritted her teeth, and recalled Elisa's lesson. "I must bathe," she insisted, standing up. "I still smell of the dirt in Hyde Park."

"Your bath and water is being brought upstairs now," Caroline said. "I must also prepare. I trust I can leave you unattended in this matter?"

"I have apologized, Mama. What else can I say that will assure you I have mended my ways?"

Caroline's gaze raked over Natasha. She sniffed, and left the room.

Natasha had bathed and dressed in the most conservative evening gown she possessed. It was from her first season, and most likely someone would remember the gown and comment upon its age, but she did not care. What was important was the impression she made. She wanted everyone believing her to be a gentle, modest maid with nary a thought in her head but the need to find a husband.

Beneath the gown she wore no corset, and her drawers and camisole were both made of the lightest French silk—virtually transparent and so light it felt like they were barely there. For a few wicked moments she had contemplated leaving them off altogether, but the maid who attended her was not Alice, the redheaded, dimpled young girl from Manchester, who Natasha could cow into obedience. She could not risk word of improper underwear reaching her mother, and she needed the maid's help to do up her dress.

Besides, the idea of being completely bare beneath her dress was too daring to execute right now—merely contemplating it brought a blush to her cheeks.

She prodded experimentally at her midriff. It felt strangely soft and pliable, and she bent and touched her toes, marveling at the unaccustomed range of movement. She would have to be careful to maintain the very straight back of a lady, or the entire world would know of her corsetless state.

She descended the stairs upon the appointed hour, moving sedately, thinking of Elisa's elegant glide.

Her father stood at the fireplace, holding a sherry glass, and looked up as she entered the room. "My dear, you look simply lovely," he said, with a paternal smile.

"Thank you, Papa." She rose to her toes and kissed his cheek, and he gave a funny little "hurrumph" sound. But he looked absurdly pleased.

Caroline, when she arrived, looked Natasha over, and raised an eyebrow. "No rouge, my dear?" she asked suspiciously.

"Really, Mother, is that an appropriate subject to discuss in front of a gentleman?"

It deflected Caroline. As she could find nothing else to criticize about Natasha's appearance, she was forced to turn her attention elsewhere.

After her parents partook of a small glass of sherry, which Natasha refused, the carriage was called for, and they traveled the two miles to the Dulsenay's large town home. They arrived at the same time as many other guests. Natasha kept her eyes lowered, but nevertheless managed to identify everyone who had not entered the house yet. Vaughn and Elisa were not among them.

She had not expected Seth to attend. He was still *persona non grata* in London, and no one knew the Wardells entertained him, or were helping him with his investigation. Perhaps it was just as well Seth was not here—Natasha did not know how well received Vaughn really was. If he tried to force Seth upon society, it might prove more than his sterling reputation could support, and both the Wardells and Seth would be shunned.

Besides, Elisa must surely still be abed. Natasha's heart went out to her friend. She did not know how she could have survived such a blow, herself. Elisa's courage was magnificent.

At last they had all been received by Lord Dulsenay, and moved into the long, cavernous drawing room for pre-dinner sherry. Natasha found an isolated chair in a corner made by the frame of a square arch. She accepted a lemonade, sipped the sugary concoction, and hid her grimace as she looked around at the guests. A brandy would be most welcome right now.

There was not a single person in the room under forty years of age, and certainly no one that she knew well enough to be able to speak to them without a formal introduction, or at least someone to accompany her during the conversation. She was suddenly aware of the rules and moral expectations she had been flaunting so freely for more than a year. No wonder her parents had begun to look so harried and frustrated.

It reminded her of something Vaughn had said to her, and his meaning became dazzling clear. *You are a young woman, Elisa—you do not have the power to live your own life without consequences. Not yet. You are dependent upon family for your support. It is easier for men.*

It was a bitter lesson, but Elisa had alleviated it a little with her own axiom. For women, appearance is everything.

Very well, she would play the game Elisa's way, and see if it worked any better. Certainly, her open defiance had not served her well. Would this new strategy help her win Seth? Would Seth be able to clear his name?

She started and nearly spilled her full glass of lemonade when she heard the nasally drawl of Sholto Piggot. She couldn't see him yet, but his penetrating voice carried rather well.

Natasha shrunk back in her chair, glad that she wore no corset and could bend her back a little to hide behind the edge of the archway that projected just here. She heard her mother's voice—gay and trilling with laughter, and it suddenly became very clear. She was the only unaccompanied maiden. Piggot was the only man here without a companion.

Her heart sank. She had forgotten this potential complication in her life.

Elisa's voice whispered in her mind. "Courage, Natasha." After all Elisa had suffered through to emerge victorious and with Vaughn by her side, this little dinner party was a mere hiccup in comparison.

But she would not sit idly by and let Sholto Piggot choose the ground for their confrontation. She put the glass of lemonade aside with a small touch of relief, and stepped around the arch. Her mother and Piggot were standing by the fireplace, beneath the great crystal candelabra that hung from the ceiling there. Her mother always tended to seek the greatest light in order to highlight her pale hair. But the light did not flatter Piggot at all. He looked pinched and ill, with two hectic spots of color over his high cheekbones and a very red nose.

Natasha took a deep breath and swept forward to greet him, a smile plastered on her face.

Piggot straightened up and gave her a short bow. "Lady Natasha...you do honor me with your presence. How delightful to see you here."

As if it is such a great surprise! Natasha allowed him to kiss the back of her hand, and tightly fisted the other against the need to wipe his moist imprint away. "Lord de Henscher. What a pleasure to see you once again," she told him.

Piggot's eyeglass dropped as his eyes widened in genuine surprise, and she hid her smile.

"Lady Natasha, you look delectable this evening," he said, his gaze shifting to the modest neckline of her gown. The conservative cut didn't seem to deter his wandering eye. The man had a way of looking at her that made her feel like she wore nothing at all.

She reached for a civil tone. "Thank you, my lord.."

He smoothed a spindly finger over his thin moustache. "Please, my dear. Call me Sholto."

Natasha could smell the brandy on his breath. It seemed he had a fondness for drinking. He positively reeked of it.

Her mother was beaming, her gaze tripping from Piggot to Natasha. And, like a thunderclap, it came to her. Her parents were going to force this alliance. It was marry now or be put on the shelf, and her parents would never settle for a spinster daughter. Bile rose in her throat at the knowledge. Time had simply run out.

They would marry her off one way or another…even to an effeminate, much older second son of a duke, than be saddled with her for the rest of their days.

And all at once, Natasha couldn't think of a thing to say. What could she possibly say to such an odious man, when all she had ever been taught to say in such situations were meaningless little coquetries designed to flatter the man, and draw his interest?

But then, like a breeze across a summer lake, a strong emotion fanned through the room, spreading consternation, whispers and shock before it. Natasha sensed rather than saw the collective drawing of breath as every assembled dinner guest's attention was drawn to the doorway of the drawing room. The butler stood there, waving a new guest into the room. Natasha could not see the guest because a portly earl stood in front of her. She could not crane her head to see—it was not ladylike. So she waited until the guest stepped into her view.

Relief washed over her in waves. It was Vaughn. He was nodding, shaking hands with some of the men nearby him. Of course everyone knew him. Vaughn was well liked amongst men and always had been. He lifted his hand, as if to indicate a companion and draw them forward at the same time, and Natasha felt a touch of shock. Elisa had attended after all? But surely, it was much too soon for her to be about yet? Perhaps that was why everyone was so shocked.

Then Vaughn's companion stepped into view, and Natasha's heart lurched, even as icy shock gripped her.

It was Seth.

Dressed in utterly correct dinner attire, Seth was the well turned-out gentleman she had first met at the ball. After the first icy shock slithered through her system, it was chased by a hot gladness that fizzed through her system. She was so glad to see him! She wanted to run across the room and throw herself into his arms.

Instead, she lowered her eyes, and fought to keep her face neutral. *Appearance is everything.*

She realized that Piggot watched her closely. The sharp little eyes glittered with something she could only assume was a possessive pride. How she hated him! The acid emotion swept through her, shocking her with its strength.

From her lowered eyes, she discreetly watched how the roomful of people reacted to Seth's scandalous presence. The ripples of delicious shock and rumor were widening. Women were hiding their mouths behind fans as they leaned to each other and passed along the terrible news. Men were clearing their throats, staring hard at Seth. They were freely speaking about him—no fans necessary.

It was a dangerous strategy Vaughn and Seth played. Vaughn was gambling his own reputation. He counted on the fact that they would not dishonor him by telling him his guest was not welcome. He was going to use his own position in society to ram Seth down their throats and make them accept him. But would they do it?

Natasha held her breath, unable to tear her eyes away from the pair of handsome young gentlemen, for the next few moments would be the deciding ones.

Vaughn spotted Natasha's father, and worked his way directly toward him. Natasha bit her lip. How brave Vaughn was! He intended to confront the man who would be most resistant to Seth's presence.

Her father's face turned red as he realized that Vaughn sought him out. And even though the conversation in the room continued to buzz unabated, even though it appeared that everyone was having a jolly time talking in their little groups of two or three, Natasha knew these people of old. Just like her, they were watching Vaughn and Seth, missing nothing. They would take their cue from her father's response to Vaughn. If he refused to shake Seth's hand, if he refused to acknowledge him, then they would all reject him. They would all conform to each other, they would not dare risk the same banishment they doled out to anyone who was different from them.

Vaughn reached her father, and Natasha wished she was but a few paces closer so that she might hear what he said. , Vaughn drew Seth to his side, and introduced him to her father.

Her father's face grew even more red, and there were white lines of fury etched along either side of his mouth. Natasha knew that he would not support this, and that he was about to order Seth from the room—and the house, regardless of the fact that this was Lord Dulsenay's home. Her father was angered beyond reason.

Vaughn leaned a little closer to her father, still talking, a pleasant smile on his face. What was he saying? Her father, although he was listening to Vaughn, stared at Seth. Seth looked calm enough, but just like she, Seth would know that everything depended on what her father did next.

Her father continued to stare and still Vaughn spoke. Finally, moving like a man with stiffened joints, her father lifted his hand and held it out to Seth.

Seth took it, shook it, and gave a small court bow—one of acknowledgement of a peer. Oh, but that would not be received well by her father! It didn't matter that Seth was technically of higher rank. Her father would not tolerate Seth pointing out that he considered himself on equal footing. But Natasha knew instinctively why Seth did this. He must be accepted not just as Vaughn's friend, but also as the heir of a peer of England in his own right.

Her father gave a stiff nod back. Acceptance. They had done it. Seth could not be ordered from the room now unless he committed an act so indecent he sullied his name all over again.

And her father hated it. She could see it on his face, and it made her realize how cleverly Vaughn and Seth had picked their first opponent. Vaughn already knew her father would much rather hide unpleasant facts than deal with them, most especially in a public place. Several years ago, he had learned this weakness when he'd confronted her father with Elisa at his side. Vaughn had merely to mention the skeleton in the Winridge cupboard—her father's bastard son, who remained anonymous even to this day—and her father had folded, defeated. Was Vaughn using the same tactic here? Was that what he had spoken of to her father before he'd taken Seth's hand? A reminder that his own past was no more pristine than Seth's?

It hardly mattered for right now. They had won their victory—Seth was free to mix with the other guests, and Vaughn was touring him around the room, introducing him. Natasha noticed he was quite properly introducing Seth to those of higher rank first. As there was at least one continental prince, and two dukes, it would be a while before they reached the unaccompanied ladies and maidens. Nevertheless, Natasha found she was holding her breath, and watching their slow progress around the room, impatiently waiting her turn.

Her mother and Piggot were chatting quietly, their backs turned just a little towards the center of the room. Natasha knew her mother was in no hurry to be forced to greet Seth, and would do nothing to encourage the meeting. The turned back was as much as she dared now that her husband had accepted Seth. And oh, how it must gall her!

A muted gong sounded, and the wigged butler at the door lifted his chin. "Ladies and gentlemen, dinner is served."

Frustration bit at her. She would not get to "meet" Seth in public! Damn!

Then she caught her mother's glance, full of satisfaction, and knew that she was thinking the same thing. Her mother slid her hand under Piggot's elbow. "Lord de Henscher, would you do my daughter and me the honor of escorting us to dinner?"

"I'd be delighted, Lady Munroe," Sholto said, his voice high and tight, as if he were nervous.

With a mental sigh, and a polite smile, Natasha trailed after her mother and Sholto into the dining room proper. Her heart fell even further when she saw that place cards had been laid. It was too much to hope the very staid Dulsenays would succumb to the new French custom of allowing guests to choose their own seating.

Natasha found her place, next to a bent and bewhiskered lord, who was extremely hard of hearing, and sniffed continuously.

She slid her glance to the right, her heart already dropping. The discreet cream-colored place card confirmed what she had suspected.

"Oh dear, what a delicious surprise!" Sholto exclaimed, a hand to his cheek as he peered down at the card with his name on it. He beamed at Natasha, and pushed the footman aside, who had been about to help her seat herself. Sholto slid the chair beneath her, and clumsily caught the hem of her dress in the feet of the chair. She was forced to stand and untangle the snarl. This close to her, his cologne was strong enough to choke a horse. Even worse, beneath the cologne was an unpleasant aroma. It stole the breath from her lungs and made her eyes water. She gave him a polite smile and sat once again, her heart tripping along unhappily.

As Sholto sat down, she glanced at Seth. She longed to speak to him. Her heart pounded, and she reached for her glass with a trembling hand. She tore her gaze away from him, took a sip of the cool water and set it down.

Her parents were watching her closely from their position further along the table—closer to the host, but not as close as Seth and Vaughn. He and Vaughn had been seated quite close to Lord Dulsenay himself—a mark of honor that would not be lost on anybody here.

Natasha smiled innocently at her parents before turning to Piggot. "The weather is quite wonderful, do you not agree?" she asked. From the corner of her eye, she could see the tall, dark-haired man who sat to the right of the redheaded duchess who had spoken to him so intimately at the ball. Her heart sank.

"Yes, it is delightful," Piggot responded to her question. "I was just asking your father if I could call on you tomorrow. Perhaps you would like to take a stroll about Hyde Park?"

Such a clumsy change of subject! She hid her grimace. Of course, an engagement was always preceded by a courtship, even a clumsy one.

It took every ounce of will not to look directly at Seth after her first searing glance. She knew her parents watched her, and Piggot was already suspicious. Nevertheless, Natasha was still aware of Seth sitting at the end of the long table. He already chatted with the guests seated around him. Although everyone here must surely be aware of his reputation, it did not seem to make them reticent about speaking to him.

She realized that it was precisely because of his reputation that they would be most eager to speak to him. They would find it a novel opportunity to talk to someone who was considered "wicked".

Her stomach twisted a little tighter, and she looked at the jellied appetizer placed in front of her and knew she would not eat a bite, despite the lack of a corset. She spent the entire meal, instead, responding to the odd polite comment from the men on either side of her. Sholto Piggot ate like a condemned man, and she wondered if the tiny rumors she had heard about him were true. Was his legendary family fortune all spent? Whatever the reason for his gluttony, she was glad of it. It spared her the need to converse politely with him.

Whenever she thought she could get away with it, she watched Seth. And throughout the meal, her puzzlement grew. Seth not once looked at her, not even a casual glance. He must surely have seen she was at the table, but he made no attempt to catch her eye or in any way communicate with her. She didn't understand it at all. Even though her parents hated it, Seth was now nominally accepted by polite society…so why did he avoid her gaze? She was certain he was doing it deliberately—no man could sit through an entire meal and fail to glance even once at all the people at the table.

His attention was directed at the duchess, the corners of his mouth lifted in a smile that looked more like a smirk. The earring caught the light and her heart skittered alarmingly. She wanted this man with a desperation that frightened her.

Hot resentment began to build in her breast, mixing with the excitement his proximity built in her, creating a volatile concoction that destroyed what little appetite she had left. Unbidden, memories of their earlier encounter came back to her, the way Seth's mouth had slanted against hers—the taste of him, the sweet velvety smoothness of his tongue dancing with her own. And now he flattered the duchess to his right, and refused to look at her.

Then dessert arrived, and Natasha realized with a thrill that in a few moments, the men would be withdrawing for their brandy and cigars, producing the perfect opportunity…

She accepted the bowl of ice cream placed in front of her, to give her hands something to do. She didn't like the cold dish, although ever since the man from America had introduced his new churn, it seemed that everyone was serving it. While she took tiny scoops with her little spoon, Natasha laid out her own battle strategy.

As the dishes were cleared, the men all got to their feet, and with gracious bows to their lady companions, stirred themselves into a hasty retreat to the smoking room. There they would remain for the rest of the evening to shout themselves silly over politics, horses and goodness knows what else.

Natasha waited until she saw Seth rise, then waved to the footman standing behind her. He leapt to pull out her chair. She flicked her train out of the way, and gave a big smile to the lady who had been sitting next to her deaf gentleman.

"Please tell the waiter I will partake of tea, would you? I'll return in a moment."

The woman nodded, and turned back to her female friend. Natasha hurried around the table while trying to make it look like she was merely gliding elegantly along. She had to time this properly. It must look innocent.

Seth was walking towards the door, alongside Dulsenay himself. The sea captain's head was down, as if he were concentrating on what the lord was telling him. It would not work if Dulsenay stayed with Seth. She would have to speak to the lord first—he was of the higher rank. She would be caught up in formalities and nothing would stop Seth from simply stepping around her and continuing on his way.

Natasha could feel her heart beating hard as she judged her pace. Almost there...and how to get Seth on his own?

She nearly sighed with relief as someone called Dulsenay's name, and he halted, waving Seth to go on.

She stepped in front of Seth as she came to the door. To anyone else watching it might look like she simply happened to reach the doorway at the same moment as Seth.

He stood watching her—she could feel his gaze on her, almost as if the touch of it heated her flesh. She could feel herself beginning to shake with terror and excitement. So close...

She held her hand out as a lady would upon first meeting a gentleman. "It's Harrow, is it not? We met at the Sweet Pea Ball, but we haven't been properly introduced yet."

His eyes narrowed. He made no move to take her offered hand, but instead seemed to draw back a little, as if she were poison to him. His chin lifted and settled squarely, and he spoke loudly—no one in the room could possibly avoid hearing him, including the deaf gentleman who had sat on her left. "You presume far too much, Miss."

Stunned, Natasha felt her hand drop back to her side, as Seth stepped around her and left the room.

White noise buzzed in her ears and her mind, blanketing the flurry of questions, muffling the bewildered cry building in her. She turned back to the table and saw that Piggot and her mother and father were all staring openly at her. Her mother's face held fierce satisfaction, while both Piggot and her father's were tight with fury.

They had seen. They knew she had engineered the moment, and had watched Seth dismiss her. And now, they must surely see the depth of her dismay, for she was powerless to hide something that swept through her whole body, leaving her shaking.

They had seen and noted. And they would now act to head off the threat that Seth represented to their plans.

Chapter Twelve

At breakfast, the next morning, Natasha learned that her parents and Piggot had not waited more than an hour to make their move against Seth.

Natasha came to the breakfast table starving. She had eaten so little at the Dulsenay's party that her body was rebelling now. She hastily donned a wrapper, her mind focused upon the need to eat soon.

She sat at the big table, and while the maid poured her a cup of tea, her father wiped his mouth with his napkin and cleared his throat.

"Let me be first to congratulate you, my dear, on your engagement."

She stared at her father, trying to absorb his statement, as he tossed that morning's *Times* in front of her plate. It landed as he had folded it, with the Public Announcements column face out. She could not fail to miss the item. PIGGOT – WINRIDGE were emblazoned in bold letters as the very first listing.

She picked up the newspaper with a hand that trembled. The center of her chest was locked solid by an icy mass.

A public announcement of her engagement to Sholto Piggot. Her father or Piggot must have hurried to the newspaper's offices last night after the dinner, to place the announcement before the midnight deadline.

Her engagement to Piggot was now known across all of London, which must surely be abuzz with the news.

"You didn't see fit to consult me on this matter?" she asked, looking up at her father. Tendrils of anger curled through her, around the hard knot in her chest.

He smiled benevolently. "Your mother saw how eagerly you sought his company last night. When Sholto asked permission to marry you, I accepted for you. I knew you would be pleased."

Checkmate. She could not now recant her false demeanor last night. She glanced at her mother, and saw the fierce satisfaction in her eyes. Her mother had seen through her act—or had she only seen it once Natasha had betrayed her true feelings by seeking out Seth?

She wanted to weep, but knew tears would be futile now.

"You must put on your best gown," her mother said, and her victorious joy sang in her voice. "We are to be presented to the Duke today."

"You mean, his future daughter-in-law and her rich parents will be presented," Natasha shot back. "Do not pretend this is anything other than what it really is, Mother. You sold me for a title."

Her father held up his hand as if he were about to appease her, but her mother stood up, her eyes glittering. "Very well, then," she said, her voice low. "If you prefer the gloves off, we will deal at that level. Piggott is the son of a Duke, and you have a chance to be a duchess. You have shown no inclination to do your duty by us and find a suitable husband, and Piggot is eager to marry you. At your advanced age, such an offer cannot be refused, for no others will be made. We accepted because you would not. Piggott will marry you within the month."

"Marry my dowry, you mean," Natasha returned. "He's penniless. You'll be supporting him the rest of your lives."

"That matters not at all." Her mother dropped her folded napkin to the table. "Be ready by ten o'clock." And she sailed from the room without a backwards glance.

Natasha looked at her father, but he dropped his gaze from hers and tackled his breakfast platter as if his life depended upon his finishing the meal.

He would offer her no support.

Grimly, she began the task of preparing to meet her future father-in-law.

*****

Seth bit back the anguished cry that seemed to want to explode from him, and stared at the words on the page. The engagement of Sholto Piggot and Natasha Winridge was there in black and white, no matter how much he wanted to deny it. His fingers curled into a tight fist, crumpling the newspaper, and he tossed the offending announcement aside.

If only he had not rejected her last night…that was the only way her parents could have forced the issue. He knew in his bones that Natasha would not have allowed this if he had not publicly humiliated her.

He leaned his forehead against his fists and closed his eyes against the hot swirl of guilt and helplessness. His fault, it was all his fault.

"It was for her protection," he muttered.

And now she was lost to him. The wife of a merchant, a man who didn't deserve her in the least.

He raked a hand through his already mussed hair, the action reminding him yet again that he'd drunk too much after leaving the party. His head throbbed, and his anger merely underscored it.

Last night a bottle of brandy had been followed by a carafe of cheap wine purchased at the dockside pub he had adopted while the *Artemis* was in port. Harry had mysteriously appeared as he was finishing the wine, and had helped him back to the *Artemis*.

Once on board, he'd thought that finding a woman to see to his needs would help him forget the hurt he'd seen in Natasha's face, but the French whore who had sat on his lap and fondled him so intimately only made him think of Natasha's innocent and trusting blue eyes. He'd dumped the whore on her ass, and sent her scurrying from the ship, a silver coin in her hand.

He'd found the ship's medicinal whiskey bottle then, and pulled the cork. He'd spend the rest of the night drinking away his unhappiness, and the mess that was his life. Parents who disowned him, the woman he wanted denied him, and a past he could not escape, no matter how much he tried.

Now he would not have the chance to undo the damage. Natasha would marry Piggot, have his children, and live a life of privilege.

He drove his fingers into his hair, trying to massage away the ache and obliterate the knowledge that he had brought this all upon himself.

"I see you've read the news."

Seth looked up with a start, to find Vaughn standing in the doorway of his cabin. Seth nodded, relieved to see his old friend. "Yes, I have."

Vaughn looked around the cabin, undoubtedly noticing the empty whiskey bottle, the upturned carafe. He took a step further into the cabin. He was impeccably and fashionably dressed, not a ruffle out of place, and his presence in the little cabin made Seth notice the squalidness of the cabin, and his own unshaved, bleary-eyed state.

"Maybe it's for the best," Seth muttered. "What sort of life could I offer a woman like that anyway?"

"Have you forgotten your new ambitions so quickly, Seth?"

Seth shook his head. "I dinna expect such…opposition. Even my father…" He gave a sniff. "Well, I know my place there. He wouldna lift a finger to help me. He let it happen to me, while he stood back and watched, and it all happened because of him—yet he did nothing to help me then. He'll do nothing now."

"So the only way you will get the recognition you need as the legitimate heir of the earldom is if you take it," Vaughn pointed out. Seth was grateful he did not also point out that this was the fifth or sixth time he'd heard Seth vent his fury over his father's duplicity. Vaughn was a good friend.

"Take it?" Seth snorted. "I'd need an army at my back. These people…they are so…"

"I know," Vaughn agreed. "But the Seth I knew at Oxford…he did not buckle under at the first sign of resistance."

Seth lifted his head, stung by the gentle reprimand. "I never said I was giving up!"

Vaughn smiled a little. "Then I misunderstood. My apologies."

Seth sat back in his chair, and pushed the other one out from the table with his boot. "Ah, you're a good man, Vaughn Wardell. Ye know very well I was swimming in my own melancholy."

Vaughn sat. "I know."

Seth took a deep breath and blew it out. "I just don't know what to do next. She's engaged to the fawning fop. And she only got engaged because I refused to acknowledge her last night."

"We both know you couldn't afford to do that. Not publicly. Whoever the enemy is, they see everything, hear everything. Until you know who it is that sits and rearranges people's lives to suit his own ambitions, then no one should learn of her importance to you."

"Then I am truly lost."

"I said 'publicly'. What goes on behind closed doors is a very different matter. You must let her know the truth of it, Seth. Tell her how you feel. Don't let it go unsaid. Life is too short."

"Perhaps it would be better to leave London altogether."

Vaughn frowned. "She's a strong woman, Seth. You do both of you a disservice by keeping quiet. What have you got to lose by telling her what's in your heart?"

*****

Two hours later, Seth stood in front of the Munroe's house. He'd been there an hour already. He waited behind the yew hedge that fringed the park opposite the small, elegant townhouse, where he was hidden from most passersby, and from any casual glance through the windows of the house he watched.

He had not changed from his shipboard clothes. Nor had he shaved or arranged his hair, although he had washed his face, eaten as decent a breakfast as he could manage, and drunk a quart of water to put out the fire from last night's indulgences. The choice of clothing had been a deliberate attempt to mislead. He was sure that no one but Natasha would recognize him when he was not wearing the clothes and accoutrements of a lord.

He wasn't sure what he intended to do. Waiting here gave him a chance to examine the townhouse and the comings and goings there, while he formed a plan to somehow reach Natasha, and let her know the truth. But he would have to contact her in such a way that her parents, and the odious Sholto Piggot did not know of it. And that could prove to be the biggest challenge, for even last night he had observed how closely all three of them watched the wayward daughter. They'd not let her out of their sight even once.

Fifteen minutes ago, a carriage had been brought around, signaling an outing, and Seth's attention had lifted. This may present the opportunity he was looking for.

The front door opened and he straightened, watching as Sholto Piggot emerged with Natasha.

His heart gave a sharp tug. She was dressed in a light blue gown, and looked shockingly pale. Sholto had her hand tucked well under his arm, and his own laid across her fingers. It was almost as if he was guarding against her trying to pull her hand away.

The pair made their way down the stairs, followed by Lord Munroe and his wife, and Seth's gut tightened a little. All of them together. That would make things difficult.

"Look at me, Natasha," he said under his breath.

* * * * *

Natasha could feel her mind slipping into a misty sea, unconnected from everyday concerns. She no longer cared that Sholto Piggot would marry her. She didn't care that her parents were fiercely determined to see this marriage through, even if she walked the aisle with their hands on her back. She cared for nothing and no one, including her own miserable future. It was easier not to care. Nothing she did or tried to do seemed to be able to change the course of her life by an inch, so there was no point in trying to change anything. And if she allowed herself to think about the days and years ahead, she knew she would scream, and scream and scream…

It was easier to disengage, to let the world flow around her and on its way.

When Piggot had arrived at the house, she had been listlessly waiting in the big armchair in the parlor. He had been nervously energetic, tripping over his own stammering tongue, flushed with the success of his engagement. His timidity would normally have made Natasha's skin crawl, but she was numb to it all. She did not flinch as he slid an antique engagement ring on her finger. The old-fashioned filigree metal had been cold against her flesh, but she had barely noticed it.

Now, her fingers were trapped under his sweaty palm, as he led her towards the family carriage. Her father stepped up to her side, and caught her elbow in his hand. It felt like he was trying to ensure she didn't bolt down the street, away from the carriage and her future. His fingers pinched as he tightened his grip.

There wasn't a lot of traffic on the street today. The only person nearby to witness her virtual abduction was a tramp behind the hedge across the road. He moved around the hedge, to come over to the wrought iron fence. He gripped two of the sharp finials at the top of the fence, watching them as they moved to the carriage—perhaps even he could see that she was being forced into this? But she let her gaze drop back to her feet as inertia reasserted itself. A solitary tramp would not understand her dilemma, and would not care if he did.

Her father halted. "What the hell?" he breathed.

The indignation and surprise in his voice caught her attention, and she looked up. Her father was looking across the street, too. Staring at the tramp. Then he motioned towards the tramp with his head. "Jones, see him off. We don't want him cluttering up the street."

"Yes, sir," the butler said, letting go of the carriage door he had been holding open. He flicked his hand at the two manservants standing at the top of the steps, and they hurried down to join the burley butler as he moved across the cobbled street.

Natasha peered at the solitary man behind the fence, wondering what had offended her father. Then the tramp shifted his gaze to look at her directly. Sharp gray eyes pinned her to the pavement, the glittering gaze felt like an accusation.

Seth.

All the fogginess in her mind evaporated, like mist blown away by a fresh sea breeze. Her heart leapt high and hard. She felt her body stiffen to alertness, even as she blinked away the last of her inertia.

Seth was here. Why? Why would he be here if he'd rejected her last night?

The truth slammed through her, stealing her breath, in one dizzy heartbeat. She stared back at Seth, at his hands curled into fists around the pikes on the fence, his knuckles white. His eyes blazed.

She understood then that his repudiation of her last night had been a ruse, that somehow, in some obscure way, he was protecting her. She didn't fully understand how, but knowing he had not really rejected her was all she needed for now. How could she have been so blind?

Relief and something akin to excitement rushed through her. She pulled away from her father and Piggot's grip, rushed around the carriage, and crossed the street. She heard her mother call out behind her, and marveled that her mother would dare stoop to such crass behavior in public. Natasha picked up her pace. She was running now, and flew passed the butler and his two men. Thank goodness she had not donned a corset this morning!

There were discarded boxes at the foot of the fence, and she clambered up them until she could grip the railings of the fence herself. Seth's hand uncurled from the pike, and reached for her. She gripped his hand fiercely. She knew she had seconds at most. "I didn't understand," she said quickly. "I couldn't see why you did it."

"Why marry him?" he asked, and his voice held a rough burr, as if he had been abusing it lately.

"I couldn't see past my own hurt pride," she confessed. "And my parents—"

Two strong hands grabbed her waist. She was ripped away from the fence, and from Seth's grip on her hand, with a vicious force that she could not withstand. But she was content, for she had seen the relief in Seth's eyes. And the warm regard behind that relief. He still cared.

She staggered across the cobbles, stumbling to find her balance once more. Then Sholto Piggot was there, holding her up. Her mother gripped the carriage door as if she held it for dear life.

Jones and his men rounded the fence and grabbed Seth by both arms. Seth fought them, and for one breath-robbing moment Natasha thought he would actually get away from them. But then her father stepped in, and between the four of them, they dragged Seth to the cobbled street. The two manservants held him steady, while her father confronted him.

"Oh dear," Piggot exclaimed. His face was flushed, and he gave little flustered motions with his hand. There were people emerging from the houses around them, now. They crept closer to watch the drama

"Why are you watching my house?" her father demanded. His face was pink with fury.

Seth just looked at him.

Her father glanced at the butler. Jones was a big, heavy fellow, and totally loyal to her father. At his glance, Jones stepped forward and drove his fist into Seth's stomach. Seth doubled over despite the grip the two men had on his arms. So Jones swung his hand upwards, and it caught Seth square on the face. His head was rocked backwards, and his knees buckled. He would have fallen to the cobbles if the two servants weren't propping him up. His head fell forward again, loose and uncontrolled.

Natasha smothered the little cry of horror that pushed from her lips. Piggot gripped her arm. "You have no need to witness such things," he said, pushing her towards the carriage.

She wrenched her arm from his hand, and stayed her ground. She would not leave Seth to face the next moments alone.

Finally, Seth shook his head, and lifted it. Blood ran from the corner of his mouth. He smiled at her father, and spit. The glob of blood landed on her father's snowy white starched shirt front.

Rather than enraging her father even more, the defiance seemed to calm him. He studied Seth with a cool look, as if he were weighing matters. Then he nodded, decision made. "My daughter is to be married within the month. She has no interest in associating with someone of your…station. I don't want to see you anywhere near my daughter again. But I can see that you're a stubborn fellow, so I am going to offer you an inducement to stay away."

"You can't buy me off," Seth said. "You don't have enough money for that."

Her father nodded, as if this confirmed something he'd suspected. "Yes, I rather thought you'd say that. My inducement isn't money. Jones here and a few of his friends, are going to take you back to the dock from which you crawled here. They're going to beat you until you can no longer crawl. Then they will throw you back on your scurvy ship, have the ship towed out to open sea, and the lines cut. I suggest that a man with your obvious intelligence take the lesson I am offering and apply it."

Natasha surged forward, alarm and horror spilling through her, but Sholto Piggot held her back with considerably more strength than she had thought him capable of using. At her involuntary reaction, Seth glanced at her. She saw his eyes narrow a little, the swift mind behind them assessing quickly. He shook his head a little. Just a little.

She fell back, his message clear to her. She didn't understand fully why Seth was not defending himself, or speaking, but his tiny head shake confirmed that he had his own plans. She had to trust him…and stay silent.

Piggot was forcing her back to the carriage, back towards her mother. Even though her heart was thudding with fear for Seth, she allowed herself to be manipulated into the carriage. From the tiny window, she watched him being hauled away for his beating.

Surreptitiously, she wiped her eyes of tears with a hand that shook. She had to trust Seth, now. Trust that he would do what was best for both of them.

Chapter Thirteen

When they arrived home from the dreary visit with Sholto Piggot's father, the duke, Natasha thought she would finally be left in peace, with time to think. She had so much to think about now! And the afternoon tea party at the duke's city residence had strained her nerves. She had been the center of attention as Sholto's wife-to-be, and she was no longer willing to provide a false demeanor. She had learned the dangers of such hypocrisy just this morning.

As she pulled off her gloves and slid the pin from her bonnet, her mother gripped her arm. It was the same arm that her father had pinched, and that Sholto had pulled. She looked down at her mother's hand on the silk and up at her mother. "You're hurting me."

Her mother wordlessly tugged her up the stairs. Natasha realized she was being taken to her room, and her heart gave a little hard trip-hammer. What now? In what way had she transgressed?

She waited stoically for her mother to vent her fury and disapproval yet again. Instead, her mother lifted her hand and slapped Natasha across the face.

The blow instantly numbed the side of her face, and Natasha stood rooted to the spot, shock slithering through her with cold, icy fingers. She lifted her fingertips to her cheek, and prodded it. She could feel nothing, but her eye watered freely.

"You dare insult the Duke in that way!" Her mother's tone was low and breathless and her bosom rose and fell against the tightly corseted lace tea gown.

"Insult? I? How on earth did I insult the Duke, Mother? I barely spoke to him!"

"You spoke to no one! You sat there without so much as a smile. You refused every morsel the Duke pressed upon you. You embarrassed him, and you embarrassed us all. Your father is shamed. Shamed!"

Natasha let her hand drop, staring at her mother. It seemed that she would not even be permitted to simply comply with their wishes with minimal involvement of her emotions, they would only be satisfied with her full, enthusiastic embrace of everything they planned for her. *Seth, oh Seth, how I wish I could run away with you!*

Even as she stared at her mother, Natasha rolled that revolutionary thought through her mind again. Yes…she would run away. She would go to Seth.

"You will stay in your room," her mother pronounced, "and reflect upon your ingratitude."

"Yes, Mother," she murmured dutifully, her mind full of thoughts of Seth.

Her mother flounced from the room, and she heard the key turn on the other side. She sank down upon her bed, and contemplated the window. It was a large sash window, and on the wall outside was a strong vine…

The key turned in the door again, and her mother stood there with Natasha's maid, Hailey. "Remove your dress," her mother demanded.

Natasha rose to her feet and walked behind the dressing screen. This was a tactic her mother had employed since a time when Natasha was fourteen, and had unlocked the door by pushing the key out with the point of a knitting needle, and brought it back under the door to her side on a sheet of paper. On that occasion she had spent the afternoon with the stable boy, playing in the straw, rather than reflecting upon her lack of discipline, upon her bed. By removing all her clothes from the room, her mother was ensuring that if Natasha somehow managed to sneak past the locked door again, she would be unable to proceed any further.

Natasha silently removed the dress with Hailey's help, thankful that the screen hid her corsetless state from her mother. Reduced to her undershift and stockings, Natasha reemerged from behind the screen, in time to see her mother sweep even her wrapper up into her arms, and walk from the room. She had not left so much as a pair of shoes behind.

Natasha sat on the bed and stared at the window. She could not use it for her escape—she could not possibly roam the streets of London in her shift.

Three hours later, the door was unlocked, and Hailey entered.

Natasha smiled at her maid. Hailey carried a tray with a teapot and an unappetizing array of cold meat and cheese. It was of little matter, she had no appetite, anyway.

"You look pale, my lady. Shall I get you a blanket?"

Only a few years older than herself, Nastasha's maid had been a good friend to her over the years. She had few enough friends amongst her peers, for her mother had always been nervous about familiarity and intimacy. Her family spent the majority of the year in northern England, at her father's estate. That was where she had met Vaughn and Elisa.

"Have my parents gone to bed?" she asked Hailey.

"No, miss. Your mother has retired for the evening, but your father is still awake. He's in the study. Did you wish to speak with him?"

"Hailey, would you do me a favor?"

Hailey looked up, her brow furrowed in a frown. "Of course, my lady."

"When my father goes to bed, will you come back here and let me out?"

Hailey gasped and put a hand to her chest. "I would lose my position." The words were little more than a whisper, and the girl's cheeks flushed with color.

Natasha took the maid's hand. "Hailey, you are the only one I can trust. I need to see Elisa—the Marchioness of Fairleigh. I need to speak to her."

"I could send word to her for you."

"My parents would not allow it. They know Vaughn and Seth are close friends."

Hailey shook her head. "I can't risk it, Lady Natasha."

"Hailey, my parents are forcing me to wed Sholto Piggot. You have seen Mr. Piggot with your own eyes. Would you be content, having him for a husband?"

Hailey dropped her gaze to Natasha's shoulder. "It is not my place to say, miss."

"I can not marry this man. It would kill me to do so. I need to speak to Elisa and Vaughn. I need their help, and they are the only people who can help me now. If you do this for me, I will never forget it. You will stay with me for the rest of your life. You will not regret it, I swear it."

Hailey chewed on her bottom lip. "You will take me with you when you leave here?"

"Yes, I swear it. You have my word."

"All right. I shall return at midnight. That should give your father ample time to drink the carafe of wine he requested."

Natasha hugged her maid. "Thank you, Hailey. Thank you so much."

* * * * *

Natasha threw Hailey's worn, ragged cloak on over her shift. The cloak came to her ankles and hid everything except her bare feet, but Hailey's shoes were too small for her. She slipped out the window, holding tight to the vine that hugged the brick wall. She did not dare look at the ground looming below. Instead, she focused on making her way down the vines. Once again on steady ground, Natasha fled into the fog-filled night, heading for Vaughn and Elisa's. They did not live so very far apart, but Natasha took her time, making sure that no passing carriage saw her—although at this time of night there was barely any traffic. The streets were dark, save for the few gaslights flickering, barely lighting the way.

A forceful wind breezed through the thin cloak she wore, and the even thinner shift. She had stripped off her stockings, for they were slippery underfoot on the cobbles and paving she hurried across.

She must get to Seth with Vaughn's help. She had to talk with Seth, to tell him how she felt. Then she could make plans for her future. Perhaps she could sail to Ireland with him, and start a new life. For a moment she allowed herself the luxury of envisioning what that life might be like. She would be content with anything if she had Seth. Even a small cottage on the Irish Sea. No servants—well, Hailey of course, but just a handful of help…and children. She would love to have many sons and daughters. She knew what it was to grow up alone, an only child, starved for companionship.

Gilroy answered Natasha's knock immediately—almost as if he had been waiting for her to arrive. He opened the door wide for her as soon as he saw her. "Please come in, Lady Natasha. You look quite chilled."

Vaughn met her at the study door. "Natasha," he said, taking her hands in his, looking over her shoulder as though he expected someone else. "What's happened?"

Embarrassed at the late hour, she shifted on her feet. "I have to see Seth. He came by earlier this morning, and I'm ashamed to say my father saw to it that he would not come back. I fear Seth may be injured, or worse. Have you spoken to him today?"

"What do you mean by your father making sure he wouldn't come back?"

"My father ordered his butler to beat Seth, quite badly. Seth could do nothing."

Vaughn swore under his breath. "Maybe we should go to the *Artemis* now."

"It won't be there. That's what I'm trying to tell you—"

Vaughn put his finger against her lips, and again glanced over her shoulder. "Later," he told her. "Let's go." He took his coat from the peg by the front door, and called for Gilroy. The butler appeared swiftly. "We're taking the buggy, Gilroy. Have it brought around, quickly."

"Yes, sir." Gilroy went off to do his bidding.

Vaughn fingered the cloak Natasha was wearing, and tugged at the strings holding it together. "Take it off. You can wear Elisa's." He reached for the thick velvet coat hanging on the peg next to his, then his eyes widened. "Good god, where are your clothes?"

As the cloak slithered aside, Natasha wrapped her arms about herself, suddenly cold. "I was locked in my room, and my clothes taken." She slipped into the luxuriously warm coat that Vaughn held out, and when she faced him once more, his face was neutral again, but his lips were tightly pressed together. "Are you angry with me?" she asked.

He shook his head. "Not you, Natasha. Wait until we're in the buggy."

The buggy was an open-topped one, and Natasha was glad of her borrowed coat. She snuggled into the warmth, while Vaughn took the reins. He clicked the horse into motion, and settled into his seat, and glanced at her. "Did Seth say anything to you this morning?"

"There was no time. My father pounced on him so quickly. Four of them held him down." She shivered suddenly.

"You must know, Natasha, that Seth cannot afford to let the world see any attachment between you. Until we know who it is that plays with us, we must assume that anyone might be that person."

"That is why you would not let me speak in your house? You do not trust even your servants?"

Vaughn's lips thinned again. "Only the people in our house—including the servants—knew that Seth was there, the night they broke in the window."

"Oh." She frowned.

"For the same reason, Seth can trust no one. He took an enormous risk, coming to you this morning."

"He paid for it," Natasha murmured. She glanced at the road they were on, noticing it properly for the first time. "This isn't the way to the docks."

"No," Vaughn agreed, but would say no more.

Twenty minutes later, Natasha heard the sound of lapping water, and the creak of rope against wood. Somewhere ahead of them, she knew, must lay the Thames. Then the heavy fog swirled and broke apart for a moment, and she saw the thick masts of a great ship, behind bushes and shrubs ahead of them. Then the fog closed in around them again.

Vaughn halted the buggy, and helped her out. He led her around the bushes, and up a wooden ramp. A dock, she realized. One of the little private docks found all along the banks of the Thames—used for small boats and watercraft. But moored next to this one, looming large out of the fog, was an oceangoing cutter, dwarfing the post it was tied up to. "This is the *Artemis*?" she asked, whispering. "How is it that it's here? It's surely too shallow for such a ship…"

"Normally, yes, but this section of the river is deeper than most, and Seth is an excellent navigator." Vaughn brought her to the foot of a gangplank that rose up in a steep climb to the deck of the ship, high above them. "Seth is waiting for you, I'm sure."

She paused with one foot on the steep gangplank. "You are not coming aboard?"

"I'll return in the morning."

"What if Seth needs you? Needs help?"

Vaughn just smiled. "Good night, Natasha."

She wanted to latch onto his arm and insist that he come aboard with her, but Vaughn was already walking away.

She swallowed, and climbed the gangplank. She was glad of her bare feet, which gave her a sure grip on the narrow planking, which seemed precarious despite the boards nailed across it at regular intervals.

As she stepped onto the ship's deck, a door opened and a large figure walked out into the fog. Seth wore similar clothes to the ones he'd worn this morning, but these were even more ragged. His hair was mussed, like he'd been abed, and he looked very much like a pirate from one of her novels.

As he came closer, she noted the bruises on his cheek and the cut on his lip. But that was all. Confusion swirled in her.

"But they took you away to beat you! How is it that you're here, and untouched?"

"Hardly untouched," Seth growled, touching his mouth.

"But…my father ordered…I don't understand…I've been so worried!"

Seth gave a grin. "After fifteen years in a penal colony, did ye not think I'd've learned by now how to duck a fist?"

"But there were four of them!" Her voice was growing strident, but she could not help it. "I watched them drag you away."

"Four is nothing," Seth said gently. "I've had to fight off six in my time. But I couldn't do it until your father was not around to see it, or he would have made sure of my departure. After I dealt with them, Harry and I sailed the *Artemis* up the river. We had to take it out of the docks, because you father would have checked to make sure his men had followed his orders and towed the ship out to sea."

She resisted the urge to run to him, to tell him how scared she had been for him, how happy she was to see him, now…and how desperately she did not want to marry another man.

Seth brushed off his sleeves, looking uncomfortable, almost embarrassed by his casual clothing. She thought him incredibly appealing in his rags, the shirt showing a great deal of his chest and forearms. The pants formed to his body, and his feet were bare. How wild he was compared to any other man she knew.

Silent moments passed. Natasha could hear the pounding of her heart, and wished that he would say something. Anything.

"What are you doing here?" he asked, his gaze shifting over her slowly.

"I couldn't stay away. I needed to see you, to make sure you were all right."

"And now you have."

There was nothing she could say to that, nothing that would counter it. Except the truth. "I don't want to go," she confessed.

"Then don't." He was before in her two strides, pulling her up against him, kissing her with an urgency that matched her own. She clung to him, holding onto him for dear life.

When he broke the kiss, he put her at arm's length. He was positively beautiful, this sea captain of hers. "I like you in your sailor's clothing," she said.

He chuckled and pulled her close. He smelled like heaven, the fragrance both heady and arousing. "Did your ma not tell ye it's unsafe to be out alone at night?"

"You know as well as I do that my mother would have a fit if she knew I was here."

"Then we'd best get you below deck before someone notices."

She hesitated. She knew exactly what that meant. He would make love to her, here aboard his ship. Her maidenhead would be taken by a sea captain—a man who had been wronged by the people who should have loved him the most.

"I can take you home if you'd like," Seth said softly, as if he didn't want to startle her.

"No," she said quickly, taking his hand.

Seth led her through a narrow doorway, onto steep stairs that led to an equally narrow hallway. He opened one of the doors leading off the hallway, and she stepped through, gazing around. The cabin was clearly his stateroom. It was a clean, relatively tidy room, but very sparse. It held only bare essentials, including a wide bed with odd, high sides, and a desk with little rails that ran around the edges. Of course, that would stop things rolling off in rough conditions. The desk had a clutter of rolled-up papers, and a lamp that hung over it from a chain on the wooden-beamed ceiling above. The lamp was turned low, and there was a candlestick on the shelf above the head of the bed. The shelf also had a little rail.

At the foot of the bed was a sea chest, hand-carved and battered from use. The brass escutcheon plate gleamed in the low light.

But her gaze kept drawing back to the bed. The rest of the cabin glowed with wood paneling, yet was bereft of any color or decoration. The bed, though, reflected the essence of the man beside her, covered in rich, lush fabrics in dark colors. It looked inviting and warm. And masculine.

It was slightly rumpled, from where he must have been resting before she came aboard. Excitement and fear raced along her spine. Tonight she would become a woman.

Seth unbuttoned his shirt, shrugged out of it and tossed it aside. How beautiful he was, a contrast of hard muscle and smooth olive skin that captivated her. Sholto Piggot would not look like this man. Few could hold a candle to Seth Harrow. And for tonight, he was hers.

Natasha pulled her loose hair aside, unfastened Elisa's coat, and slid it from her shoulders. She dropped the coat over the chair behind the desk and turned to see Seth staring at her. "Prepared, are ye?" he asked, gazing at her shift.

She bit her lip, wondering if the truth would serve her this time. It had seemed to make Vaughn angry, rather than understanding. "My mother locked me in my room, and took my clothes away from me."

Seth crossed his arms, studying her. "But you still found a way to come to me."

She dropped her gaze to her toes. "You think me a loose woman…"

"No." He was there, in front of her, lifting her chin. He stared into her eyes. "No, Natasha. I think of you as brave, courageous beyond belief. Stubborn and willful. And a pure delight." His lips curved softly as he pulled her close.

A moment later her shift sagged around her, slid to the ground to puddle about her feet. His gaze moved over her. She felt self-conscious and exposed, but then his gray eyes met and held hers. "You are breathtaking, Natasha."

She could not help but smile at his compliment. Then he kissed her, lifting her in his arms, and laying her down on his bed. He untied his pants and pushed them down his long legs.

The breath lodged in her throat, as she saw his long, thick length, aroused and rising past his navel.

She had never seen a man naked, but doubted that many looked like him. Realizing she was staring, she pulled her gaze back to his face.

He smiled at her expression. "'Tis fine, Natasha. Ye can look all ye want."

She could feel herself blushing furiously. "I'm so new to this. I want to be good for you, Seth, but I'm afraid I won't know what to do…"

"Hush." He slid onto the bed beside her, his eyes never leaving her face. "This is a first occasion for both of us, you know."

"You? But surely, you've had…I mean…you must have…" She fell into confused silence, and Seth's grin became a low chuckle.

"I'll not abuse ye poor soul, Natasha. There have been women aplenty in my life. But never one like you."

"You mean…virgin, don't you?"

"Aye, maidenhood is part of it."

"And what is the other part?"

"We'll leave that for another time," Seth murmured, leaning forward to kiss her. His lips were soft, warm, and gentle, coaxing open her own. She remembered the shock, and Seth's strong erotic reaction when she had responded to his kiss before, and she thrust her tongue forward, to meet his own.

"Mmm..." He lifted his head from hers. "Who taught you to do that?"

"You did. I mean, you did it to me, so I thought..."

"Ye need to stop thinking, lass." He pushed at her shoulder, so that she was forced to lay with her back flat against the sheet. "You need to stop thinking, and start feeling instead." He threw his thigh over her hip, and straddled her, and she caught and held her breath as he rose before her. He looked strong, the muscles of his chest and arms were bulging, the flesh tanned and glowing in the dull light. "Ye can't enjoy yeself if ye are worried about what ye doing."

"I can't help it," she confessed. "How can I ensure you...enjoy yourself, if I don't worry about it?"

Seth leaned forward to kiss her mouth, quickly, and with little passion. His hair swung forward to caress her cheek. "Then let's get that out of the way, shall we?" he said, the proper English gentry accent back. "Natasha, may I say what a wonderful time I've had this evening? It was most enjoyable."

She started to giggle, and realized that she sounded like a schoolgirl. So she tried to suppress the giggle, which only made it come harder.

Seth grinned, too. "Ye don't like my accent?" he complained, with mock severity.

"I like it fine. Any way. All ways. Sometimes you sound like every other lord in the country, and sometimes you sound very Irish, and sometimes, like when I first came aboard, you didn't sound anything like either of them. It's an accent I haven't heard before."

"Australian. What you were hearing was an Australian accent. It's a mongrel, made up of the accents of every poor bastard that's ever set foot there, and that's a mash of countries from around the world, including the lower-class English and poor Irish." He grabbed her wrists where they lay on her torso, and picked them up. "Is there an accent you prefer?" he asked. "Whatever you want, will be my pleasure."

"Just be yourself, Seth," she said quietly. "Don't 'put on' an accent for me. Not for me."

He stared at her for a long moment, then lifted her wrist so that he could kiss her loosely curled fingers. "I will," he said softly. Then his smile returned, along with a devilish glint in his eyes, as he lowered her arms so that they were stretched over her head. "Take hold of the rail there," he said quietly.

She felt for and found the narrow bed head rail he spoke of, and curled her hands around it.

"Now, you're not to let go, ye hear?"

"Why? What are you going to do?" she asked, alarmed.

"I'm going to teach ye to feel instead of think. So your hands must stay on that rail, no matter what. Agreed?"

"Agreed…I think."

"Yes, or no…or I pack ye up and send ye on your way. Agreed?"

"Agreed." She swallowed on a throat gone very dry. "What are you going to do to me?"

"Oh, this and that," Seth growled. He brushed the hair from her face, and ran his thumb over her lips. "What I want you to do is concentrate on what my hands are doing. That's all."

"Just your hands?"

He grinned. "For now." His hands caressed her cheeks. "Feel that?"

"Yes, of course."

"Focus, 'Tasha, my love, focus."

Her heart jumped at the endearment, and she stared up at him, but he seemed oblivious to her sudden leap of excitement. Instead, his hands moved down to her throat, tracing the line there. "Feel what I'm doing," he told her. "Close your eyes."

She stared at him, unable to comply and close her eyes. It would leave her far too vulnerable in a situation where she didn't know what would happen next.

Seth's hands paused. "Close them…or I could blindfold you, instead, if you like."

Obediently, she closed them. Immediately, she became aware of the soft touch of the sheet at her back, the heat where Seth's thighs pushed against her hips, and the soft brush of his testicles against her pelvis. And the scent of him—it emanated from the sheets, the pillow, and from Seth himself—wreathing her mind in a giddy, intoxicating tendrils. Her heart picked up speed.

His hands brushed over her collarbones, making her jump. "See now, you're feeling and not thinking," Seth said, his voice a murmur.

"Yes," Natasha said, and her voice was hoarse.

The soft fingertips slid around the sides of her breasts, and for a moment she was disappointed. She had thought that he would touch them next. But his hands were stroking along her hips and belly, and she gave a low sound as her belly rippled with pleasure. The fingertips swept over the hollow next to her hipbone, and she found her back was arching in response, lifting her hips off the bed.

"God, yes," Seth said, and his voice was also husky. "Listen to your body, Natasha. Listen to what it's doing, what it's telling ye."

His weight shifted off her hips, and his hands on her ankles separated her legs, spreading them wide. It opened her up, and she could feel cooler air at the juncture of her thighs. She had grown moist and slippery there as she did sometimes when reading her novels. This, then, was part of making love. A normal thing.

His hands were sliding up the inside of her calves, stroking and fluttering, climbing slowly higher and higher. She realized that if he continued on his path, his fingers would soon be at that hot, moist spot that was now throbbing in anticipation. And a hot blush flooded her face as she recalled that Seth had already acquainted himself with that part of her anatomy.

Her whole body leapt with pleasure when she recalled that hot explosion of excitement his tongue had sent through her. But somehow, she knew that was not all of it. There was more, and Seth was about to show her.

His hands were sliding along her thighs, caressing the skin, stroking it, sending little ripples of excitement through her. She realized that she was making panting sounds, little moans and whimpers.

"Tell me what you want, Natasha."

"I don't know," she managed to say, and licked her lips.

"Yes, you do. What is your body telling you? Feel it."

She let herself sink into the pool of pleasure his hands were creating, feeling the ripples and spasms shivering through her, listening for the growing sense of what she wanted. It was an ache of incompletion. She felt it, felt the shape of it.

"Tell me," Seth coaxed.

"My breasts," she said, feeling her cheeks heat again. "I want…" But she could not finish the thought, because she wasn't sure what she wanted. Just that her breasts ached to be touched…somehow.

"Ah…" She heard him move on the bed, felt his weight shift. "Like this?" he asked, and his fingers lightly stroked her breasts. It was wonderful, and pleasure raced through her at his touch, but it wasn't quite right.

"No, not quite," she said, frowning.

"Then, this is what you mean." His fingertips slid over her nipples, tugging at them, and she gave a hard groan of pleasure as the thrill of his touch seemed to arrow right down to the spot between her thighs, where he had pleasured her that night.

"The groan of a woman," he murmured, and he seemed absurdly pleased at the guttural sound she had made. "Then, you would like this much better..."

She held her breath, waiting. Then felt the incredible touch of something warm and moist all around one nipple. When hard edges closed around it and tugged, she realized with a flare of passion that he was using his teeth and tongue and mouth on her breast. As he transferred his attention to the other breast, she gasped aloud at the exquisite tremors sweeping through her body, and her eyes opened involuntarily. "Oh my!" she gasped.

Seth looked up at her. His own eyes were sleepy, half-closed. And his manhood seemed to be thicker, harder, longer, almost pulsing with its own heartbeat.

Natasha heard her breath coming in little pants, and as she stared down at Seth's cock, she finally put the pattern together. "Inside me," she said, her voice guttural and thick with excitement. "I want you inside me."

Seth's smile was slow, one of a gourmand taking his time. "In a while," he assured her. He brought his mouth back to her breast and this time she watched him lapping at it, his tongue making the flesh gleam in the lamplight. She let her head roll back on the pillow, groaning aloud her pleasure.

His tongue slid further down, deserting her breast. Quickly, he trailed down her abdomen, until his lips hovered over her mound. He settled himself between her legs, and Natasha could feel her thighs fall apart to accommodate him, even as her face flushed hot again. But before she could protest at this most intimate caress, Seth bent his head to her flesh and she felt his tongue slide against her, lapping at the little nub of flesh that she had discovered for herself in the bath. But she had never pursued the rubbing to the point where Seth had brought her—had not known such an explosion of the senses was even possible. As his tongue made her writhe and wriggle on the mattress, she realized that it might be possible for her own fingers to do the same…

And then her thoughts scattered into incoherent fragments as the excitement swelled and beat at her with heady pulses, building and swelling and building, until suddenly, her whole body locked and held still at the apex of such incredible delight. It shuddered through her, pulse after pulse, taking her breath and her heartbeat with it.

Until finally, her energy drained, and she fell back upon the bed, her body tingling and nerves zapping white fire.

Seth moved to lay beside her and kiss her forehead. "That's feeling, lass," he said, his voice low and hoarse. He tugged her hands free of the railing, and massaged her palms, where her fingernails had dug into the flesh.

"But what about you?" she asked.

He brought her hand down to his engorged cock, and wrapped it around the thick shaft. "We're not finished yet," he assured her. Guiding her hand, he showed her how to stroke him, the gentle up and down movement, making sure her palm bumped over the edges of the crown, his soft brogue instructing her as she experimented.

She was astonished at the heat and rigidness of his shaft, and how at the same time it felt velvety soft against her hand. She was caught by delight at the way her touch made Seth groan, and the pace of his breathing increased. Then he caught her hand, and pulled it away. "Enough," he gasped.

His eyes were darkened, the centers of them dilated. His own hand he brought sliding along her thigh, leaving sizzling flesh in its wake, until his fingers slipped between the folds of flesh, into the heat and moisture there.

Natasha bucked hard against his hand, all the nerves there still sensitive and alert. He smiled at her reaction, and stroked again, making her hips tilt. She gasped as his fingers buried themselves inside her, and knew that this was the place where his cock would go. "Hurry," she said, suddenly aching for that moment.

He settled himself between her legs again, only this time, his hips lay against hers, and he propped himself up on his elbows. He looked into her eyes. "We can't hurry. Not this time."

She could feel him pushing at her entrance, and instinctively spread her legs further, bringing her knees up against his hips.

"Yes," he said, pulling at her knee and bringing her leg over his back. "Open up for me." And his cock pushed inside her, just a little. He felt enormous to her, and she gasped a little at the intrusion. Seth lowered his head, and took her nipple into his mouth, tugging at it with his teeth, and stroking the very tip with his tongue. The tingling expanded, thrummed all the way to the proud flesh between her legs. And she felt him push further inside her, spreading her.

"Feel, Natasha," he whispered.

She closed her eyes, spreading her senses out, to feel the sensations he was causing. And despite the tightness, she sensed the rightness of this entry into her body. Though there was a sudden, sharp pain, it felt right. It felt good. She could feel a pressure on her pearl of pleasure, and the low-grade pleasure it caused that was swiftly building.

Seth suddenly slid into her completely, burying himself to the hilt, and she gasped. "Oh, that feels so wonderful!"

He laughed, a low chuckled that reverberated against her chest, and made her smile. "That's what I'm supposed to say," he said, and kissed her temple. She felt him withdraw a little, then push in, and she coupled up that motion with the stroking of her hand, and saw the pattern. His thrusting caused no discomfort, for the slick moisture aided the motion. Then the pressure on her pearl became a pleasurable massage that swiftly built to a swelling wave of excitement. "Again?" she gasped, her eyes opening wide.

"Come for me," Seth gasped. There was sweat at his temples, and the tendons at his neck stood out, tight and hard. His thrusting was growing quicker, harder, which built her own pleasure.

The peak of it hit her, just as Seth locked into a tight bow above her, with a harsh groan every bit as guttural as her own had been. And she could feel him moving inside her, little thrusts and spasms.

Now I am a woman. The thought held a fierce satisfaction, as her body rocked with the force of her climax.

Chapter Fourteen

There were other couplings that night, in between quiet times when their bodies rested and their minds drifted. Towards the end of the long night, Natasha found herself rousing from sleep, awoken by Seth's touch. She lay on her side, and Seth was against her back, with his head on her pillow. His hand over her waist had laid heavy and hot, but now his hand was moving, stroking the flat plane of her stomach, making it quiver. Slowly, the hand moved up to her breasts, to tease and tickle the nipples, and stroke the soft underside of each swell.

The caresses drew her fully awake, and her body, too. She could feel herself growing moist again, just from the touch of his hand on her breasts. Perhaps he sensed her growing alertness, for his hand slid down to her thighs, and slipped inside the folds of flesh, deep enough to slide inside her. She moved her thighs restlessly, giving him better access, and she heard him chuckle behind her. His lips pressed against her shoulder, and his hand moved higher, to stroke the nub of flesh that she'd learned during the night was called a clitoris, and was a source of all pleasure for her.

She trembled at the waves his hand was creating. From behind, she felt his cock press against her, and slide inside her. She welcomed him with a hot rush of satisfaction, which pushed her enjoyment to a higher level. She encouraged Seth with murmurs and sighs of pleasure as he thrust deep and hard.

As her climax took her, she felt Seth stiffen and groan behind her, felt his seed spill into her, and let her eyes close in a dreamy, contented bliss.

A little later, she felt Seth shaking her gently. "It's nearly dawn," he warned her.

She opened her eyes to find herself staring into his face. Warmth flooded every inch of her as she stared at the man who had taken her maidenhead, and who had shown her things she had never dreamed of.

After sleep, he looked younger, the lines around his mouth and eyes not as pronounced. His hair, tousled from sleeping and other things, lay in chaotic disarray on the stark white pillow. Memories of the night they'd spent flashed through her mind, reminding her why her body ached this morning in places she'd never hurt before.

She smiled to herself. Seth was a wonderful lover, gentle, caring, considerate, passionate. Even now she yearned to make love to him again, to experience the bliss. No wonder her novels had never been able to explain the act itself. There was nothing like it from which to draw comparisons. No words were worthy enough of expressing the emotions involved, save that it was the closest to thing to heaven she had ever known.

She glanced over at the small window. The dark sky was starting to turn gray. Dawn beckoned. She should leave right now, return to her home before her parents became aware of her absence. She glanced back at Seth. He smiled slowly, and all thoughts of leaving fled.

"Good mornin'," he said, pulling her close. His body felt hot and hard, and very, very good. She kissed him, inhaling deeply his musky, masculine scent. If only she could stay like this all day…in his arms.

His manhood, like steel and velvet, nudged against her stomach and she smiled.

"See what ye' do to me, lass?"

She laughed lightly, and her fingers brushed along his hard length, feeling him thicken and lengthen under her ministrations. She suddenly understood what Elisa meant about a woman having a certain power over a man. How a single touch could bring a man to his knees.

"You're a quick study, Natasha."

She loved his soft Irish brogue. It sent a shiver along her spine. "I learned from the best."

Her declaration pleased him, she could tell by the light in his gray eyes, and he proved it a moment later, kissing her hard, his tongue slipping past her lips, stroking hers with practiced skill, stealing the breath from her lungs.

Nudging her onto her back, he parted her thighs with his knees. He broke the kiss, his eyes so dark and passionate, it made her heart skip a beat. She glanced down at his manhood, the tip of which touched her opening, which was already hot and wet with need.

Slowly he entered her, inch by inch, as her body stretched to accommodate his great size. He closed his eyes, his jaw set, obviously straining for control. She knew that she would never forget him as he was now. The way the cords of his neck tightened as he tried to contain his need.

And then he began to move, a slow, fluid motion that had her lifting her hips to meet his every thrust.

One of his hands covered her breast, weighing it before his fingers splayed, running a nipple between forefinger and thumb. The breath caught in her throat as warmth spread throughout her. Seth leaned down and kissed her there, his mouth hot, his tongue like velvet as he stroked her.

Her insides tightened like a bow, as she neared the unbelievable pinnacle.

And then it hit her with a strength that left her breathless, her body pulsing and throbbing as her climax claimed her.

Seth groaned low in his throat as he followed her over the edge, his body shuddering against hers.

When her heart finally slowed down, she looked past Seth to the window—and was reminded that she needed to get dressed. There was no time to waste. She sat up and threw her legs over the side of the bed, grabbing her shift and hastily putting it on.

Seth ran a hand down her back, sending goose bumps over her flesh. What she wouldn't give to stay here with him, to spend the day in bed, enjoying this new love. There was nowhere else she'd rather be.

"What now, Natasha? Do you go back and marry him?" Seth's voice was harsh, and she turned to look at him.

He frowned, his gaze searching hers.

She bent down to kiss him. "How can you ask that? You know my father arranged the marriage against my will."

"Your father will never allow you to marry me," he said in a harsh voice. "He will never see me as anything but a convict."

She wanted to reassure him, but how could she when she knew her father better than anyone? Seth was right. Her father would never allow her to marry him.

"I won't keep you with me, Natasha. Not unless we're married. I won't let the world shun you as it shuns me."

She squeezed his hand. "I'll go back to my home, to my parents, but you come with me, Seth. Together. We finish this together."

He watched her for a minute, saying nothing. She saw the emotions flicker across his face, and knew he seriously considered what she was saying, but she also saw the stubborn set of his jaw. "I cannot return with you. Not now, not when you are already in danger. We must keep this private. No one must know. Just promise me you will not marry him."

"I swear I will not." Natasha heard footsteps on the deck above. Vaughn had arrived. She flung on Elisa's coat, and buttoned it, then spared a final glance at Seth. Should she tell him what lay in her heart? Did she have a right to speak it? She glanced at the bed she had slept in, and knew that she was his wife in deed, if not in fact, and the right was hers.

She smiled at him. "I love you, Seth. Only you."

And she saw his stunned expression as she shut the door behind her.

Ten minutes later, as she sat safely in Vaughn's carriage, Natasha chewed on her lower lip. She had seen Seth's face when she had declared her love to him. Shock, and disbelief. Had she made a mistake by declaring her feelings?

Every ounce of her being protested at leaving Seth and the *Artemis*, but Seth was right—she must bide her time. There was someone out there that could do real harm. She had only to look at what had happened to Vaughn and Elisa for proof.

The carriage stopped just around the corner from her house. She exchanged Elisa's coat for Hailey's cloak, pulling it tight around her, and kept her head lowered as she made her way to the back of the house. She dare not try the servant's entrance, for too many would be up and stirring by now.

Instead, she climbed up the ivy, hoping her footholds did not give and send her plunging to the ground below. By the time she had made it to her room, she was out of breath, and her hands ached from holding onto the ivy. Daring one last glance down to make sure no one had seen her, she opened the window and climbed into the room, to find Hailey sitting nearby, sound asleep in a chair.

The maid snapped to attention the minute Natasha tapped her shoulder. "My lady, I was so afraid you would not return in time." She lowered her voice. "Thank God you are home now." Hailey hugged her tightly. "Here, let us get you out of that shift and into a nightgown."

Within minutes Natasha was in her nightgown, snug in her bed, and falling asleep, visions of Seth and the night with him filling her thoughts.

A shrill cry woke Natasha from a sound sleep. She sat bolt upright, and tried to steady her pounding heart.

Had the cry been her mother's? It seemed it may have been.

Feet pounded down the hallway outside her room as servants raced toward the sound.

Natasha clutched the blankets to her, wondering what had happened. Had her mother discovered her secret? Had she or a servant or perhaps a neighbor seen her climb back into her bedchamber this morning?

Doom filled her. She scrambled out of bed, grabbed her robe, and tied it haphazardly. She wrenched at the door, and almost slammed into it as the knob refused to give way under her hand. Of course, of course, the door had been locked.

She pounded on the door, and shouted, and finally, someone turned the key and let her out. But they had gone before she could even open the door to find out who had paused long enough to help her.

She rushed down the hallway and stumbled down the stairs to the public rooms below.

She came to a skidding stop, her heart jolting in horror. Her mother, whose back never touched the chair, who would sooner die than be seen sitting on the ground, even at a picnic, now sat slumped in the doorway of her father's study, her skirts indecently showing her ankles.

"Mother!" Natasha rushed to her side, but her father's valet, Nigel, held her back. "Lady Natasha, please, I would ask you to go to your room. This is not something you should see."

A maid held a vial of salts to her mother's nose and she stirred, a terrible sob tearing at her throat.

What could possibly be so horrible that it would cause her mother to faint and sob in public?

She surged against Nigel's arms, enough so that she could see further into the room.

It had been snowing in the room. That was her first thought. Snow lay in a small drift across the floor. Then her mind connected up what she was seeing. Down. Small, wispy feathers. And lying at the edge of the mound of feathers, one of her mother's beautiful tapestried cushions. It lay flat, the tapestry ripped apart. The drift of feathers was the stuffing, which had been cast across the floor like confetti at a wedding....

She saw someone lying flat on the floor, legs sprawled, and one of her father's favorite whiskey glasses lying on its side nearby…and a puddle of blood that had pooled beneath the person's…body.

She recognized the shoes, the feet, and the black suit.

Her father. In that moment she knew her father was dead.

Natasha sagged as a wave of dizziness washed over her, and Nigel steadied her.

"I don't understand!" she wailed.

Tears welled in the older man's eyes and he shook his head. "Your father has been shot, my lady."

"Shot? But who?" She couldn't get her mind to function properly. Her father couldn't have been shot. Oh, people were shot all the time, but not her father, not in this house…

"Who else, but the very man who was here yesterday. It's a pity we didn't kill him then."

Seth?

"That's impossible." She shook her head.

"I'm afraid it's the truth, my lady. Your father was holding a note signed by Seth Harrow, demanding satisfaction for the insult yesterday."

"Mr. Harrow was not here last night."

"He must've come in the wee hours. Your father woke around two in the morning, and I brought him a glass of warm milk. He was alive then, when I retired. Your mother found him just a moment ago. I am so very sorry."

*****

The sun had well risen, casting long shadows on the deck of the *Artemis*, as Seth dressed in his gentleman's finery, preparing for the day ahead.

He was usually an early riser, but this morning his mind circled around the small miracle he had experienced last night.

As he had been preparing for this journey, back in Australia, he had braced himself for the grim, unpleasant tasks facing him in London. He would never have predicted finding such happiness in this fat old whore of a city—yet he had.

I love you, Natasha had said. He could hear her sweet voice still.

She loved him. He had seen it in her eyes—the softness, the compassion, and yes, the love.

It had been a long time since anyone had looked at him like that. It had been just as long since he had felt anything like that for another. The penal colonies had no time for the softer emotions, and ruthlessly stamped out any such inclination. The guards had not cared, and soon enough, the prisoners themselves ceased to care. All that mattered was survival at any cost.

But now everything had changed. For all that he tried to deny it, he had a lot to live for, and a lot to prove, if he was to win Natasha's hand.

And he would.

Whatever and however long it took—it didn't matter. Natasha Winridge would be his wife.

"Seth, get up here!" Harry yelled from the top deck.

Seth frowned. Harry never yelled. His heart hammering, Seth rushed from his stateroom, up the steps and onto the deck.

Harry pointed to the shore.

Just beyond the *Artemis,* a group of men were coalescing on the little dock. Many of them wore blue uniforms and tall hats.

His stomach tightened. Bobbies, and lots of them, and they were headed for his ship. Why else would they be here?

How had they found him? Well, it wasn't as if he'd hidden the ship. It was impossible to hide an oceangoing vessel on the Thames. He'd simply moved it to where it was not expected to be.

He eyed the approaching huddle of bobbies, and wondered what trouble Natasha's father had stirred up for him this time.

Then his heart turned cold as another awful possibility occurred to him. Natasha's sojourn with him must have been discovered. Her father no doubt had called the authorities. He wasn't sure what law he had broken, bedding the daughter of a noble lord, but he was sure that her father would find a way to punish him for the deed.

Very well then. Seth took a deep breath. He'd acknowledged the risks he courted last night. Even as he'd watched Natasha climb the gangplank, and realized that she had come to him, and what the natural conclusion to her visit would be, he'd accepted everything that came with such a night of pleasure. The joys and pleasures, the shining moment she had confessed her love for him, and also the consequences.

So he turned squarely to face the policemen.

"Harry," he called softly. "I want you to go to Lord Fairleigh's house. Tell him to meet me at Scotland Yard as soon as possible. And tell him to bring the best barrister money can buy."

Chapter Fifteen

"The cargo is rotting away, Seth. All that food. It's a bloody shame, but I have to make a decision." Harry's fingers tightened around the bars of the jail cell, for he knew as well as Seth where that food had been bound—Ireland, to fill the stomachs of hungry friends. Seth had no intention of returning home empty-handed.

It was a day since Seth had been arrested for the murder of Lord Munroe. The charge had been a cold shock to him, and he had spent the time in the cell trying to understand how anyone would profit from the Baron's death. It didn't make sense.

But the note found with the body was all the damning evidence the English needed. It gave Seth the only visible reason for killing Munroe.

The problem was, he'd never written said letter, yet no one believed him. Seth knew his future was bleak. He was already personally acquainted with the wholesale injustices the court system could dish out. He knew better than to believe that truth would win through, or that justice would be served.

The rough treatment he'd received at the hands of the police officers and bobbies hinted at worse to come. They'd already decided he was guilty.

And poor Natasha. Would she believe he had nothing to do with her father's murder?

Damn, he should have sailed straight to Ireland.

And now Harry was providing more bad news.

"Word is already out," Harry continued, "and creditors are arriving left and right. The *Artemis* needs to weigh anchor, Seth. What do I do?"

Seth ran a hand through his hair, his mind racing. "Where in the hell is Vaughn? Did you tell him exactly what I told you?"

Harry looked hurt. "Of course I did."

Seth grimaced. "Sorry. But I'm stuck here and can't do anything."

Harry relented. "I know. Should I head for Ireland, Seth? Get it done for you? I can round the crew up in jig time. They're spoiling here, too, cooling their heels in the taverns. They'd be glad to leave. It's too cold here."

Seth sighed. Problems. Too many problems. And how could he handle any of them while he was here in this cell? And where was Vaughn?

Now that his friend was late, he could measure how much he'd been counting on Vaughn taking care of things for him.

Well, he'd just have to rely on himself. It had served him well enough for fifteen years. It would have to serve this time, too.

And he'd never again reach out for help, or friendship.

Or love.

He gripped the bars. "Don't leave yet, Harry," he told his first mate. "Give me a little time. I get to speak to the judge tomorrow morning—I may yet be able to shrug this off. If I'm not out of jail by tomorrow evening, you should head for Ireland, and deliver what food you can. You know well who to seek there—we've spoken about it often enough."

"Aye, I know it well," Harry agreed.

"After you've made landfall in Ireland, you can consider the *Artemis* yours. You can go where you want, do what you want. I'd advise you to head back to Australia, but as you'll be the captain, that's your decision to make."

"But I can't do that!" Harry protested, his hands clutching at the bars, too. "What'll you do when you get out of here? Even if it is later than tomorrow?"

Seth gripped Harry's hand. "Harry, if I can't talk my way out of this by tomorrow evening, then it will go to trial, and I will be found guilty. They think I killed a lord of the realm, Harry. They won't throw me in jail this time. They'll hang me."

* * * * *

When Vaughn had arrived at the house, he had been mysterious about the reasons why Natasha should come with him—he would not share his purpose even with her.

She had not wanted to go with him, the hot swirl of emotions she had been suffering since she had seen her father's body had blanketed her thoughts and cast her body in lead. She wanted to stay in her room.

But Vaughn had glanced around for witnesses, servants, then placed his hand on hers. "Please, Natasha. This is very important. You must speak for your family in the matter I must deal with—your mother cannot."

"Our solicitor is taking care—"

"No, Natasha. He is handling your father's affairs. He cares not a wit about yours. Come with me."

And so she had come. There had been no resistance to her leaving. Her mother, her face as white as the funeral lilies adorning the house, sat huddled before a roaring fire in the drawing room. She did not stir, nor look at her when Natasha told her she was leaving for a while. Even Aunt Susannah, in the corner by the fireplace, merely glanced up before returning to her bible.

Vaughn's directions to the driver as they climbed into his carriage gave no hint, either. "Rumpole Mews," he said shortly.

Once they were underway, Vaughn settled back in the seat and studied her. "I'm sorry about your father, Natasha. He was an honorable man. He always tried to do the right thing. That's more than you can say for many of his peers."

Tears stung at the back of her eyes, but she blinked them away. Of all the platitudes and sentiments she had heard the last day and a half, Vaughn's was the most sincere and honest. He had captured her father's spirit in a few short words.

"Thank you," she told him when she thought she could safely speak.

He nodded, and tugged down his waistcoat and she realized that he was feeling awkward.

"Why did you bring me?" she asked. "What could you not tell me at the house?"

"You and I both know that Seth did not murder your father. He could not have done this deed, and we both know why."

She nodded.

"But that is something that cannot be publicly admitted. Because we cannot speak of it, all anyone else will see is that Seth had ample reason to kill your father, and that he was more than capable of murder."

Her heart squeezed, and her breath left her. "Seth would not do such a thing—"

"I said he was capable of it, that is all," Vaughn interrupted. "Most men are capable of murder if their passions are roused enough, and Seth has more passion than most. And that is what the judges will see. So I need your help, Natasha."

"Of course," she said simply. "Whatever you ask of me."

"I'm about to ask for quite a bit," he warned.

She shivered. "Whatever you ask," she affirmed, "I will do."

The rest of the journey was silent, which gave Natasha time to wonder what it was that Vaughn was about to demand of her. The leaden swirl of guilt and grief subsided a little. She was helping Seth, and if she helped Seth then it was possible that the real killer would be revealed and her father's death would not go unpunished.

"I hope they throw the murderer in jail for life," she muttered. "No, I hope they transport him to Port MacQuarrie and he dies breaking rocks after years of misery at the hands of the guards."

"Oh, they won't leave it at that," Vaughn said. He looked at her sharply, as if he were surprised, or uneasy. "If they find out who murdered your father, they will hang him."

A cold sleeve sheathed her heart, and squeezed. "But…they think Seth did it."

"That's right," Vaughn agreed softly.

The carriage came to a sharp halt, punctuating his simple answer.

Natasha stared at him, her skin prickling painfully. She made no move to leave the carriage. "They'll hang him?" Her voice was strained.

"If he's found guilty."

"But…but…last time he was innocent, and they sent him to Australia anyway!"

Vaughn rested his forearms on his knees, and clasped his hands together. He stared into her eyes. "That's why I bought you here. You must trust me on this, Natasha."

There was an earnestness in his voice that Natasha could not interpret. She shivered. "I said I would." But her voice lacked conviction.

Vaughn nodded. "Come with me, then." He pushed the door open, and helped her down to the cobbles.

They were in a pleasant mews that contained a row of elegant office apartments. Behind her, Big Ben struck the hour with a sonorous note, and she realized they were in Whitehall, close by the Houses of Parliament. And somewhere, even closer, the courts. She shivered.

Vaughn led her inside the nearest office. The coachman already had the door held open and his tall hat hid the nameplate.

They stepped inside the warm, well-lit room. A clerk at his high bench turned at their arrival, and slid off the stool, and came towards them, wiping his inky hand with a rag. "My lord, may I help you?"

"I have appointment with Mr. Davies," Rhys said.

"A moment, m'lord, I'll let him know you're here." The clerk hurried to a door at the back of the room, tapped lightly, and stepped inside and shut the door. Natasha looked up at Vaughn, hoping for some hint of what was about to happen, but his face gave away nothing.

The door opened, and the clerk hurried back again. "This way, please, my lord, my lady." He bowed, and waved toward the door, which had been left open. Natasha saw bookshelves, heavy with leather-bound volumes, but nothing else.

Vaughn led her through the door, into the large room beyond it. Her attention was caught by the large mullioned window and the view of the Thames behind it, then she saw the man who was rising from behind the table, and her delight at the view, her thoughts, all slithered to an icy-cold halt.

The man could be her father! He was identical in all ways except age...this man was nearing his thirties, if he was not past them. The hand he held out to Vaughn lowered, and his eyes narrowed, as he stared at Natasha.

She clutched at Vaughn's arm, her knees a little weak. There was only one explanation for the man's resemblance to her father.

"I might have warned you, Natasha, but I thought, if you'd known, you might not come with me," Vaughn said quietly

The man's eyes, so like her father—and her own—narrowed more as Vaughn spoke. He addressed Natasha directly. "Adding what Vaughn just said to the fact of your uncanny appearance, I must conclude that you are Natasha Winridge, the only *legitimate* child of the late Lord Munroe," he said matter-of-factly, coming closer to her to study her.

This was her brother. The half-brother who had been born to a Welsh actress. The brother her father would never acknowledge. "I don't know your name at all," she said, and felt her cheeks bloom with color. "They never told me your name. I only learned of your existence a few years ago, and that was…well, because of Vaughn."

"Rhys Davies," the man said, smiling, showing two deep dimples. The lack of a title made the name sound plain, bare. He gave a short, almost mocking bow. Perhaps he understood her thoughts. If her father had acknowledged him, he would now be the new Baron Munroe.

Vaughn settled Natasha on a chair before the table and straightened. "Rhys is one of the best barristers in London," he told her.

"Don't let the old war dogs along the Bowery hear you say that," Rhys responded. "As far as they're concerned, no man can be a good barrister until he's in his dotage."

Natasha recoiled a little at the bitter tone in his voice, and he saw it. He gave her a wry smile. "Forgive me, but Vaughn prodded an old ache. I am not acknowledged among my peers because of my 'youth'." He shrugged, as if he were dismissing it. "But then, it's something I'm used to."

She felt a touch of sadness. Her father's failure to acknowledge Rhys had clearly left a deep wound in him, one that would never heal now that her father was dead and could not amend that rift. She understood the sense of loneliness he felt, for the last few years she had felt it herself. None of the unmarried women she knew seemed to even think like her, and she knew very well her family was horrified at her struggles for independence, for a freedom she could not seem to grasp.

Yet for the last few days she had found that freedom and independence, contrarily, in Seth's arms.

She looked at Rhys now with an uncompromising stare. "Are you as good at your role as Vaughn says, Mr. Davies?"

He blinked, and looked at her thoughtfully, as if he were reassessing her. "Yes, I am," he said at last.

"Then that is all that matters."

"Rhys has a record for championing the underdog and winning," Vaughn said, taking the chair beside Natasha, while Rhys returned to seat himself behind the table.

Rhys lifted a brow. "What possible underdog could you need to champion?" He pulled the writing chest towards him and picked up the quill.

Natasha straightened her shoulders. "I am afraid I am the bearer of bad news, Mr. Davies. My father, or rather, our father was killed yesterday."

Rhys looked from Natasha to Vaughn, his expression indecipherable. "This is not news to me, Miss Winridge. Forgive me when I add that the fact strikes me as neither good nor bad. And I still fail to see why you need my services."

"How much of the matter do you know?" she asked.

"Only what was reported in the *Times*. I am not intimate with any members of your family."

"They've arrested a man for his murder. Seth Harrow."

"This I've also read," Rhys said coolly. "I thought it strange that the *Times* didn't indicate why he was arrested." His eyes seemed to pin her to her chair. "You know why, don't you? That's why you're here."

Vaughn stirred. "You should know, Rhys, that Seth Harrow is actually Seth Williams, heir of Marcus Williams, the Earl of Innesford."

Rhys frowned. "I didn't know Innesford had a son."

"He was convicted of treason and transported to Australia as a Fenian, fifteen years ago," Vaughn explained.

Rhys' eyes widened just a little, the only reaction he had given to any of the shocking facts they had provided him so far. He looked at Natasha. "And why would the son of Innesford want your father dead?"

"He had no reason. He didn't do it. He couldn't have."

"And why do you seek me out? By rights, Williams should approach me for representation. It is not strange that the daughter of the victim works on behalf of the accused?"

"I have become...involved with him." Her cheeks warmed under Rhys' steady regard. "My father opposed the match so vigorously, I was locked in my bedchamber to keep me from him."

Rhys glanced at the sheet of paper beneath his quill, then dropped the quill, and pushed the writing chest away again.

"That gives Williams ample reason to kill your father," Rhys said softly. "So there must be more you need to tell me."

Natasha could feel her cheeks blazing now. "The night my father died, I... I...was with Seth."

Rhys absorbed this as if it were simply one more fact to add to the story. "Do you have proof that you were with him the whole time?" he asked.

Her humiliation was complete. "Mr. Davies, you dare question my word?" she returned heatedly.

Vaughn laid a hand on her wrist. "I took her there, Rhys. And picked her up. And there was a first mate onboard, too, who would have seen her arrive and leave."

Rhys nodded. "You must forgive me, Miss Winridge, but the questions I've asked you so far are mild compared to those the prosecuting barrister will direct towards you."

Natasha felt her heart stutter to a stop. She flashed a glance at Vaughn, her eyes wide.

"She cannot appear in court," Vaughn declared, quickly.

"Ah." Rhys pursed his lips. "Then we are at the heart of the matter, aren't we?" He looked at Natasha again, assessing her. "I read of your engagement to Sholto Piggot, the son of the Duke of Marlberry, a few days ago."

Natasha kept her gaze steady. "My parents arranged the match behind my back and without my consent. When I read the item in the *Times* I was as surprised as you."

Rhys considered this for a moment. "I wager you were even more surprised than I, Miss Winridge." His smile was utterly charming, capped by an irresistible dimple in each cheek.

Natasha found herself smiling back. "I'm sure I was, Mr. Davies."

He sat back. "Would you like some tea, Miss Winridge? We may be here for a while, and I have many questions to ask you."

"Does that mean you will take the case? You will fight for Seth?" Her breath stilled as she waited for his response.

"Yes, Miss Winridge. I will take on the case. Vaughn has the rights of it. This is a case no other barrister in London would demean himself enough to take on, and I *like* the tough fights." Again, the irresistibly charming grin, which seemed to have more than a bit of the devil in it. "You strike me as a sensible, levelheaded lady, and that will help enormously, for we have a lot of work ahead of us, and you will find much of it uncomfortable because it will require you to be perfectly frank, perfectly candid about yourself and your relationship with Seth Williams—with my client. Is that agreeable to you, Miss Windridge?"

She smiled a little. "Only if you call me Natasha, Mr. Davies."

He considered this. "Under the circumstances, you'd better call me Rhys." He held out his hand to her, in a man-to-man gesture that she understood immediately. If he had been acknowledged by her father, she would have spent years already calling him Rhys. And she liked the gentleman's form of agreement, so she took his hand, like a man, and shook it.

And for the first time in two days she felt her body awaken and her spirit stir. Finally, she had hope.

Chapter Sixteen

Natasha had heard terrible stories about Newgate Prison, but the reality was far worse. Once it had been a gate into a much smaller London. Now, the prison towered over one of the poorest, most squalid sections of London Natasha had ever seen. Black filth seemed to cling to everything, including the white-faced, ragged people huddled on the pavements that turned to watch the carriage go by with hopeless eyes.

The stench was indescribable, and each time it wafted through the window, Natasha recoiled. She looked at Vaughn, holding her handkerchief to her mouth.

The corners of his mouth shifted into a grimace. "It's wretched, isn't it? Would you have suspected such a world exists, walking the manicured rows of Hyde Park?"

"Is this the rough world men constantly seek to hide from us women?" she asked.

"It is a tiny fraction of it," Vaughn admitted.

"Why hide it at all?" she demanded. "Why not do something about it? How can you see this and not be shamed?"

"I do what I can," Vaughn said evenly. "Elisa and I have established an orphanage, out in the clean countryside. There are over one hundred children there already."

Natasha stared at him. "You didn't tell me."

He grimaced again. "Charity of such a practical sort is rather frowned upon by the gentry. We didn't want to have to explain ourselves over and over again."

She nodded. He was right. People like her mother wouldn't understand at all. They would be puzzled by such an act.

The carriage stopped at the forbidding building, Vaughn helped her out, and escorted her towards the gaping maw of the prison. Rhys arrived in his own hack, and reached the gate at the same time they did. Rhys spoke to someone behind a smaller grille, quiet words she could not make out. Then the gate opened, sliding upwards with a rumble of hidden machinery and a squeal of un-oiled metal. Rhys waved them through—clearly, he was familiar with the prison. If he had spent his career defending the hardest cases, then he may well have ventured here in the past.

The gate dropped down behind them with a shudder that Natasha could feel through her slippers, and she shivered. Seth was here, in this place?

She lifted her skirts and stepped over filth she was in no hurry to identify, and followed Rhys to a narrow stair that cut into the wall of the tunnel they were in, and ended at a stout door. Rhys pushed the door open.

Inside, the room seemed quite normal. There was a raw wooden floor, to be sure, and a roughly hewn counter, but the windows were whole, and there was a stove in the corner that belched a welcome heat.

There were many people in the room already, and Natasha was dismayed to see her mother, her father's butler, and Sholto Piggot talking to an officious-looking man, who was nodding and scratching things down with a badly trimmed pen.

Of all the luck, Natasha thought. She tried to edge behind Vaughn, to hide herself, but it was already too late.

Her mother's face tightened and her lips pursed when she saw Natasha. "What are you doing here?" she demanded in a loud voice. It seemed that since her father's death, her mother had lost any self-control or sense of propriety. Even her usually immaculate appointments were sloppy, poorly tied or fastened, and with no finishing details like lace edging showing anywhere.

At her mother's loud exclamation, everyone paused to look up or look around at Natasha.

Then her mother gave a low, choking moan. "You…" she gasped, staring at Rhys. Her face turned ashen and her hand went to her chest. She seemed to stagger a little, and Jones, her father's butler, caught her and held her upright.

"You have nothing to fear from me, Lady Munroe," Rhys said. "My father chose to be absent from my life. You need not share the blame."

"What are you doing here?" Caroline whispered. "Why, why? To torture me in my hour of mourning?"

"I am here to speak with a client, madam. That is all. I am a practicing barrister at the Old Bailey." There was an unforgiving chill in Rhys' voice. "The Queen's Bench," he added, when Caroline's puzzled expression did not change. "The criminal court of London."

At that moment, there was a clash of steel and the sound of a heavy door shutting. From an inner doorway, three men emerged, the center figure moving heavily and awkwardly. It was Seth, and his arms and ankles were shackled, and tied to his waist with thick chains. He looked badly beaten. One of his eyes was swollen almost shut, and ringed with blue and purple flesh.

But his eyes were alive, snapping with the simmering edges of temper, and Natasha was inordinately pleased to see it. Seth simmering with fury was the man she had come to love—the man full of passion, life, and the will to face anything.

"Oh, Seth, what happened?" she asked, moving towards him.

At the same time the guards snapped to attention beside him, their hands on their long rifles, Natasha was halted by a hand squeezing her forearm, the nails digging in sharply.

She looked back. Her mother had found the energy to spring after her and yank on her arm. Her mother pulled her back now, with a strength that gave lie to her white face and weakness of a moment ago.

"You stay away from that murderer, or so help me god I will keep you prisoner in your room for the rest of your life," her mother muttered.

Rhys gave Lady Munroe a cool stare. She blinked, and dropped Natasha's arm.

Rhys glanced up at the constable manning the high desk. "I need to speak to the prisoner in private. He is to appear at the Bailey tomorrow. I must be allowed to prepare for the case."

The constable nodded. "You can have the usual room, Mr. Davies, sir. The guards'll see him settled." He nodded to the two guards on either side of Seth, and they hurried him through another door and away, almost lifting him off his feet as his bound ankles wouldn't let him move fast enough.

Natasha clenched her teeth against the need to protest at his treatment. If he really were guilty of murder, she would want him dragged around in chains, too.

She glanced at Rhys. "I will come with you," she said quietly.

Natasha's mother gasped, and looked at her in horror. "What have you done, Natasha?"

"Lady Munroe," Vaughn said quietly. "Do you not want to know the truth of your husband's death?"

"I already know the monster who made me a widow," Caroline snapped. "And I'm here to ensure he's properly hanged."

Vaughn shook his head a little. "Then, if you insist on such shortsightedness, I will leave you to go about your business. Good day, Lady Munroe." He gave a short bow, and turned to slide his hand beneath Natasha's. "Rhys, would you show the way?" he murmured.

Rhys took them through a dank, dim corridor of raw brick walls that seeped moisture. Some way along that corridor, the light from a strong lantern shone from an open doorway, and it was into this doorway that Rhys ducked, and Vaughn and Natasha followed him.

Seth was still standing between his guards, who looked stoical enough to remain in their place for the rest of the day if necessary.

"You can go," Rhys told the guards, placing a very large carpetbag on the plain wooden table in the middle of the room.

"But he's a murderer, Mr. Davies!" one of the guards protested.

Rhys pulled from the bag an enormous revolver and placed it squarely on the table. "I'll be quite safe," he assured them. "Why don't you two fellows just step outside the door, then? You can hear if anything goes amiss." He flipped them a coin each.

"Me thanks to you, as always, Mr. Davies, sir," one of the guards said, tugging on the brim of his cap. The other pocketed the coin with a nod. Both of them left the room, and Rhys gave a big gusty sigh.

Natasha went to Seth, but he held out his hands, holding up the fingers of one, warding her off.

"No, Natasha, I'm filthy and smell to high heaven thanks to those damned cells. Not until I've bathed for a week will I touch you." He gave her a smile. "But it's fine indeed to see you, my sweet one."

She stopped just short of him. "Oh, Seth, did you think I would not come?"

He glanced at Vaughn, then back at her face. "It would not have surprised me if you'd found this all too overwhelming to face."

"You think so little of me?" It emerged almost as a whisper. Her throat was tight with unshed tears. "You think I would rather see you hang than face this?"

Seth shook his head a little. "I'm a bitter, twisted man inside, 'Tasha. Transportation teaches ye that ye can't rely on anyone but yourself. Forgive me, but I thought I'd never see ye again, and it was like slipping back into those black clouds that I live with all those years."

"Well, I'm here," she said, straightening up and dashing away her tears with the back of her hand. "And I've bought help. I would like you to meet Mr. Rhys Davies, Esquire, a barrister of the court of London, who will defend your case before the Queen's Bench tomorrow."

Vaughn tugged on Natasha's arm. "Let him sit down, Natasha. Step back. Come."

She allowed herself to be drawn away, and Rhys brought the single hard chair that was clearly intended for him around to Seth's side of the table. "Sit, Mr. Williams. I know well the conditions in the Newgate cells, and have come well prepared. Sit."

Seth shuffled over to the chair and sat carefully, the chains clanking in a way that made Natasha moan and turn her head away.

"I can do nothing about the chains for now," Rhys explained, digging into the carpetbag. "But, here."

He stepped around the table, and held out a silver flask. "A small measure of restorative brandy." He held out his other hand. "Fresh bread, to fill your stomach."

"Lord above, food," Seth muttered, and grasped the small loaf with his manacled hands, and tore into it, eating hungrily. Rhys propped the flask on his lap and returned to the bag. He produced an apple, which he left on the table, a hair comb, a small pile of clean, folded cloth, and a corked bottle. "Water," he explained when Seth eyed it. "Can you listen well enough while you eat?"

"Certainly," Seth said, uncorking the flask.

"Your friends here have—"

"Natasha is not just a friend, is she?" Seth interjected.

Rhys looked up from his ledger, and blinked. "If you're implying—"

"The eyes, man. The eyes," Seth added impatiently. "You've both the same sire, or I'm no judge of men."

Rhys absorbed this without expression. "That is correct," he said at last.

"Yet you're going to defend me, the man that's supposed to have killed your father?"

"Strange as it seems, yes," Rhys answered quietly. "Natasha can be very convincing."

"What did she tell you?" Seth demanded.

"I told him the truth, Seth," Natasha said gently. "Nothing else will withstand the trial ahead."

"More truth," Rhys answered quietly. "May I continue?"

Seth sighed and pushed his hand through his hair, the other following it, bound by the manacles that clinked softly against the chains hanging from it. "Why not?" he said, at last. "This world grows stranger by the moment."

"In 1824, in Harrow, Ireland, you were found guilty of the murder of two English soldiers during the Riot of 1823. You were transported to Australia for a sentence of seven years. Correct?"

Seth glanced at Natasha and she saw him swallow. "Yes," he said at last.

She hid her dismay. She had quite forgotten the past that dogged Seth's heels. Murder. If the world thought him capable of murder once, they would do so again.

Rhys led Seth through the highlights of his fifteen years in Australia, then turned to the death of her father.

"I spoke to the bobbies that attended the Lady Munroe's calls for help," Rhys said. "I learned that LordMunroe fell upon his pocket watch, smashing it. It was stopped just past the hour of two o'clock." Rhys looked up from his page. "Where were you at two o'clock two mornings ago, Seth?"

Seth glanced at Natasha before looking at Rhys once more. "I was aboard the *Artemis*."

"Can you prove it?"

Seth nodded. "Harry, my first mate saw me at midnight when I went to my cabin."

"And at midnight you…went to sleep?"

"Yes."

"Alone?"

Seth stared at Rhys, unblinking. "Yes."

Rhys stared right back, challenging the lie.

Natasha felt sick to her stomach. Seth was a convicted criminal. He would swing for this murder if she didn't speak the truth aloud and in public. And if she did reveal the truth, all of London would know of her scandalous behavior. She would be ruined, but Seth would be freed. Turmoil swirled within her.

She saw that Vaughn was watching her and remembered, suddenly and unexpectedly, the night he had faced the world with Elisa at his side, and dared them all to reject them. Only moments before, in the middle of the ballroom floor, while the entire cotillion had watched them, he had spoken to Natasha and exposed to her his love for Elisa and his fear for what that love would bring down upon them.

"True love has an inevitability about it, Natasha," he'd tried to explain, and she had seen the weariness in his eyes, the stress. "I'm quite powerless to stop it, and I know that both of us are going to pay a terrible price for it. But Natasha, I don't want to stop it. I will pay that price to keep Elisa in my life. I know you don't understand it, that right now you're too full of hurt. But one day, you will fall in love and then, you might be able to look back on this moment and understand what I'm telling you. I just hope you never have to face the choice I'm making this night."

And Vaughn had turned to face the world, with Elisa by his side, and by some small miracle, had found acceptance.

He was looking at her now, and she knew that he was remembering the same moment. The corner of his mouth turned up a little. Sympathy. But he would not help her make her decision. He knew that she must do that.

She looked at Seth. He, too, was staring at her, and she read his message as clearly as if he'd spoken. "Keep your silence."

She shook her head. She could not. Silence would kill him.

"I was with him, Rhys. You know that. All of you know that. And it seems we must tell the world this fact if Seth is to survive."

Seth closed his eyes and clenched his jaw.

Rhys turned to her. "Are you sure, Natasha?"

"Don't, 'Tasha, love," Seth said softly. "Don't. Not for me."

"If not for you, then who?" she demanded, turning to him. "I love you, Seth, and I don't give a damn what the rest of the world thinks, anymore." She laid her hand on Rhys' arm. "How do we do this, Rhys? How do I get myself heard?"

He nodded. "I'll arrange it."

"No!" Seth cried, trying to stand, and sending the flask flying and the chains crashing about him. The sound was enough to bring the two guards rushing into the room, to grab him by both arms and restrain him.

"We'll need to see the warden immediately," Rhys demanded. "And is there a police chief here?"

"Yes, sir," one of the guards said.

"Bring the prisoner with you," Rhys said, packing up his copious carpetbag once more. "Natasha, Vaughn, please follow me."

Rhys returned them to the office. Natasha saw that her mother and Sholto Piggot were still there, and even as her heart sank, she was pleased. The more people that heard this, the better. Like Vaughn, she intended to declare the truth to the world.

Nothing less would save Seth, now.

They were all staring at her and the group emerging from the inner workings of the prison, now, and her mother was fanning herself, lifting her curls. "Oh, my…" she exclaimed in a die-away voice that Natasha knew now was false. The strength of her mother's grip on her forearm, earlier, gave lie to the helpless widow. Even now, her mother was playing games, concerned about appearances.

Rhys was facing a man in a blue uniform with brass buttons, who sat at the high desk. "Sir, concerning the murder of which my client, Seth Williams, son of Marcus Williams, the Earl of Innesford, has been accused, I have new information."

"You are Rhys Davies, the barrister, are you not?" the police chief interrupted.

"Yes, sir."

"What is a barrister doing down in these parts? Shouldn't you be sending a lawyer?"

"The circumstances are somewhat extenuating, sir," Rhys explained, with a wave of his hand. "Are you familiar with the case?"

"Familiar enough. I arrested the man."

"Good. Then, you'll be aware that the time Lord Munroe died was just after 2 a.m., yes?"

"That'd be correct." The police chief rested his hand on his chin, clearly intrigued by Rhys' manner and words.

"Sir, this young lady, here, can account for the accused man's time that night, and prove he did not kill Lord Munroe."

The police chief's sharp gaze swung to Natasha and she held up her chin and stepped forward. He lifted his hand in a signal that she halt. "Mr. Davies, I think it best we clear the room, don't you? Let's listen to what the lady has to say in private."

"No," Natasha said firmly. "I want everyone to hear it, sir. I want there to be no doubts about Seth's innocence in this matter."

The police chief considered this, and nodded. "Very well, then. Please continue, Miss."

Seth surged against his guards. "For god's sake, Natasha, no...don't."

She gave him a smile, and looked back at the police chief. "Seth Williams, or as you know him, Seth Harrow, was with me the night my father died. All night."

"Oh, my dear lord," Sholto Piggot exclaimed, his voice trembling.

"You lie!" her mother cried. "My good man, my daughter is lying for reasons beyond comprehension. I had her locked up in her room, all night."

The police chief looked to her, and lifted his brow.

"My maid let me out later that night," Natasha said, as calmly as she could muster. "When I returned just after dawn, I climbed the ivy outside my bedroom window. Send someone to check—you'll find the ivy pulled away from the wall in a dozen places."

"I will," the police chief said. He turned on his high stool, and flicked a finger at a couple of the uniformed men sitting at the tables behind him. "And talk to the maid, too," he added. They saluted and hurried out of the room. The police chief turned back to her. "The ivy will only prove you climbed in or out of your room. It doesn't prove the night you did it. Did anyone see you on this…escapade, miss?"

She thought about it. "Seth's… Mr. William's first mate. Harry, I think he's called." Natasha took another step forward. "Sir. After what I have said here today, I will never be accepted in society again. My family will disown me. I will lose everything I have. And I may still lose the man I love. I could have simply kept my silence and avoided that cost."

Vaughn cleared his throat. "Sir, as Miss Winridge has already committed herself to this confession, I should also point out that I drove her to Seth's ship that night, and picked her up again in the morning."

The chief stared at him, the shaggy eyebrows lowering. "Did you now, Lord Fairleigh? Well, here's a fix, for certain."

"It's a fix that's easily resolved," Rhys said. "Get Williams to write the words found on the note in Lord Munroe's hand. Compare the writing. You have the note, do you not?"

"As it happens, yes, I do." The chief stirred himself. "Someone take the chains off that man. Hurry about it, lads. Get him some ink and a pen. Let's get this matter settled."

The chains were unlocked and taken away, and Seth flexed his hands and feet, rubbing the flesh, as they brought pen and paper, and a pot of ink. He sat at the table and looked at the chief. "I don't know what words you want me to write," he said.

The chief, who had his arms crossed, watching Seth, nodded his head. "Glad you asked, laddie. I'd have been worried if you'd sat and writ the note without pause." He looked down at the scrap of paper in his hand, and read out the words, and Seth wrote them quickly. He held the sheet out to the chief, who reached down and took it from him. He looked from one to the other, and sucked his teeth. "Well, this'd be a pretty kettle of fish. It appears we're without a suspect."

*****

Seth stepped out past the porticulled gate, and took a deep breath. Vaughn laughed a little. "It's hardly fresh around here."

"It'll do. It'll do more than well enough," Seth said. He found he was rubbing his wrists again, and dropped his hand. He could still feel the manacles there, even though they were gone. He looked around the yard that fronted the prison gate. "Where's Natasha?"

"Her mother hurried her off straight after you wrote the note." Rhys stepped out beside them and hefted his carpetbag.

Seth held out his hand. "I owe you my life."

Rhys shook it. "You owe me my bill, which will be large enough. Your life is your own. I just did my job." He looked over his shoulder. "I have a cab waiting for me. And it looks like

Lady Munroe is waiting to impart some choice observations with you, so I'll leave you good folk to sort out the aftermath.

"I'm glad I'm not a recognized member of that family." He grinned. "Natasha will have a hard time of it now."

"No, she won't," Seth said with a growl.

Rhys cocked his head a little. "Perhaps not," he agreed. "Well, I do have a practice to run…"

"Send me your bill," Vaughn said quietly.

Seth saw that Lady Munroe was indeed waiting for them. "Good, let's get this settled," he said, and headed in her direction.

He heard Vaughn hurry after him, but didn't wait, and didn't slow his pace. He faced Caroline . "You can lock her inside the carriage, or her room, but it won't keep Natasha from me. Not forever. Don't you see, Lady Munroe? I'm not taking her from you. She's leaving all by herself."

Caroline looked a little startled. "Natasha isn't with me. She went ahead, in Lord de Henscher's carriage." She simpered. "After all, she is engaged to be married to him."

Seth blinked. "He will still insist on marrying her, after all this? Despite her confession?"

Caroline blushed, and looked down at her toes, and muttered something.

"What?" Vaughn demanded, by Seth's shoulder.

Caroline lifted her chin again, and revealed her rosy-colored cheeks. She was clearly mortified. "I said, Natasha is too highhanded. He had to practically force her into his carriage."

"*Force*?" Seth repeated.

"Well, he *is* going to marry her!" Caroline repeated.

"What do you mean by force?" Vaughn pressed.

She looked confused, and flustered. "I don't know," she said, pushing at her hair in a nervous way. "He bundled her up and pushed her inside."

"Did she say anything? Was she protesting?" Seth pressed.

"Does it matter? After all, she is— " Caroline began.

"Yes it matters, damn it!" Seth exploded. "If de Henscher is a man who can't stand the idea of a woman who doesn't come to him untouched, then he's quite likely to punish her for it."

Caroline paled. "But…"

Seth felt a tugging on his filthy shipboard shirt, and looked down. A just-as-filthy lad with big brown eyes held a folded note out to him, and held out his hand.

"Vaughn, I have no coin," Seth muttered, as he unfolded the note. He heard Vaughn give the lad a copper as he read the note. Then his hearing, his heart and his chest locked in agonized contractions as the meaning of the note slammed home.

You didn't leave when I told you to. Now you pay the price.

"Natasha. He's got Natasha," Seth croaked. The agony in his chest, his heart, made him double over. He looked up at Vaughn, unable to get his chest to unlock and let him breathe properly. "It's Piggot. It's been Piggot all along."

Chapter Seventeen

Vaughn grabbed the note and read it. He nodded. "My carriage is right here. Let's go."

Seth managed to take a breath. One more, then straightened up. "Which way did de Henscher go?"

Caroline had both hands to her cheeks. It was impossible she could understand everything that was happening, but enough of the tension in him conveyed itself to her, that she was now even more flustered. "Why would I tell you, a common criminal—" she began.

"For heaven's sake, woman," Seth cried. "de Henscher killed your husband. The man you just shoved your daughter towards. *Tell me which direction they went!*"

Caroline began to tremble and tears filled her eyes.

Seth held out his hand. "Point then, if you can't find the words. I'm going after her, and I need a direction. Just point."

She pointed.

"Come on," Vaughn urged, running for his carriage. He shouted directions at the driver as he climbed in, and the carriage was already turning as Seth hauled himself inside. He positioned himself so he could see the traffic ahead of the horses.

Vaughn was frowning. "What's the connection between you and de Henscher?"

Seth gave a dry laugh. "He was my shipping agent here in London."

"You mean...de Henscher is in *trade*?" Vaughn seemed surprised.

"I've been shipping goods from Australia to him for years." Seth ran a hand through his hair. "It's de Henscher, though he always signed by the name Sholto Piggot. How could I not have guessed that?"

Vaughn considered it. "Indeed," he said, "he has much to lose—even fifteen years ago, when your father voted for trade restrictions on goods to Ireland that competed with local industries. It's a fairly well-known secret that the family is penniless. He would have lost everything." He looked at Seth steadily. "Didn't you say that the soldiers broke into that Fenian meeting that night almost as soon as it started?"

"Yes."

"Is it possible they knew about the meeting ahead of time?"

"It's possible. They've had more than their fair share of traitors over the years."

Vaughn tapped the windowsill, thinking. "It is possible the soldiers broke into that meeting with the single intention of arresting you?"

Seth jerked at that. "But why? To do that, they'd have had to have known who I was, that I'd be there…"

Vaughn leaned forward. "I think you'll find, if you were to question your father, that Piggot was somewhere in the background at that time, unnoticed, absorbing information. But for now, let's assume that he was. He had you imprisoned to force your father's hand." He glanced out the window. "We're heading for Vauxhall."

Seth clutched the window frame. "Vauxhall! Piggot has a warehouse there."

"Address?"

Seth gave it, and Vaughn leaned out the window to give the driver the address. He shut the window and sat down again.

The blood was pounding Seth's temples. "I will kill him, Vaughn. I swear it."

Vaughn removed his jacket and rolled up his sleeves. "And I will not stop you, my friend. The man has taken much from us both, and he will not live to see another day." Reaching beneath the velvet-covered seat, Vaughn lifted up a box. Lying inside were two pearl-handled dueling pistols, which he began to load.

Seth lifted a brow. "I would ask what those were for, but I suppose I don't need to."

Vaughn's lips quirked. "I never leave home without them."

"Lord Wardell, there is a carriage just ahead," the footman called out, slowing the horses.

Seth recognized Piggot's abandoned carriage immediately. The wheel lay shattered, and footsteps were clearly seen outlined in the dirt road. "The warehouse can not be far," Vaughn said, handing one of the pistols to Seth as they jumped from the carriage.

They raced over the small rise ahead, and the Thames, sparkling in the late afternoon sun, was spread before them. On its shores, close by where ships could load and offload cargoes, lay an enormous brick building with few windows. None of the massive double doors were open.

A pistol shot rang out, and the bullet whizzed past Seth's head. Then another shot.

Vaughn let out a groan behind him. Seth turned, his heart in his throat. Vaughn lay on the ground, clutching at his leg as blood welled around his fingers.

Seth dropped down beside him, ripped off the sleeve of his shirt and handed it to Vaughn. At that moment, Vaughn's driver came running. Seth motioned to him to be cautious, and he scurried closer, bent over almost double.

"I have to go," Seth ground out. His whole body seemed to be tugging him towards the warehouse.

The driver took the sleeve of Seth's shirt and began to wind it around Vaughn's thigh.

"From the furthest door to the left. There's a man-sized door within it. Do you see it?" Vaughn asked, his voice ragged with pain. He held up his pistol. "Take this one, too."

Seth shook his head. "You keep it."

"He has two. You'll have to outshoot him. Are you good enough?"

Seth glanced at Vaughn. "Natasha's in there with him. I'll be good enough." Then better sense made him add, "And if I'm not, and Piggot steps out of this building alive, you take him with yours. Agreed?"

"I haven't the strength left to argue." Vaughn propped himself on his elbows. "Go."

Seth raced for the warehouse, his heart pumping loudly in his chest. He had faced many an enemy in his time, but none of them had held someone so dear. If anything happened to Natasha, he would tear the man limb from limb with his bare hands.

No more shots were fired as he approached, and Seth had to assume that Piggot had left his position and was somewhere else within the bowels of the warehouse. Seth approached the smaller man-sized door, and edged it open with his foot, squinting into the darkness.

No sound, no movement.

He stepped fully inside the building, and only now noticed the chill of the late afternoon air on his bare chest. There were wooden boxes and crates stacked everywhere, with no uniformity, no sense. The air smelled musty and almost damp.

As his eyes adjusted to the dark, he saw ahead of him that there was a roughly formed corridor made by the crates. He padded down the soft soil that was the floor of the warehouse, moving silently, clutching the pistol.

He filled his lungs with air. "Natasha!"

Silence. Then, faint scuffling.

"Seth! I'm he—"

Horror washed over him. The cutoff call could only mean Piggot had silenced her in some way.

He inched forward down the long corridor. Her voice had echoed and bounced in the cavernous building, but he thought it had come from just ahead, and to the right. As he progressed, he checked behind each crate that he passed.

There was a tiny space behind the next crate. He crept forward, then peered around it, his heart thundering.

In a small clearing made by badly stacked crates, Piggot stood with Natasha in front of him, staring with wild eyes towards the passage. He held a pistol to Natasha's temple, and another pointed towards Seth.

Seth stepped around the crate, his own pistol at his side.

"I've reloaded. Don't take a step closer," Piggot warned.

"The note was not a good idea, Piggot," Seth told him. "You must have known it would immediately point to you. Or is it, perhaps, that you *wanted* us to know who you really are?"

"I'll kill her if you take one more step toward me!" Piggot's voice was shrill.

"All those years of scheming and manipulating, of being so clever, and not having anyone to applaud you for your efforts. It must have burned you up knowing that no one would ever get to appreciate the work you had put into preserving your lot."

He was within twenty yards of the man. Piggot was sweating profusely, his hand shaking. "I'll kill her!"

"Not if I kill you first."

"I mean it!"

Natasha was staring at Seth, her eyes wide and glassy with shock. He must have hit her to silence her, before. Seth's resolve hardened. "All right then, kill her. Then I'll shoot you," he told Piggot.

"You'll kill me anyway!" Piggot screamed, his shrill-like voice rising to the rafters, startling birds out of a nest tucked there.

Just a little bit more pressure was needed, Seth realized. "It's not like she'd ever love you, Piggot." He sneered. "You're not man enough for her."

With an outraged cry, Piggot fired.

And missed.

Seth rose from his dodging crouch, and raised his pistol. He only had one shot, and everything suddenly seemed clear and bright all around him as he watched Piggot bring the pistol at Natasha's temple around to bear on him. Seth pulled the trigger, already knowing his shot was true.

The shot took Piggot in the center of the forehead, and for a moment he tottered backwards, a surprised look on his face, before his body realized that he was dead. He collapsed against one of the crates.

Natasha flew into his arms, and Seth tried to push her away. "I'm not suitable for ye," he said, plucking at the jail-stained trousers.

"But you're wrong. You are exactly the man I have been looking for all these years, and now that I found you, I won't ever let you go…" she said, and wound her arms around him.

Seth closed his eyes, and inhaled her sweet scent.

Peace. At last.

Epilogue

Harrow, Ireland. Christmas Day

Natasha glided into the drawing room of Innesford Hall, and looked around at the people she loved most in this world. For this shining day, they were all assembled in her house.

Seth, her handsome husband, sat beside Vaughn and Elisa, telling them about their pending trip to Australia.

She could hardly wait to see the land Seth talked about so often.

Seeing her, he stopped in mid-speech and stood. "Here she is now."

Elisa, round with child, came toward her, arms wide. "There you are. I was concerned when we arrived and Seth said you were not feeling well. Are you feeling better now?"

Natasha hugged her dearest friend, relieved they had finally arrived to spend the holidays with them. "I feel much better, especially now that you're here. I have missed you."

"And I you," Elisa said, taking Natasha by the hand and heading toward the others.

"I'm so surprised you chose to travel in such a condition, but I'm very glad you did," Natasha told her.

Elisa waved her hand. "I'm not about to go into decline for nine months because of a perfectly natural process. I'd rather see my friend."

Natasha sat down, and her husband stepped behind her and took her hand in his own. Seth cleared his throat. "We have news that we wanted to share with you."

Vaughn lifted a brow. "And?"

"My mother will be arriving this afternoon. She has decided that she would like to stay here with us."

"That is wonderful news," Eliza replied, smiling at Seth.

Vaughn's brow lifted higher. "And what, pray tell, moved your mother from the unforgiving harridan that refused to attend your wedding or acknowledge you in any way at all, to sudden concerned mother…and mother-in-law?" he asked.

"Ah. As to that…" Seth paused dramatically, to sip at his Madeira.

Vaughn crossed his arms, and Elisa sat with her lips pursed and her eyes sparkling with joy.

"Oh, Seth, stop teasing," Natasha told him, pulling on his hand.

Seth relented. "It seems she's wanting to be here for the birth of her grandchild."

Vaughn's lips curved into a dazzling smile. "Grandchild?"

Natasha blushed to the roots of her hair. "Indeed, I am to have a child in the spring."

"That is wonderful news!" Elisa clapped her hands together. "Our children will be friends, just as we are."

Seth sat on the chair beside Natasha, her hand still in his, and she glanced over at him. The smile had slipped from his face.

"What is it, my love?" she whispered, concern flooding her.

He shook his head. "Happy," he said at last. "I'm happy, as happy as a man can be. I wish I could reach back in time to the lad who got marched up that gangplank in shackles, and tell him it would all be worth it—that he must go through this to find the happiness at the other end."

Vaughn touched Seth's glass with his own. "I don't think it would have made any difference then, Seth, if you'd known."

"Why not?" Seth said, a bit sharply.

"Because the lad then didn't know what he wanted, didn't know his place. He couldn't have taken happiness if it had been offered to him, because he didn't think he deserved it. You had to go through that to learn there are people in this world who believe in you and love you. You had to go through it to find out that you're capable of giving that love back."

Natasha squeezed Seth's hand again, and kissed his cheek, careless of the fact that they weren't alone. "I love you, Seth."

To her delight he pulled her into his arms, and kissed her back thoroughly. "And I love you, Lady Innesford."

Enjoy this excerpt from

Forbidden

Chapter One

1835, Fairleigh Hall, England

Vaughn Wardell, Viscount Rothmere, only heir of the Marquis of Fairleigh, stepped from the carriage and looked up at the three-story manor he hadn't seen in nearly two decades. Fairleigh Hall hadn't changed at all. The grounds were still immaculate, and the impressive manor rivaled any in England.

He hated the sight of it.

The years he'd spent at Fairleigh Hall had been the worst of his life. Now, at the age of twenty-nine, he had returned to this hideous heap of stone to save his future.

His gut clenched as it had when he heard the outrageous news. The thought was a despairing one: Kirkaldy, his mother's final gift, might be lost to him.

Little more than a glorified hunting lodge near Edinburgh, Kirkaldy had been his mother's only untainted possession. The days there, far from Fairleigh Hall and his father, had been the best of Vaughn's young life. At Kirkaldy, his mother had been carefree, even joyous. For that reason alone, Vaughn intended to plant himself like a weed here at Fairleigh Hall, a weed that refused to be pulled and discarded, until Kirkaldy's ownership had been determined.

Taking a deep breath, he walked up the thirteen steps to his father's home.

Vaughn had no trouble imagining the disapproval his father would convey upon his return. He'd learned years ago there was no pleasing Rufus Wardell. The only emotion Rufus had ever openly shown him had been when he'd announced Vaughn would be leaving for boarding school. A cruel smile had curled his father's lips as he'd laid out the details of what would become twelve years of purgatory, hidden behind the walls of one of the best public schools in England. Though nearly a decade had passed since he had graduated, those memories still appeared in his dreams from time to time. They would wake him in the middle of night, to cold sweat and a hurting heart, the bed sheets tangled around his legs.

The memory subsided as the door was opened. Joshua, his father's trusted valet, stared at him. "Good lord! I mean, Lord Vaughn." The valet's expression softened. "You've come home?" There was a buried hope in his tone.

Vaughn's chest tightened with fondness for the old man. While Vaughn had been growing up there had been countless occasions when he had been locked in the attic for yet another transgression. It had been Joshua who had slipped food, blankets and tallows to provide light through the long nights when not even his mother's pleadings had moved his father to release him.

Vaughn laid a hand on Joshua's shoulder. "I'm not here to stay," he said gently.

This time the disappointment in Joshua's eyes was easy to read. He stepped back, covering the emotion with formal pride. "Come in, my lord."

Vaughn handed over his coat, hat and gloves and strode through the broad entrance hall into the circular foyer that dominated the center of the building, where he halted. He turned a full circle on his heels, taking in the cold marble surfaces and massive round columns that lined the foyer in regimented pairs. They were dazzlingly lit by the glass dome on the roof that bathed the foyer in natural sunlight, showcasing the polished, untouched perfection of the green-flecked marble. The foyer was widely admired across five counties for its elegant, unusual design. Whenever his father loosened the purse strings enough to entertain, the foyer was thick with guests dotted about the floor and the stairs, tucked into the recesses between the columns, gossiping.

But while everyone had appeared to enjoy the spectacular room, Vaughn's recollection of the foyer was a bitter one that caught at his throat. His gaze lingered on the staircase that swooped in a spiral to both upper floors. His pulse skittered at the sight of the thick stone balustrade on the first floor. That was where he had stood as a frightened ten-year old, his fingers trying to dig into the cold stone, watching his mother leave in the middle of the night.

She'd promised to send for him, with as many kisses and hugs as she could manage before hurrying to escape the house. She had smelled of lavender, and her hand against his cheek had been warm and delicate.

That had been the last time he'd seen her alive.

"Your father is at dinner. Shall I announce you?" Joshua asked, startling Vaughn and bringing him back to the present.

"And ruin the surprise?" Vaughn asked, already heading toward the high-arched French doors. Taking a calming breath, he opened the double doors and stepped inside.

The room was long and dim compared to the foyer. There was a row of tall sash windows along one wall, and their limited light fell on a collection of large portraits and mediocre landscapes hanging from the picture rail on the other. Between was an ocean of expensive oriental carpets, pinned down on the edges by heavy, hand-carved buffets and occasional chairs. All of them framed the focal point of the room: a long Georgian mahogany dining table that easily seated thirty people.

There were not that many people dining this evening. In fact, there were only two. One was a woman sitting at the right of the head of the table, her back to Vaughn. This could only be his father's new fiancée, Elisa.

The woman who had ripped Kirkaldy from him.

She was to blame for all of this. It was because of her he had been forced back to Fairleigh Hall to confront Rufus.

The sight of her erect back filled him with a sudden sharp fury he hadn't suspected he held. His whole body tightened with it. She was ruining his life, taking away from him the only precious memories he owned.

Vaughn blinked, astonished at the power of the emotion that bubbled up inside him now that he was at the point of confrontation for which he had been bracing himself.

His attention was drawn to the short man sitting at the head of the table. Rufus Wardell was staring at him, his gray brows furrowing together into a frown Vaughn remembered well. Rufus' permanently red cheeks bracketed a big nose. Small muddy brown eyes sat above them. Even at sixty, Rufus' hair was thick, but it was coarse and dirty gray. With his short, rotund shape he might have appeared boyish, but because of the cruel light in his eyes and the cynical twist to his lips, Rufus looked more like a maniacal cherub.

He studied Vaughn as though he were trying to place him. And he probably was. Vaughn was over six feet tall. He was broad across the shoulders thanks to hours as an adolescent taking his frustrations out upon various professional pugilists. There was nothing of the boy who had left Fairleigh Hall so very long ago.

After an endless moment, surprise crossed Rufus' face. He'd finally recognized him. "What the hell are you doing here, boy?" Rufus asked, his rasping voice bereft of any warmth.

Though Vaughn had anticipated his reaction, it still stung. There would be no welcome here, he realized. "Thank you for the nice welcome, Father. It's a pleasure to see you, too."

It apparently disturbed Rufus Wardell not at all that this was the first return of the child he tossed out without regard nearly twenty years ago. No conscience appeared to stir him at the arrival of the son he had inexcusably wronged.

The anger squeezed Vaughn's throat and chest and nearly closed off his breath. He'd hoped there would have been some doubt, some chance of redemption, but there was none.

"Well, out with it!" Rufus glared at Vaughn. "You obviously have something on your mind, or you would not have traveled so far. Pray tell," he added with patently false politeness, "to what do I owe the pleasure of your company?"

"I'm not here to be polite, so you'd needn't extend yourself," Vaughn assured him.

"Then get out. I'm dining with the woman I intend to marry and your presence is not welcome." Rufus shot a look at Elisa, who sat in perfect stillness at the end of the table, her head bowed in imitation of a modest woman.

Vaughn's friends had been quick to advise him just how short on modesty this harlot was. He took a deep breath, trying to quell the hot tide of resentment rising in him. "It is about her that I am here," he said. He stepped around the end of the table to face Elisa, and swept into a low bow. The courtesy came automatically, as did the phrasing: "My lady, we have not had the pleasure of being introduced..."

...and then, he looked at her properly for the first time. Shock slithered through his veins, dispersing all the fury, resentment and indignation in one breathless moment.

As her large eyes glanced up at him, wide with apprehension, he stared at her, taking in her face and apparel, trying to estimate just how old she was. Blue eyes the same glorious shade as a bright summer sky stared back at him as she gave a hesitant, nervous smile. The smile drew his attention to her full, pleasantly pink lips, and the white teeth behind.

Her skin was softly touched by the sun, but flawless, and as he took her hand and bowed over it again, he noticed the cheeks bloom with hot color at his attention.

Absurdly, her coyness sent a thrill of pleasure through him.

He could not help but smile as he stepped back. She ducked her chin, unable to look at him directly. It was then he noticed the head of gleaming blonde curls the color of wheat. A silky ringlet tipped forward across her shoulder at her movement, and he resisted the temptation to brush it gently back.

She was so young...and sweetly, stunningly beautiful.

The thought occurred to him with a shock that momentarily obliterated the sting of his father's cold welcome. With it came confusion, because although he had not heard how young his father's fiancée was, Vaughn was more than familiar with the rumors of her sordid past.

This was the woman who had brought on the death of her husband by her lover's hand? All of London had been abuzz with the news.

"Boy, you've grown tall and insolent," Rufus snarled. "I didn't pay good money all those years for you to learn bad manners."

Vaughn dragged his attention back to his father. "I'm paying my respects to the future lady of this splendid home." And he turned back to Elisa once more, to study her.

"You are most welcome, Vaughn. I am pleased to meet you at last," she responded with a tiny smile. Her voice was a low contralto, soft and unexpected.

He nodded one more time, before stepping back.

He had intended to leave the room, to let his father have his intimate dinner. It would be wiser to retreat for a while and regroup his defenses now his father had shown no punches were to be pulled in the trial that lay ahead.

Instead, he lowered himself into the chair opposite his father's fiancée. "Thank you, I will have a brandy," he told Rufus, answering the question a good host would have asked.

Rufus' upper lip curled and his eyes narrowed. He looked up at the manservant standing by the door of the dining room and jerked his head. Silently, the man glided to a buffet laid with decanters and crystal to pour the drink.

Vaughn glanced at Elisa again.

She delicately cut her meat into small pieces, lifted the fork and slid a piece into her mouth. A visible pulse beat at the base of the long column of her throat.

The servant placed the brandy in front of Vaughn. Rufus began to eat again, attacking his plate with furious gusto. With every loaded forkful of food he would take a big mouthful of claret. The red liquid dribbled from the corners of his mouth as he chomped away.

Vaughn looked away, his disgust growing. Surely the man would try a bit harder in front of his intended? How could she contemplate marrying this gruesome imp? Or perhaps the money was worth it to her…

He looked back to the silent beauty on the other side of the table. He still could not believe this was the same woman of whom he'd heard tell. The gossips had spared him no detail: a bride at seventeen, wed to an aging count. A mother at nineteen and a cuckolded wife the same year. Then, swiftly, she had set about giving her husband his own set of horns. The gossips had been firm in their approval of her husband's reaction to her supposed whoring. He had taken the only honorable course of action an aggrieved husband could; he'd challenged her lover to a duel. No honor had been lost because he'd been killed. In fact, society had gathered about his grieving family and presented a solid, united front to anyone who dared to abuse the deceased lord's memory.

That had been years ago. In the aftermath, Elisa's name had quickly disappeared into shamed obscurity. No good woman or honorable gentleman would speak of her aloud in polite company. It had only been the relaxed bawdy banter around a late night card table that had alerted Vaughn to the fact Elisa had re-emerged from her exile. His card companions that night had thought it a superb jest his own father had proposed to her. Vaughn had gone along with the joke at the time, thinking the pair deserved each other.

The contradiction between her appearance and her past was indeed confusing.

She was pushing at a piece of the meat on her plate with her fork, and Vaughn wondered if she did so to avoid looking up and seeing him watching her. Was she aware of him? By her sweet looks, he would have judged her an innocent, but her reputation told him she probably knew and understood every hot thought running through his mind.

Vaughn sipped at his brandy thoughtfully, alternately watching Rufus eat and Elisa toy with her food. She really was a lovely creature, he realized. He was not at all surprised two men had fought to the death over her.

She touched her mouth with her napkin, then lifted a fingertip to slide it across her lips a second time, without the linen. It was unconsciously graceful and sensuous. Vaughn's body tightened with an old familiar ache, intensified beyond reason like a taut bow string stretched to the limits of endurance, vibrating with tension and packed with potential power to explode…

The realization slammed into Vaughn with the shock of ice water.

He wanted her.

And the wanting was not a casual, passing impulse. It was burning in him, pushing aside thought, reason, caution.

Vaughn stared at her, feeling his heart thump erratically, and the beat echo in his temple. What was happening to him? Had he lost all good sense?

Why an electronic book?

We live in the Information Age—an exciting time in the history of human civilization in which technology rules supreme and continues to progress in leaps and bounds every minute of every hour of every day. For a multitude of reasons, more and more avid literary fans are opting to purchase e-books instead of paperbacks. The question to those not yet initiated to the world of electronic reading is simply: *why?*

1. *Price.* An electronic title at Ellora's Cave Publishing and Cerridwen Press runs anywhere from 40-75% less than the cover price of the exact same title in paperback format. Why? Cold mathematics. It is less expensive to publish an e-book than it is to publish a paperback, so the savings are passed along to the consumer.
2. *Space.* Running out of room to house your paperback books? That is one worry you will never have with electronic novels. For a low one-time cost, you can purchase a handheld computer designed specifically for e-reading purposes. Many e-readers are larger than the average handheld, giving you plenty of screen room. Better yet, hundreds of titles can be stored within your new library—a single microchip. (Please note that Ellora's Cave and Cerridwen Press does not endorse any specific brands. You can check our website at www.ellorascave.com or

www.cerridwenpress.com for customer recommendations we make available to new consumers.)

3. *Mobility.* Because your new library now consists of only a microchip, your entire cache of books can be taken with you wherever you go.
4. *Personal preferences are accounted for.* Are the words you are currently reading too small? Too large? Too...**ANNOYING**? Paperback books cannot be modified according to personal preferences, but e-books can.
5. *Instant gratification.* Is it the middle of the night and all the bookstores are closed? Are you tired of waiting days—sometimes weeks—for online and offline bookstores to ship the novels you bought? Ellora's Cave Publishing sells instantaneous downloads 24 hours a day, 7 days a week, 365 days a year. Our e-book delivery system is 100% automated, meaning your order is filled as soon as you pay for it.

Those are a few of the top reasons why electronic novels are displacing paperbacks for many an avid reader. As always, Ellora's Cave and Cerridwen Press welcomes your questions and comments. We invite you to email us at service@ellorascave.com, service@cerridwenpress.com or write to us directly at: 1056 Home Ave. Akron OH 44310-3502.

Ellora's Cave
Romantica Publishing